Sex, Lies & Stellenbosch

Eva Mazza

Melinda Ferguson Books,
an imprint of NB Publishers, a division of Media24 Boeke (Pty) Ltd
40 Heerengracht, Cape Town, South Africa
PO Box 879, Cape Town 8000, South Africa
www.nb.co.za

Cover design by Maggie Davey and Alexandra Turner
Editing by Shelagh Foster
Proofreading by Linda Da Nova
Set in Sabon LT Pro
Printed and bound by CTP Printers, Cape Town

First published by Melinda Ferguson Books 2020
First edition, fourth impression
Fifth impression 2021

ISBN: 978-1-928420-37-8
ISBN: 978-1-928420-41-5 (epub)
ISBN: 978-1-928420-42-2 (mobi)

For
Girlfriends, especially the first four: T, M, C & C
BBD
& my daughters, all four

Part One

One

Her cheek peeled reluctantly from the pillow. A union forged by drink and drool; the latter, an unglamorous snail-trail from the left corner of her mouth. Eyes wide open. *What's the time?* Jen turned her body gingerly onto her side. Her phone read 05:00 am. The party was over! *Crap! I'm in the dog box, that's for sure.* Only after she'd made the enormous effort to move her face back onto the pillow's clammy wet spot to check whether her husband was asleep, did she remember she had locked him out of their bedroom. *Double bloody crap!*

Needing to pee, she sat up and waited for her head to catch up with her body before placing her feet on the floor. Using the bedside table to ease herself off the bed, she staggered stilettoed in the dark to the bathroom.

"Shit!" she cursed, butt sliding into the wet toilet bowl. She clutched the sides to avoid slipping any further. *John always leaves the effing seat up!* She flushed, then stumbled to the basin to splash water over her face.

The fear felt like ice.

What had she done? And where was John?

She chose to ignore her best friend Frankie's string of WhatsApp messages. *Probably apologising for being such a bitch. Frankie could go to hell!*

Jen threw her stilettos across the room, unlocked the door and padded towards the lounge, tripping over the rug and nearly landing on her face on the way.

"I'm still drunk," she moaned aloud as she collected herself, grabbing a bottle of still water from the fridge and gulping it down.

"John?" she called. "Are you there?"

No answer. She moved towards a shadow of a man asleep on the couch. *Larry the Lecherous Lout.* Stirring, he grabbed at her.

"You need to go home now, Larry." Jen pushed his hand away and stepped outside. A gentle breeze stirred the hot air and she shuddered at the prickly perspiration under her armpits. *Where the hell is John?*

Candlelight flickered in the tasting room. All was quiet, but perhaps he was in there, asleep. An owl's last call heralded the dawn.

Bloody reckless to pass out with a candle burning!

Jen moved towards the entrance, the candle beckoning her in. "John?" she whispered, gently pushing the door open. A man was seated on a bench in the shadowy far corner, his head thrown back, eyes closed and mouth agape.

Good God! It was like road kill. She couldn't help herself; she didn't want to look, but she had to. Revolted and intrigued, she stood there, incapable of moving, of anything.

The man's one hand seemed to be cupped around a woman's breast while the other held the back of her head.

"Yes, baby," he groaned.

Baby!

And then it dawned on her. That man was her husband of twenty-four years! *Jen do something. Anything!*

"John?" Her voice sounded foreign.

Wide-eyed now, he looked straight at her. The idiot remained seated. *He must be in shock.*

There was an agonisingly long pause. *Aren't you going to stop her?*

She must have communicated this telepathically because both their eyes shifted to the kneeling woman, commendably (or so Jen thought) using her mouth to effectuate her adulterous husband's happy ending.

"What the hell do you think you're doing?"

She had always imagined a stronger, more dramatic reaction to such a revelatory scene of deceit and treachery.

The woman's head jerked away from her husband's groin. Jen felt ridiculously relieved when she saw that John-John wasn't standing at attention. *He's mine!* Breasts spilled out from an unbuttoned top.

Distracted by the sight of the porn-star mammaries, Jen wasn't yet aware to whom they belonged.

Then.

"Patty?" she asked, as if she had stumbled across her after many years. She turned to her husband. "Patty? The wine rep?"

Two

It was John's fifty-fifth birthday bash; a birthday that would have been overlooked but for Brigit, the eldest of their offspring and the apple of her daddy's eye. It was Brig's idea to surprise her father, yet as much as they'd tried keeping it a secret, he had found out. Brigit was disappointed, but Jen was happy the cat was out the bag; surprises weren't something she was comfortable receiving, let alone organising.

Things had gone awry after the speeches; a pity, since the party had got off to such a good start. It was Jen's fault entirely. If only she had stuck to her prepared speech. Well, it wasn't really *hers*; Brigit had written it. *Blame it on the champagne and shooters.* Maybe if she hadn't drunk so much, she wouldn't have reacted the way she did. Brigit had always said that Jen couldn't take a joke, that she had no sense of humour. *Tonight, I proved her right.*

Looking back, Jen's sense of humour failure could be traced to her gold stretch pants. Normally she paid no attention to Brig's jibes. Since she could remember, Brigit almost always found her mother embarrassing, invariably resulting in some snide remark which she had learned to ignore. However, the eldest's disparaging comments about her outrageously expensive too-tight pants had hit a nerve because, well, they were embarrassingly true.

"Oh my God! You're not wearing that tonight, are you?" She asked in the demeaning tone reserved solely for her mom.

"Yes, I am," Jen said, pouring herself into them.

John came to his wife's defence, which was rather sweet of him as the two loved to tease her. "Brig!" he bellowed from the bathroom. He'd strutted through to their bedroom, bath-towel wrapped dangerously low around his hips, and planted a kiss on Jen's cheek. "Mom's aim is to look hot; it's an age thing, hey love?" he teased, looking her over appreciatively.

"What is it with men and women in tight pants?" Brig ridiculed.

"No, it's not my aim!" Jen lied as their daughter watched her struggling to close the zip. John moved in to give her a hand, which Jen smacked away.

The mirror reflected her delusional wannabe-hip forty-nine-year-old self in pants intended for someone decidedly younger. Maybe John's birthday had triggered fears of her imminent fiftieth. She had told the shop assistant she was sick and tired of looking like a boring middle-aged farmer's wife and the young woman had assured her the pants did the trick.

"Actually, my aim is to look hip." She'd managed to get the zip up. "I'm tired of looking like a mom."

"So, you decided to shop at Forever 21?" Brig chortled appreciatively at her own joke and, as usual, John joined in.

It was true, Jen wanted to look sexy. Instead, she looked like a desperate cougar at a university digs's sex fest. She'd watched her husband as he prepped for the party. *He's effortlessly hot.*

In truth, it wasn't effortless. John spent three afternoons at gym and two mornings cycling or jogging through the vineyards, every week, without fail. It had paid off. Unlike many of his friends who had developed paunches, he devoted a lot of time to his appearance.

"More time than I do," Jen had bitched to her book club friends.

"Count yourself lucky," Shelley had retorted, and the rest of the group agreed. "At least you have something to work with. Some of us have to use our imaginations."

Jen had cringed at the thought of poor Shelley having to perform her wifely duties.

"You still look hot, Daddy," Brig said, then turned to her mom giving her the once over. "Just don't tuck your shirt in, k?"

Jen hated the way Brigit would shorten okay to 'k'. *It's not like it's a thirteen-letter word, for heaven's sake. And it's so bloody condescending!*

However rude her daughter was, she valued her opinion. "Why not?" Jen asked, lest she became the laughing stock of the party. Her eldest looked at her dad and rolled her eyes.

"Cleavage, push-up bra, butt and crotch... Leave something to the imagination. You don't want to look like you're really trying, do you?"

"You've already established that I'm really trying! By the way, does my new haircut also look like I tried too hard?"

"You look great, love," John said, turning from the mirror and dabbing cologne onto his freshly shaved face. "Don't listen to Brig. You're gorgeous."

Jen gave him a peck on the cheek. "Why thank you, John," she said, then playfully stuck out her tongue at Brig.

"I personally like your hair darker and longer," Brigit said while tugging Jen's top out from her pants as if Jen were a three-year-old. "But if a mousey bob blows you away, then hey, who am I to comment?"

Jen inhaled deeply. She tried hard not to allow Brig to get under her skin. *Definitely not tonight.* They'd got along so much better these past few weeks, both preoccupied with John's birthday preparations.

"Well, Brig, you look as chic as ever. Now if you'll excuse me, I need to fasten my shoes."

She hoped she would be able to carry them off. *Farm girls don't wear heels; they wear practical flats* – her mother's favourite line when Jen was an adolescent. Judging from the look in Brig's eyes, it was obvious that her daughter concurred.

Jen had meant it when she said that Brigit looked chic. She had developed a unique style; understated, but elegant. She wore her hair short – a throwback from her swimming days at school – and was one of the few women who could wear a boyish hairstyle without looking butch. In fact, she never had a shortage of admirers; there was something so feminine about her that complemented her masculine crop.

Brigit had chosen tight black satin pants that tapered to just above her ankles and a loose-fitting black top with a subtle gold shimmer that plunged sexily at the neckline. Her accessories were understated: a gold cuff for her wrist, a long black and gold necklace that hung low to her belly and small studs in her ears. She wore an unusually big ring on her middle finger, drawing attention to her manicured nails.

Her look was simple yet sophisticated. The exact opposite of Jen's.

"Don't forget this," Brigit said, handing over a typed speech before leaving the room.

Jen tucked the speech into her pants pocket, and her shirt back into her pants.

"Cow!" she mouthed to John.

"Don't be like that, Jen," John said. "I think you look shaggable, especially bending over to buckle those heels, baby." He rubbed up against her. "John-John agrees. Here, feel. He's standing at attention."

Jen playfully pushed him away and turned to give the birthday boy a quick peck on the lips.

"Now, piss off," she teased. "You *and* John-John. We have a party to go to, and I believe it's yours, you dirty old man."

Three

John hadn't celebrated his fiftieth, choosing to take the family on holiday instead. It seemed that a bash for his sixtieth was not on the cards either, as he'd often said that the thought of celebrating old age was depressing. Brigit had come up with the idea of a surprise fifty-fifth party for her dad. "It's halfway between fifty and sixty."

Jen thought it a great idea. She loved dancing and she loved a party. She also felt that it was important to mark his birthday with friends who had touched his life, and hers; friends they'd practically grown old with.

Old! She didn't like to think of herself as old, but forty-nine sounded pretty decrepit.

That night at the party, music from the eighties and nineties had blasted from the speakers. A handful of people frolicked around the dance floor, looking like throwbacks from the era of shoulder pads and Swatch watches.

Jen gyrated with her girlfriends. Over the years, John's

friends' wives had become her besties. Their tipsiness had made them zealous to show off their Zumba moves. Not that any of their husbands noticed; they were drinking at the bar, probably commiserating over Stellenbosch's latest drama, the Steinhoff scandal.

Despite Brig's disapproval, Jen had been complimented on her outfit, giving her the confidence she desperately needed to carry off the contentious stretch pants and the killer heels. Gladys, their housekeeper was the first to offer praise. "You look so young, Jen. I thought you were Brigit."

Jen kissed her on the cheek. "Thanks, Gladys, but I don't think Brigit will be happy to hear this."

Her friends thought her new haircut and colour took off ten years, and the padded push-up bra (the best invention since the nineties) did an impressive job under her sheer white top. *At least someone had the intelligence to put those awful eighties shoulder pads where they mattered!*

Lecherous Larry had already given her bum a squeeze, which Jen took in the spirit of things. Lee, John's best friend since childhood, had taken the time to tell her how beautiful she looked.

The music came to an abrupt halt – Brigit's orders – and everyone was summoned to listen to the speeches. Brigit delivered a well-constructed and polished speech, as expected. *She is, after all, in broadcasting.* Pete, on the other hand, was reliably incoherent. Drink and nerves were never his best combination and he was filled with both.

Next was John's turn. He started by thanking his friends, and made some lewd joke about growing old. He then moved on to his family, first mentioning his parents, who were unable to attend (after years of animosity, they had a cordial but distant relationship). The best were left for nearly last: their children, waxing lyrical about Brigit and how proud he was of her. He went on to talk about Pete and what a wonderful man he had become.

Yep, I certainly have a soft spot for our boy. Father and son, however, had a strained relationship which Jen had hoped would improve now that Pete was employed full-time on the farm.

She straightened up as John began to speak about her. "What can I say? I know it's a paradox, but I'm a happily married man," he quipped, rather shyly. Jen smiled at him. He said how lucky he was to have had her by his side for twenty-four years of marriage, and how admirable it was of Jen to have stuck by him. She looked down rather coyly. The guests clapped, but John silenced them. "Well, she has nowhere else to go. Isn't that right, darling?"

Her head jerked up and her coy smile faded fast. *He's turned a very private and potentially contentious issue into a joke!* John quickly saved himself, "Why would I want you to go anywhere, baby?"

Oh my God! Shut up. You're only making things worse. He turned to his friends. "See how hot she looks?" A few wolf-whistles from the men.

"Stop, guys!" Jen feigned laughter. "You're just encouraging more of this ridiculous…" The whistling got louder.

"You've really gone the extra mile tonight, especially in those pants." He had drawn the attention of one hundred pairs of eyes to her gold stretch pants. He winked at Brigit and her laughter egged him on. "Brig thinks her mom's too old for them, but I think she's one hot mama, don't you?"

"Here's to you, Mrs Robinson," said Pete's friend, Max, a boy of twenty-two! Lecherous Larry began to chant, "Cougar! Cougar!" Jen looked at her girlfriends for some help, but they too had joined in. Everyone, except Pete, who knew his mom only too well, had become participants of Larry's ridiculous chant.

My pants look shinier in this light! They seem to be tighter too.

"Kudos to you, Jen. Your husband's a lucky man." Thank God that silenced everyone. Jen craned her neck to see who her saviour was.

Patty!

The farm's sexy wine rep.

A rush of gratitude towards her. "Thank you!" Jen mouthed.

When he'd hired Patty, John had said that she was just what they needed to sell their wine. Jen had been a little concerned, especially since her friends had warned her to "keep an eye on that one". But she had decided it was better to be friends than enemies with the devil, and once she got to know her, she quite liked her. She especially liked her now. Her girlfriends could say what they liked about Patty: that she looked like a whore (she certainly dressed like a stripper) and that her boobs were fake (so were most of theirs) but she secretly admired her; she was afraid of absolutely nothing and no one. Despite her humble roots, mingling with the Stellenbosch elite – notorious snobs – never fazed her. Well, it looked that way.

John pulled his wife towards him for a conciliatory kiss then handed her the mic. Now, embarrassed at the attention drawn to her outfit, Jen surreptitiously buttoned up her shirt. She stood in front of the sea of faces, a fixed smile supressed her seething. She was angry with everyone. They had encouraged John to make her the butt of his jokes.

She looked down at the prepared speech. *Where would I have been without you, John? You were and still are my knight in shining armour.*

Oh my God! Really? I can't get these words to leave my mouth. Not now. She had wanted to speak before John, but Brigit had insisted on the order of things. She inhaled deeply before she began, and now other words spilled effortlessly from her. "As John said, we've been happily married for a number of years. That's no paradox, John. I've obviously been happy, and you've been married." This elicited loud clapping and cheering from the guests. John laughed and squeezed Jen's hand gently. "And for the most part, it's been absolutely scintillating for me. Let's see: John expects his breakfast at nine every morning. Nothing too heavy, maybe an egg or some oats, but definitely two cups of coffee to kick-start the day."

Somebody shouted, "After your morning shag, I hope!" It was Larry, of course. *He's such an asshole.* Jen freed her hand from John's and crumpled up Brigit's speech. She threw it at Larry. It bounced off his head and landed at his feet. Everyone laughed.

"No, Larry, John chooses to mount his *tractor* until twelve thirty, which is unequivocally lunch time." More raucous laughter. It felt good. Jen was on a roll. "John likes to have a cooked lunch, don't you, darling? Because being a farmer and working the land works up an appetite. And before you allow your dirty minds to wander, it's not sexual; that appetite's usually for chicken and a salad, or fish and chips."

John stood there, mouth gaping. *Where was Brig,* Jen wondered. She began to feel unsteady on her stilettos. "We have many hobbies, don't we, John?" The guests seemed to be hanging on every word. "You love to gym, cycle and run, and I enjoy complimenting you on the results of your gyming, cycling and running." Only light laughter from the guests. "My aim was to look hot in these pants, I confess." The guests were silent. "Clearly Brigit, they're a huuuge fail. Where *is* Brig?" A sea of faces turned in unison to look for Brigit.

John stepped forward.

"I haven't finished, John," Jen said firmly. "Everyone needs a good laugh and I'm glad I could oblige." A few claps. Then her eyes locked on Lecherous Larry and his group of friends. "You guys need a laugh, thanks to your buddy, Jooste. It ain't easy watching shares plummet. I guess it's the same for me, I took a gamble on these very expensive pants and boy, did I lose."

Total silence.

Frankie signalled to her to wrap it up. Jen reached out her hand to John, but he ignored the gesture. *Okay, if that's how you want it.* "Well, they say that growing old means becoming set in your ways. For John, his passage to sixty will be a breeze, as he has been set in his ways for the last twenty-four years. As for me? Well, it seems you're right, John; our marriage contract guarantees that I'll be by your side or in the kitchen until rigor mortis sets in."

Boom!

Jen couldn't remember much after that, except for her friend Frankie standing in front of her, hands on her hips.

"Jesus, Jen," she spat. "What got into you?"

"John pissed me off!" she said defensively.

"No shit? Reminder: It's his birthday!"

"Ya, well I don't enjoy being the butt of his jokes." Her breath caught in her throat. *Why doesn't Frankie get it?*

"Maybe you should've tried laughing. You're obviously insecure about shit or you would've just taken it for what it was, a little comic banter."

She looked at Shelley for support. "Come on, I was hysterically funny."

"Sorry, darling. I have to agree with Frankie" Shelley shrugged. The rest of the group looked on, saying nothing.

"Why?"

"All I know, is if I had said what you said, Frans would throw me out."

"Did none of you hear what *John* said?" Jen's voice was shrill.

"You overreacted. And then you got mean." Frankie turned and walked away.

"Some of us've lost millions on Steinhoff shares. You wanna talk about insensitive!" That was Anne. She hated Jen and the feeling was mutual.

"I didn't know. Sorry!" Jen lied.

As if that wasn't enough, Brigit had marched up to her mother, spewing under her breath, "You couldn't have stuck to the speech we wrote, could you?"

Sounding like a belligerent child, Jen said, "*We* didn't write it. You did!"

"Oh, for fuck's sake, Mom! I give up with you."

She felt the tears well in her eyes. What *had* she been thinking? And what now? Too embarrassed to face their guests, she opened a bottle of the farm's renowned Chenin Blanc and crept, unnoticed, into their bedroom, locking the door behind her.

The party continued despite her absence. The music blared. She could hear the guests clapping and laughing. As she got drunker, so the music seemed to get louder.

Jen vaguely remembered Gladys knocking on her door to tell her she was off to bed and that she would be in to tidy up in the morning. "Thank you, Gladys," Jen managed to say cheerfully before she heard someone shout over the music, "I feel like a fucking thirty-year-old!" It was John. The guests cheered. She knew she was in deep shit, but at that point she was too drunk to care. Anyway, she was feeling very sorry for herself. Her absence didn't seem to matter to him, or anyone else. The Stellenbosch ranks had closed in; so, she sucked the last drop of wine straight from the bottle and passed out.

Four

Brigit, beyond furious with her mother, had grabbed her overnight bag and her keys from her childhood bedroom and stalked out of the party, hoping to miss the revellers. She was intercepted by Lee on her way out. All she bloody needed; she had successfully avoided him thus far.

"Brigit!" He moved in to kiss her cheek, but she pulled away. He pretended to ignore her paltry behaviour. "I've been trying to get your attention the whole evening. Brilliant party you organised."

Brigit smirked. "Yes, really brilliant, Lee. Mom's speech was a total disaster."

Lee laughed. "No, it wasn't."

Brigit stared at him, disbelief in her eyes.

"Okay! She stuffed up a bit." He whispered conspiratorially, "I think she's drunk."

Brigit was in no mood for jokes. "Well, fuck her!" She could see Lee flinch. Stellenbosch kids were brought up to respect their parents.

"I can see you're taken aback, Lee. But seriously, fuck her! I'm out of here."

Lee tried to stop her, but she knew he knew better than to interfere. She'd take the N1 home. It wasn't as dangerous as the N2 at this time of night.

Once home, she caught the lift to the tenth floor of her apartment. Keys ready, she unlocked her door and stormed in, dumping them and her bags on the floor. She stomped into the kitchen to pour herself a gin and tonic, furious with her mother for ruining the party, for her at least.

The alcohol had the desired effect. She kicked off her shoes and went through to the lounge and sank into the leather sofa that Jen – ever the frustrated interior designer – had bought her as a house-warming present. Her mother had been determined to have a hand in decorating Brig's apartment.

Her mind wandered to the night's events. The more she thought about it, the angrier she became. She had to concede that it generally was difficult for her mom to please her, but she had really tried with Jen this time. Even if the party had been Brig's idea, Jen's keenness to help was graciously accepted, although Brig had been clear that she was in charge of the evening's proceedings. Brig had arranged the invitations and the disco and had delegated the catering and of course the décor to her mother. She had wanted her dad's birthday to be perfect, and tonight her mum had sabotaged the whole affair.

Brigit rose from the sofa. She needed her pyjamas. It was late, and she was exhausted. She had intended to sleep over at the farm, having anticipated a late night. Now she had to drive back to Stellenbosch for tomorrow's Sunday lunch. It was, after all, John's actual birthday. It seemed like a good idea at the time, but after what had happened, she really didn't feel like seeing Jen. *It's not about you, Brig,* she reminded herself. It didn't seem fair to hurt her dad's feelings by cancelling. She'd have to go. *Well, at least Lee won't be there*, she thought. Everyone was used to Brig ignoring her mum, but she couldn't ignore her godfather, that would seem rude.

Just then a message from him came up on her cellphone.

"Want to know if you're back safe."

She answered with a thumbs-up. She should've answered, *you were just in my thoughts*.

"Party's still going strong. You shouldn't have left, Brig."

Fuck him! She was angry with him too. Angry with the world it seemed. She thought back to her chance meeting with Lee only yesterday. She had bumped into him in the city and they'd had a spontaneous lunch at a nearby pub. Although godfather and goddaughter were not that close, Brigit knew that he had always adored her, and she loved him dearly too. It was raining heavily, and he had offered to give her a lift to her apartment. He was curious to see her new place and he had asked if he could come up for a quick look around.

They had been drinking, so they were both more relaxed than usual around each other. Lee took off his shoes on instruction from Brigit, who was very protective of her cream carpet. He showed himself around her small but very chic home, complimenting her on the décor. Jen's unsolicited generosity and help with the interior had resulted in an apartment worthy of being photographed for *HOUSE&HOME* magazine.

When Lee returned from his walkabout of her bedroom and study, she invited him to sit on the sofa next to her. He did, and looked up at the framed photograph dominating the opposite wall.

"Great picture that!" he said.

It was a black and white print of a naked woman, her face in shadow.

"Thanks. A photography student took it for his final-year project. He was awarded a first, so he gave me a copy."

"So, it's you." There was a moment's strained silence, then Lee asked if she had any of her dad's wine lurking in the apartment.

"Of course, I do! But shouldn't you rather have a coffee? You're driving back home and I'm sure you've exceeded your quota."

"Tonight is poker night with the boys," he said. "I'm not driving home. I'll leave my car at work and shuttle back with them."

"Ah! That's why you look so smart." He seemed pleased with the compliment. She wondered if Frankie shopped for him. He looked dapper in black ankle pants and a linen shirt with the top button unfastened to reveal a few stray chest hairs. His five o'clock shadow gave the impression that he hadn't had time to shave, yet she knew his whole appearance had been carefully considered. He was one of the few of her dad's friends who still advertised his marital status by wearing a thin gold band.

On returning with a glass of red wine for him and a gin and tonic for herself, she found him standing at the glass doors to her balcony, admiring the view.

"Here you are, Uncle," she joked, handing him his wine.

"Great view you have here, spoilt brat!"

"*I'm* paying the rent. I'm not relying on Daddy's generosity anymore."

Lee had smiled. "Well good for you."

"I've got to say, I scored a luck. This flat was going at such a great rate. Something about an overseas investor wanting a tenant who would look after it as if it were her own." They looked at the skyline in silence. Then Brigit said, "You see that building over there?"

"Which? The Finance Building?"

"Yes."

He took a sip of his wine after clinking his glass with hers.

"Allegedly it has a decadent gentlemen's club on the top floor!" Brigit said matter-of-factly.

Lee spluttered, nearly choking on his wine. "Really, how do

you know about 'gentlemen's clubs'? Are you employed there?"

"Ha ha. Wish that my life was so interesting. Nobody can really confirm it, but being in media, we get to hear just about everything. It's apparently quite the place to go to. If you have money, you can buy discretion, drugs and a no-strings-attached fuck."

Lee pulled a face. "That word doesn't sound good from your mouth."

"Sorry," Brigit said sarcastically, "but I'm a grown woman."

"I know. I'm sorry." He suggested they sit down.

They sat opposite one another this time.

"So, Brig, no boyfriends?" he asked.

Brigit didn't answer immediately. She wasn't sure whether to share her secret with him. "I've been nursing the wounds of a three-year relationship with my lecturer."

"Three years! So, you were seeing him while you were at university?"

Brigit confessed, "Yes. As you know, it's completely unethical for both to fraternise. He could've lost his job and I could've lost my place at university. So, it was a long, secretive and exciting relationship until I graduated."

"Well, surely now you can date in the open? Or is he married, or old, or both?"

Brigit laughed at Lee's multiple-choice question. "None of those. He has commitment phobia; dating a student suited him. It meant a no-strings-attached relationship. The minute we could date openly, he lost interest. Apparently, he's a seasoned seducer of students."

She remembered how flattered she was by him. "All the students seem to flaunt their sexuality in the same way. But you, your beauty and your own sense of style is way beyond your years, Brig." Shit! She had just turned twenty. She was ripe for the taking.

23

"Everyone adored him; they still do, I guess. So, I was flattered," she continued. "And I was smitten. He made me feel so adult, I'm kind of spoilt now. Young boys are just so pathetic with their stupid hard-ons and their pre-coital banter!"

His blue eyes softened. *Those eyes.* Brigit thought they were her godfather's most endearing feature.

"I'm sorry, my darling. This is something that you obviously spoke to your mom about. She does know, doesn't she?"

Brigit could feel her jaw tighten. "You *are* joking, aren't you? Mom and I are notoriously not close. Also, she is such a prude when it comes to relationships and the 'right' thing to do."

"I think you should be a lot more forgiving of your mom," Lee said softly. "She loves you dearly."

Brigit snorted. "I know I sound like a child, but I have mommy issues. My therapist thinks they're actually daddy related but I'm not buying into her theory." Then, as an afterthought, "While we're on the subject of parents, you won't tell Daddy about Pierre?"

"Who's Pierre?"

"The lecturer! He'd kill him."

Brigit had kept Pierre a secret. She had no girlfriends she could confide in and anyway she knew the consequences if it ever got out. As for John, she would never have told him, even now. John would kill any guy who broke his baby's heart.

Lee laughed. "Now you're the one joking. I'm not going to say anything to anyone; especially about spending time here with you this afternoon. It feels kind of inappropriate."

Brigit smiled at him. *All men were boys, no matter their age.* "I know that you feel uncomfortable, but why should you? If Mom met your son for lunch…" She burst out laughing. "Not a good example. Mom would never meet Clive for lunch or go to his apartment for an aperitif. Okay, your secret's safe with me."

Brigit walked unsteadily into the kitchen to get Lee another

24

bottle of red, returning with the bottle and a glass for herself. Ever the gentleman, Lee took the wine, opened it, then poured her a glass, handing it to her as he spoke. "Shit, Brig, take it from me. It's so difficult, this parenting stuff. And as for marriage, that ain't easy either. It's no wonder kids might come out of it a little scathed. But you must know that your mom and your dad – both of them – have your best interests at heart. They really do." Brigit frowned. "They do," he iterated.

By the time six o'clock came, they had drunk the entire bottle of wine and Brigit was plastered. She had moved back on to the couch and had snuggled up next to him, resting her head on his shoulder. "Thanks for listening," she slurred.

"Pleasure my girl." She had felt Lee's awkward attempt at a feel-better pat on her shoulder. It made her giggle a little. "Can you not call me 'my girl'? I'm an adult."

"You're right. I'm sorry. But you called me Uncle!" He grinned and then his face became serious. "Hey, I'd better get going." He glanced down at his Rolex. "I'm going to be late for the guys. Last poker night before your dad turns fifty-five." He was about to stand but Brigit was up before him. She hitched up her peasant skirt and straddled herself across his lap. Drunkenly, she placed her arms around his neck and leaned in to kiss him.

He turned his mouth away from hers.

"Don't," he said. "Please don't do that, Brig."

"Why?" she asked. "It's what I want."

"I don't think it is what you want. And it's not what I want." He spoke to her like her father did when she was a child.

She climbed off his lap. "You don't want me?"

"Brigit, you're young enough to be my daughter." Brigit rolled her eyes at him. "Do you want more reasons? I have a whole list for you. Christ, I held you in my arms when you were born. I'm your godfather! Your dad is my best friend and I respect your mom enormously. And you. I respect you."

Brigit felt foolish. Lee held her chin and turned her face towards him. "Look at me, Brig. Please don't think this is easy for me. I'm flattered. I'm a man, an old man. And you're gorgeous. But don't forget I'm married. Can you imagine the hurt we'd cause all round if any of... *this* happened?"

Lee left the apartment quietly. Brigit lay on the couch, embarrassed and humiliated, even though he had tried not to make her feel that way. Except for their brief encounter at the party, she had managed to avoid contact with Lee. Knowing that it was only polite, she texted him back, making light of her temper tantrum: "Glad it's going strong. I know I shouldn't have left, but it's what I'm known for, so best I don't disappoint."

The thought of Sunday's lunch exhausted her. *I just can't face an argument with Mom and, knowing me, there will definitely be a fight.* What was the point? Her father's birthday would be ruined a second time. She resolved to cancel with him first thing in the morning.

Five

Patty had sobered up. She knew this because performing oral sex on her boss had begun to make her queasy and a lot less lusty. However, the outcome kept her motivated to finish what she had begun.

As her mind began to clear, she realised the impact this could have on Jen should she ever find out. She liked her; it just baffled her how blind Jen was (or pretended to be; the jury was out). But Patty knew that, for the most part, it was easier to turn a blind eye than confront the truth. Perhaps she would've done the same if she was in Jen's well-heeled shoes?

"John-John wants you, baby," he groaned. "Can you feel how hard he is?"

I should have known! she thought as her mouth wrapped around John-John. John's type named their dicks to apportion the blame should they be accused of any sexual impropriety.

She wanted to gag. Luckily Patty was a girl who was good at blowjobs – expert in fact. So, John and his insatiable prick's demands weren't anything she couldn't handle. Her boss wasn't any different to the many men with whom she had come into contact. They probably dreamed of her in the very same position she was in now, and tonight was John's lucky night. Or so he thought. One of the main reasons for employing her, he had said, was because he was convinced that his clients' prurient thoughts would increase their wine sales figures exponentially. And how right he was. She was creaming it. Unlike Jen's friends, she had to work to live, so she had always used what talents she had to her advantage.

She regretted not having drunk more. Alcohol made her think less, and thinking about Jen had made her feel guilty. She was the only one who gave Patty the time of day. They had chatted occasionally, and she had invited her to a movie once. Patty had declined because she didn't want to cross any boundaries between her work and her personal life, but she'd been grateful to her for her kind gesture.

The furore Jen's speech had caused had given Patty the gap she was waiting for. She remembered being surprised by Jen. She had shown some guts. *Good for her! "Nowhere to go." How dare John? Then he draws attention to her pants! Horrible pants, admittedly, but still.* Jen had retaliated. She had spoken out in front of the Stellenbosch gentry, and that's why Jen was ensconced in her bedroom and Patty was fucking her boss.

Patty remembered being pulled from her seat. "You'll have to be my partner for the evening!" John had shouted drunkenly over the loud music. "My wife has locked herself in our bedroom and we can only assume she has passed out."

Patty obliged. "Is she okay?"

"I don't know," he shouted back. "Frankie says she had a word with her about the speech so maybe she's feeling a bit embarrassed. I did try, but the princess is not coming out of her chamber." He laughed. "It's my party and I feel like a fucking thirty-year-old!"

The revellers on the dance floor whooped in delight.

"Here, feel my abs." He grabbed Patty's hand and placed it on his stomach. "Not bad for fifty-five?"

Patty humoured him. "Not bad at all, John."

John laughed at her and grabbed two shot glasses from one of the waiters circulating the dance floor. "Come! You need to catch up. Two for you, Madam." Patty obliged and downed both glasses. She knew the mix would have an immediate effect, but she didn't care.

"Do you want me to show you something harder?" said John.

Patty moved in closer to him, whispering in his ear, "I don't know, John. You've been desperate to show me something hard from the first time we met."

"Come on, Patty. You exaggerate."

Patty lifted her manicured finger to his mouth. "Ssh. I haven't finished."

John looked back at her expectantly. She smiled. "I guess it's on these occasions that one should be more indulgent, especially since you've made me very drunk. And I haven't bothered to get you a present."

They teased each other on the dance floor until most of the guests left. Patty remembered Frankie giving her the hairy eyeball and rejecting Lee's attempts to get her to leave the party. With everyone finally gone, John grabbed Patty's arm and led her across the lawn to the tasting room. It was there that the real fun began.

Patty was too busy focusing on getting John to climax to hear his wife enter. If he hadn't lost it, she wouldn't have realised that something was wrong.

Jen was virtually inaudible. "What the hell do you think you're doing?"

She thought it was her conscience speaking to her, as it often did. She did have morals! When she finally realised it wasn't her voice but Jen's, she jumped up, then stupidly tried to recover some decorum by attempting to stop her boobs from falling all over the place. Patty shuddered. This was not the outcome she wanted. She recalled the way Jen had said, "Patty?" as if she had been stabbed in the back. *What was that Shakespearean line? Oh yes, "Et tu, Brute?"* She couldn't get past that image of her, vulnerable and betrayed. *Yes. Me too, Jen. I'm sorry.*

John was caught with his pants down. Literally. *Fuck! Fuck! Fuck!*

He hadn't heard Patty laughing. When he eventually did, he barked, "Jesus Christ! What's so fucking funny, Patty? Jen has just walked in on us! Christ!" He pulled his pants up and zipped his zipper. He rubbed his temples. *What have I done!* Patty had stopped laughing. *Thankfully.* When he finally looked at her, he saw that her top had been buttoned up and her breasts were back in place. After all that had happened, he still couldn't help thinking how fucking hot she was.

"Sorry, nervous reaction, I guess. Well, aren't you going to run after her?" Patty asked.

John sat with his elbows on his knees, still rubbing his temples. "I can't. That would just cause a scene. She's hysterical. Give her time." He was advising himself it seemed. He'd seen Jen's face. Shit! He felt so bad for his wife. He had hurt her. It was never his intention to hurt her. He loved her. What the fuck had he done?

Patty's heels clicked on the stone floor. He looked up to see her bend over the candle and blow it out. One blow. They hadn't managed to finish what they had started. He had been cheated out of the best blowjob and he was pretty sure there would never be another chance with Patty. *What the fuck is wrong with me?*

As if reading his mind, Patty said, "You're a sociopath, John. Your wife has just caught us red handed and you're looking at me like that. Have you no shame?"

He rubbed his scalp vigorously and said, "I know. I know! I can't help it. I feel shit, Patty! You don't have to tell me how shit

I feel. I know." He looked tortured. "But…" She folded her arms just under her breasts, pushing them up, making them look even bigger. "But I feel shitter for John-John."

"It's very off-putting, you know?" He watched as she smoothed out the wrinkles of her pencil skirt.

"What's off-putting, Patty?" There was nothing off-putting about her. He recalled the night's events: how she had pushed that very same skirt slowly up over her voluptuous hips. He had always perved over her butt. And now he had seen it, squeezed it, grabbed it.

"Naming your dick," she said.

She made him feel ridiculous. All he wanted to hear was how horny he had made her.

Maybe if she'd told him, he wouldn't feel so incredibly shit. "You drive me wild. Even with the crap you've caused."

"Really, John! It's all my fault? You plied me with drinks, remember? I was drunk. I could say *you* took advantage of me, Mr Pearce."

John was starting to feel vulnerable. His wife was out there somewhere, betrayed and hurt. And Patty? Was she implying…? "Uh-uh; you lifted your skirt to tantalise me. What was I supposed to do?"

Her full lips parted into a broad grin. He was mesmerised. *Those lips were around my cock,* he reminded himself. Then, *Jen saw. You stupid sick dick!*

Patty interrupted his thoughts. "You ordered me to show you my butt, remember."

Jesus! How could he forget? He leaned back against the wall, pausing for a moment before he spoke. "I can't help wondering why you agreed after months of batting my advances?"

"I never agreed. You made me very drunk. You took unfair advantage of me, John."

Was she being serious? "Bullshit. You were so ready, your

31

panties were off."

"I never wear panties." She shifted her bottom so that she was sitting on the table top.

He remembered his mouth on her, the taste of her and his fingers anxious to explore her. He had brought her to a climax more than once. "Sorry to be the one to break it to you, Patty, but if you're thinking of joining the #MeToo group, you don't qualify." He laughed sardonically at his own joke. "You were so wet I could've bottled your juices." She had tried not to, but he had noticed her flinch. His tone had become ugly, he was unsure why.

"Too crude for you?" he asked. She didn't answer. Her deadpan expression made him even more uneasy. "Come on, Patty. I was joking."

"Do you talk to your wife the way you speak to me, John?"

"What's that got to do with you?"

"Nothing. Just wondering. It makes me sad that poor Jen doesn't know the real John Pearce."

"Jen knows the real me. We've been married for twenty-four years. We love each other. She's a good wife and an excellent mother. What we did, you know it's not love."

She stood up to leave. He tried to stop her. "You're as to blame. You seduced *me*, Patty. I'm married. And you ask me if I've no shame. Where's your shame?"

He felt Patty prise his fingers one by one from her arm. Her eyes bore into his as she spoke. "If you're trying to tell me that you and little Johnnie…"

"John-John."

"Whatever, John, really! If you're trying to tell me that I am the only person you've broken your sacred marriage vows with, then you insult my intelligence."

John frowned.

"Secrets turn into ugly truths when exposed. I'll start with your constant sexual harassment of me."

"Jen's hardly going to believe you after seeing you suck my dick."

"You're right." Her voice sounded strangely upbeat. "That's why I'll have to tell her about your once-a-month poker evenings." John's eyes widened. Prompted by the attention this evoked, she continued. "I think this information may hurt even more because every one of your friends goes down with you, don't they, John? While your wives do book club, you all frequent an illegal sex club in Cape Town."

He moved his face threateningly close to hers as he spoke. He noticed she stood her ground. "You wouldn't do it. You'd go down with us. You'd have to tell Jen how you know."

"Of course, I would. It would be worth it. Working at the sex club didn't make me a slut, John. Working for you did." She turned to leave.

"You'd be fired and then you'd have no income. Nobody's going to employ you. You've got more to lose than you think." She didn't answer.

He shouted after her, sneering, "You wouldn't dare! You'd have nowhere to go."

Six

Jen didn't know why she had run. She hadn't given it any thought until she'd realised how tired she was getting. She had crossed the farm's boundaries and passed over three of the neighbouring vineyards. *Fight, freeze or flight – that's what they called it.* She had chosen flight after standing frozen for what seemed like ages.

It was only when she passed a group of farm labourers and their families making their way to church, that she realised that it must have been – depending on how one regarded it – as late or as early as seven in the morning. She saw their panicked faces as she approached. The sight of her dishevelled hair and swollen eyes meant choosing whether to greet her (thus acknowledging that they'd seen her and that something was certainly wrong in the perfect world of the white madam) or to ignore her (a show of blatant disrespect and a disregard for social standing).

Jen solved their dilemma by greeting them. "Môre," she chirped as if it were normal to run barefoot through vineyards

35

in last night's dress-up. They stood aside to let her pass. "Môre, mevrou," they mumbled back.

As she passed them, one of the children asked, "Is mevrou orright?"

His father jerked his arm to silence him. They were serious and cordial now, but Jen knew that by tonight they would be feasting on her transgression.

Under normal circumstances she may have noticed the ripening grapes: a glorious season in the winelands and the most popular time to photograph.

She had a flashback to her husband and Patty. He had called Patty, "Baby"! Baby was reserved for her. *Well, that's what I thought.* She suppressed the urge to vomit. The image of the two of them together brought Jen to an abrupt halt. Her legs could take her no further. Her phone dropped as she doubled over, gasping for breath. She fell to her knees to retrieve it. Her hands shook as she dialled her best friend's number.

Frankie picked up immediately. "Have you come out of your room, Rapunzel?"

"Frankie!" Jen sobbed.

"Jen! What's wrong?"

Jen couldn't speak for her sobbing.

"Okay, Jen, I'm sorry I was such a bitch to you last night." Jen could hear Frankie sigh a little impatiently. "But you embarrassed John. On his birthday. You embarrassed us all." Jen became even more inconsolable. "It will pass, Jen. John will get over it. We all will."

"Frankie, I saw John..." She couldn't finish her sentence.

"Jen. I can't hear you."

Jen tried again. "I saw... I mean, I caught John. He was with someone!"

Silence.

"Frankie, are you there?" She checked her phone.

"With that whore?"

A flashback to Patty's boobs. Spilling everywhere.

Jen's sobs affirmed Frankie's suspicions.

"The fucking bitch!" She sounded furious. Good. Jen needed an ally. She needed someone on her team.

She laughed miserably. "Her boobs aren't fake by the way."

Frankie ignored her friend's attempt to make light of the situation. "I tried to warn you about Patty. We all tried to warn you! I told you that women like her are marriage wreckers. But no, *you* liked her."

Jen slumped down with her bum in the sand. "Please, Frankie. Stop lecturing me."

"She's a wannabe, from some shitty place. She wants what you have, Jen."

Jen drew circles in the sand with her manicured finger as she spoke. "I could've said the same about you when you started dating Lee." She didn't mean to say this. Her words had just spilled out.

Jen heard Frankie inhale deeply. "Ok, I'll let it go because you're emotional. I never wrecked a relationship to marry Lee. Ag! I don't know how to explain it to you. You can just see she's a slut. I don't know how you missed it."

"I'm trusting?" Was she trusting or just plain blind?

"I banged on your door last night; I sent you text messages."

I know. Which I chose to ignore. "I thought you wanted to lecture me again. About my speech."

"Jen. She was all over John. I couldn't stay at the party the whole night. God knows I tried, but Lee needed to get home. What with his diabetes, he's such a party pooper! I even told him to go home without me, that I'd Uber. He insisted we leave together. He said you were a big girl and that you could take care of yourself."

Jen's heart burst with love for her friend. She hadn't had many friends growing up. In fact, Frankie was the only best friend she'd ever had.

"I really appreciate you trying to keep an eye out for me. You're a good…" Frankie cut her off.

"The two-timing son of a bitch! How could he do this to you? You must be furious."

"I'm sad, that's all."

"Well, I'll kill him for you!"

At least she had someone in whom she could confide; someone who would help her through this. "Frankie, I'm really grateful that you kept an eye out for me," she repeated.

"As I said, Jen, I couldn't stand to see that slut all over John. He's my best friend's husband. It's the least I could do. You'd do the same for me, my friend."

She certainly would. Right now, though, she was confused as to what to do. *What do women do in situations like these?* she wondered. It's not like she could turn a blind eye to what she had seen.

"What am I going to do?"

"You're going to get the bitch fired, that's what."

"You know how I feel about cheating, Frankie. We've had this discussion before. I've always said that's where I'll draw the line." Jen paused. She had never articulated the rumours she had heard to anyone, not even Frankie. But she knew people must have heard them. This is a small town after all.

"I've never spoken to even you about this, Frankie. There've been rumours about John. You must have heard them?"

"You don't think this is a once off?" Frankie asked.

"I don't know what to think. All I know is how cheated I feel. I don't know if I can stay married to him. I mean what am I supposed to do? Do I divorce him? Jesus, Frankie. What the hell am I supposed to do?" Jen burst into tears again.

"Jen, you're forty-nine! You're not going to divorce him and make it easy for him and difficult for you. Best believe, once he's single, he's not going to be mourning your loss. Older men are much more appealing than older women. Trust me, Jen. I have cum-ed in this area. Pun intended."

Jen laughed despite her misery.

"Look, forget about rumours. There are always going to be rumours. Do you think there aren't rumours about Lee? Or Frans? Rumours will remain rumours unless you decide to expose them. And you don't want to do that, Jen. As for last night; it's a once off. John is a good husband and father. You know he loves you. And you love him."

"Does he? He's a good way of showing it."

"Come on. Lines always blur. Think about what you're saying. Are you going to allow some floozy to enjoy the spoils of years of hard bloody work? The sacrifices you've made as a wife? And what's going to happen to you once you're divorced?"

Jen was silent.

"Jen, what do you think?"

"I don't know, Frankie."

"I do. You'll be waiting for the scraps John and his indecently hot young bride decide to toss your way."

In the past, Jen had wondered why Frankie was so committed to staying married, despite the affair she had confessed to having. Frankie was a realist. She had a great lifestyle. "Lee gives me everything I want, except good sex," she'd once told Jen. "At this stage, average sex is a minor detail compared to the bigger picture. I holiday overseas, I stay in the best hotels, I drive a great car and I never have the stress of work or finances. Lee is one of the most successful and powerful men in South Africa and people respect me by association. They know I'm nobody from a small town in Bum Fuck Wherever. They're prepared to overlook this only because I'm married to Lee. I'm not stupid enough to give it all up for multiple orgasms? The right marriage, my darling Jen, brings respectability, no matter your past." She had chuckled wickedly, "And you know I have a terrible past."

Frankie's voice interrupted Jen's thoughts.

"Jen? Are you still there?"

Jen was still sobbing.

"Pull yourself together. Fix this."

"I don't want to be like my mum." Jen's mother had lived all her life with an adulterous husband, her dad. His affair had been common knowledge in Stellenbosch. Her mom had chosen to overlook the fact that she had a duplicitous spouse. Their marriage had been loveless. She didn't want this. She had said as much to John. He knew her terms and he had broken them.

"I have told you this before, Jen. You may see it as weak, but the way I see it, your mother didn't make the 'other woman' an honest woman. She would've if she'd divorced your dad. That woman would always remain a slut as long as your parents stayed married."

Jen interrupted her. "But at what cost, Frankie? Surely morals come into play at some point? And what about principles? They have to count for something."

"Morals and principles! Please! Your mum upheld a standing in the community and, by remaining married, she chose to maintain the lifestyle that both of you deserved."

Another image of John flashed in front of her, his head tilted upwards, legs splayed open. Patty's head between his thighs.

"The only mistake your mom made was not finding herself a lover. But who knows, maybe she was a lot more discreet than your father was."

Seven

J ohn stood at the tasting room door and watched Patty as she
walked away. He didn't know who to stress about more, Jen
or her. She had climbed into her Toyota Yaris, the company
car the business had bought as part of her package. He watched
her drive down the farm's dirt road (as always, she drove slowly
to avoid killing any animals should they cross her path). She
turned left towards the main gate on the R45 and then she was
out of sight.

What just happened? He so wanted to see if Jen was okay,
but he needed to process the disturbing exchange he'd just had
with Patty. If he didn't know any better… Had he been set up? It
certainly seemed like it. *Fuck!*

He hadn't forgotten his friends' reservations on hearing that
Patty had been poached by him. They hadn't been happy, and they
told him as much. "She knows things about us," Larry had said.
Besides her having a wealth of information that could be used
against them, exposing this 'gentlemen's' club (which probably

had links to Cape Town's underworld) could result in all sorts of… Or was he just being paranoid?

Poker night had started off as a legitimate monthly card game; it was Frans who'd turned it into 'poke-her' night. He'd been going to a gentlemen's club in the city for quite some time. It was he who had suggested that they spice up their regular boys' night, assuring everyone that it was discreet and upmarket – at a price, of course. They were wealthy enough to buy discretion and they were all keen to bring some excitement into their lives. Being in a group somehow made it more acceptable, should their wives ever find out.

So, poke-her night it became. It was, as most of these clubs were, at an undisclosed address in Cape Town. John didn't know how Frans got wind of the club and he didn't really care. It was a consolation that it wasn't one of those run-of-the-mill strip joints that every asshole went to. The club was at the top of an office block in the centre of the city and each time they went, they were given a different password to gain entry. The building housed a well-known finance company, the owner being one of the members of the inner circle of Stellenbosch. The lift had 'Penthouse' marked on it, but a key was necessary to gain access to that floor. That key and the password were given to clients by the security guard on the ground floor in exchange for a very generous tip.

The lift doors opened to a fountain at the centre of a glassed-in entrance exhibiting a spectacular view of Cape Town's skyline and its dazzling nightlights. It was a breathtaking backdrop, and when John's group first saw it they were relieved that their lavish surroundings diminished the potential sleaze that other adult clubs elicited. The interior was decorated with mirrors and chandeliers. The upholstery was black velvet and leather, which, set against the glass and chrome, created a modern and masculine feel.

The women, porn-star sexy, had been carefully chosen to enhance the décor and to titillate. Mirrored tables offered lines of ready-cut coke for an extra fee. John never did the drugs. There was no way he wanted to lose control. He needed to ensure that he wasn't going to land up in a compromising position in front of his friends. He was there for the fun; always careful to keep his shit together, as tempting as all this was. It seemed Lee felt the same.

The others were different. They behaved like caged animals let loose; wilfully blind to the fact that the girls who were propositioning them were just doing their job. On that first night, most of them had blown at least twenty thousand on drugs, drink and hardcore sex.

After that, they – except for Lecherous Larry – had learned to exercise some restraint and stuck mostly to the poke-her game: strip poker, where each man was partnered with one of the girls. If someone lost, his partner had to shed a piece of clothing. By the end, most of the girls were half naked. The winner could choose to keep his winnings or hand them over to the club in exchange for 'time out' with his partner.

John and Lee had always liked winning, and if they did, they kept their windfall. John would quash any guilt he felt about these illicit poker nights by handing his winnings over to an elated Jen.

The woman at the front had commented on this one night. "You're the only guy I know who lands up going home with money." She gave him his wad of cash.

"And you're the only girl I know who's fully clothed in here," he said as he counted it.

"Those are the conditions of my employment," she'd smiled.

"Well, how much do you charge to remove them?" He flashed the wad of cash at her. She could probably smell whisky on his breath. He had had too much to drink, that's for sure. But there was something about her that he was prepared to pay to see.

Her smile faded fast. "That's not what I do, Mr Pearce," she said, her voice cold and assertive. "Thank you for your patronage this evening. I'm told your shuttle has arrived. Have a safe trip home."

Though she'd shut him down that night, as the months went by John learned his boundaries with her and they chatted more frequently. She told him her name was Patty.

"How does a nice girl like you end up in a place like this?" he'd once asked her playfully.

"I can ask you the same question, Mr Pearce. How does a nice guy like you land up here?"

"It's obvious, isn't it?" he'd laughed. "I'm a bored old man out with my mates looking for some fun. And you? Well? You must have an interesting story."

It was more desperate than interesting. Patty had been through a nasty divorce. She'd walked out with nothing. A small price to pay for her freedom. Desperate for work, she was told about a job that had become available that was strictly off the record. An exclusive gentlemen's club needed a woman who was a little older, attractive and who wasn't interested in sex for money. Patty's terms of employment were strictly no sex with the club's patrons, clean habits and a huge amount of discretion.

"There's not much out there for a sales rep who hasn't worked in five years. This was the best I could find, and I'm grateful," she'd told him.

That was how Patty had come to work for John. And since then, she'd spent months avoiding her employer's sexual advances. And last night she had finally succumbed to him. *My dream has morphed into a fucking nightmare!* he thought.

John was now, more than ever, determined to find Jen. He had to placate her. Patty was bad enough; he didn't need to add a scorned, vengeful wife into the equation. He began to run across the lawn to their farmhouse. *I hope to fuck she's managed to hold it together; that she hasn't phoned her book club cronies and spilled her guts to them.* Stellenbosch loved a scandal. Worst of all, his children would be privy to the most embarrassing details about their father. He'd always managed to be discreet about his transgressions. Until now.

Jen didn't hear John come in. After showering, she lay on their bed in a towelling gown, hair dripping, her eyes swollen from crying.

John walked in a little while later, towel wrapped tightly around his waist. She knew he had showered in the spare bathroom.

"You at least had the decency to scrub Patty off you." She looked past him as he sat on the side of the bed and gently rested his hand on hers.

"I'm sorry," he said. "I really didn't mean for this to happen. I was pissed, and she came on to me. You weren't around. Jen, she put her hand on…"

Jen's sudden reaction startled him.

"Please, John, I don't want to hear it! What I saw was bad enough. I don't need you to give me a blow-by-blow account of the event." With a smirk that looked more like a pained grimace, she added, "No pun intended."

She could see that John was hurting for her. This gave her hope, especially when he said, "I know. Maybe nearing sixty is weighing on me more than I thought. I felt wanted, Jen. You haven't really wanted me like that for a long time."

He began to cry. Jen couldn't believe what was happening. He had tried to stop himself, but he had failed. His vulnerability made her heart spill over with love for her cheating husband and she wrapped her arms around him.

"I was such a shit to you, John. My speech was out of line." She kissed him softly on his forehead. "And you're right. I haven't been a very good wife, have I?"

"No, you haven't, Jen. If I have to be honest, you've been distant. Even so, that was a shitty thing I did last night. Can I try make it up to you?" They held hands, both deep in thought.

"Who, besides Frankie, saw you with Patty?" Jen asked.

"I don't think anyone saw me with her. Everyone had left. Why? Do you think Frankie saw something?"

"Frankie texted me about you two. Look." She showed John her phone messages.

John scrolled through them.

"Damn it! Well, text her back. Tell her everything is fine."

Maybe I shouldn't have phoned Frankie. But she is my best friend. She had felt all alone. "I told her!" She watched John's face contort. She tried to placate him. "I was distraught. I needed somebody to share this with, John. She's my best friend and she was looking out for me."

He clenched his jaw. "*Really*, Jen? Frankie will tell everyone. Word will get out. And our kids? Do you want them to hear about this?" Jen didn't answer. "What were you thinking?"

He had gone too far. Hit a nerve. She jumped up, tossed her gown aside, put on her bra and panties, and threw on a dress and sandals. "As much as I take some responsibility, I think it's safe to ask you what *you* were thinking? *You* compromised your reputation and your image with the children. I caught the two of you together. I saw you! Do you have any idea what that was like for me, John?"

John's tone softened. He got up and walked towards her. "I know. I know. I'm sorry, Jen. But Frankie!" He tried to touch her, but she brushed him off.

"Frankie's my friend. She saw the two of you and she tried to warn me." She paused before adding, "Who knows who else saw you. Damn it, John! And what else you've been up to." She grabbed her bag.

"Where are you going?" he asked. "It's my birthday. Brig and Pete are coming for lunch, remember?"

"As you said last night, I have no place to go."

"Come on, Jen, I was joking. Can't you take a joke?"

Resolute, she straightened up and looked him in the eyes. "Not when I'm the butt of your jokes, John. No, I can't."

He rubbed his hair, as she knew too well, when he felt stressed. She wanted to relent. He looked so helpless. But this wasn't one of their normal fights. She had seen him with another woman. He had broken her trust. And her heart.

"I really need to think right now. Away from you. Away from the kids."

"Come on, Jen. Baby, don't go. Please." Her laugh was pained.

"You called Patty 'baby' too. Do you say that to all the girls you fuck?" Jen hardly swore. It jarred when she did, and her husband's head jerked back slightly. Anyway, she liked the idea of getting away. The irony of actually finding somewhere else to go pleased her.

"I reckon after what I've just been through, I deserve to be massaged and pampered. I'm going to check in to a lodge at Delaire Graff." John knew what that was going to cost. "Yes, John, the unaffordable one I've been dropping hints about. I'm going to use your credit card because I reckon I deserve this indulgence."

She knew this time he had no choice. "Okay, ba, um... Jen... and the kids?"

"What about the kids?" She was defiant.

"What do I tell them?"

"I'm sure you'll think of something. You always do."

Eight

John lay on the bed, towel still wrapped around his waist, legs dangling off the edge. His phone rang. Glancing at the caller ID, he saw it was Brigit. He pressed the silence button. John couldn't talk to her now. He was feeling too emotional.

He heard Jen slam the door of her ML, a car that most of her girlfriends drove; except Frankie, who drove a Porsche Cayenne. Lee always wanted to be one up on everyone, and he had been, even at school. John squeezed his eyes shut as he heard the clutch grind into reverse. He inhaled deeply. The tyres screeched before she drove away.

He remained on the bed for what felt like a long time. His phone rang again. This time he had to answer. It was Jen.

"Yes, my love," he said gently.

"Your wine rep just called me! Has she no shame?"

Fuck! He knew it.

"Are you there, John?"

"What did she say?" He sat up.

"I didn't answer. I have nothing to say to that slut."

Thank God! he thought, lying back down.

"I want you to call her. Tell her to leave me the fuck alone. Do you hear me? She must leave me the fuck alone!" Jen sounded hysterical.

"I'll phone her." Damn right, he would. *The fucking bitch.*

"And while you're at it, fire her, John. I don't want to see her ever again."

John couldn't fire her. Not right now. She'd already alluded to sexual harassment. He'd be up for unfair dismissal. The only sensible thing to do was to wait this one out. His mind raced. *She'd threatened to tell about the club.* He was certain she'd act on it.

"I can't fire her, Jen."

"You can't, or you won't?"

"Jen, Patty could sue me for unfair dismissal. She could also turn this thing around and label it sexual harassment."

"Well, John, pity you didn't think about that before she had you in her mouth." Jen's tone changed. It was threatening and resolute; a tone John had seldom, if ever, heard her use. "It's either her or me. And if you don't fire Patty, things are going to get really messy in Stellenbosch. Another golden boy's reputation sullied. I can just see the headlines."

"Don't do anything impulsive, Jen. Please. I made a mistake." He heard her scoff at 'mistake'. "Fuck, Jen please just give this time to settle. At least give some thought to our kids." Hopefully they would make her think more rationally. "I love you, Jen. Believe me, if anyone's sorry, it's me."

He looked at his phone. She had dropped the call.

John wiped his sweaty palms on his towel. How was he going to get rid of Patty? The only way she would leave was if he offered her a cash settlement; a very hefty one, one that would make her disappear with her jaw all but wired shut.

He didn't hesitate. He was exhausted after a thoroughly shit end to his party, but somehow his anger had given him a second wind. He dialled Patty's number.

"John?" Patty said, as if she had been waiting for his call.

"Listen, Patty, I'll cut straight to the chase. Don't contact my wife again. She's gone through enough shit without you harassing her!"

"Hello, John."

She sounded a lot calmer than he was. "I called her to apologise."

In fact, he thought she sounded amused. This irritated him even more. He had no time for games.

"Do you think sorry's going to fix things? You've made it worse."

A WhatsApp message beeped in his ear. He read it before it disappeared from his screen. "You ok? Trying to reach you. Can't face lunch or Mom. Do you mind if I bail?" Another potential fire he'd have to put out. An ongoing battle of wills. It was easier not having to explain Jen's absence; he'd use Brig as an excuse to cancel lunch with Pete.

"Of course sorry won't fix it," Patty said. "I wanted to explain what happened. How drunk you made me."

John stopped her. "Like you had no choice. Don't you fucking accuse me." He stopped. Time to shift the focus of the conversation to Jen. "Jen told me to tell you to leave her the fuck alone. Her words. If Jen swears, you know she's really pissed off." He paused. His voice became softer, more controlled, as if he were reasoning with a child.

"Patty, I can't let things get messy. I don't want to hurt my children and, believe it or not, I value my marriage. Patty? Are you still there?"

"Well, seems a bit late for that, doesn't it, Mr Pearce?" she laughed.

John held his temper. "Look, I'm gonna need you to leave. You're brilliant at your job, Patty and this will have a huge effect on sales, but Jen's demanding I fire you."

"I can't just quit my job, John. Where would I go? You said it yourself. While we're on the subject of 'values', I value the money." Was there panic in her voice?

It seemed to John that he was at least moving towards having a reasonable discussion with her. He could hear her inhale deeply and imagined her tits rising. She was calm when she said, "Look, I also feel uncomfortable working with you after what happened last night."

Maybe this was easier than he had anticipated. "I agree. Then you'll go?" He sat up smoothing out his hair.

"Not so fast. Not without a settlement."

"Okay, fair enough." John wanted this done and dusted as soon as possible. He wanted to concentrate on fixing his marriage, and getting Patty out the way was a huge start. "Three months' salary and I'm prepared to pay you the average commission you earned over this period last year."

Patty laughed. "Oh, John, do you honestly think I'm going to go away for that measly amount? You do realise just how messy things can get?"

John's bath towel loosened as he got off the bed. He readjusted it firmly around his hips, determined not to pander to her. "Well, going to a gentlemen's club isn't such an unusual thing, Patty. I'll admit to it. Granted, it's going to be a rough few weeks, what with my friends and their wives, but I didn't do anything bad. I did what all boys do."

"If the threat of exposing you doesn't frighten you enough, I'll carry on working for you. I have a very thick skin. How your wife will react to me still being around, a constant reminder of your lust, is really your problem."

"Don't. Please, Patty."

Patty's tone hardened. "How will she cope, I wonder, with the scandal?" She laughed loudly at the thought. This only incensed John. "Like I said before, I'll have to tell her how you've sexually harassed me at work. I wonder if Pete will attest to this? There seems to be no love lost between you two. And a heads up, I think he's on to you by the way. And I'll sue you, John, and you'll have to pay me for unfair dismissal *and* sexual harassment."

John sat down hard at the edge of the bed. The bitch had him by the short and curlies. He tried to appeal to her softer side. She was, after all, a woman. "Patty, don't you give a shit about Jen? Think about her. She's been a friend to you. If anybody doesn't deserve this, it's her."

"Do I deserve to be given the short end of the stick, huh, John? The truth may hurt Jen, but a little bit of a wake-up call might save her from complete humiliation and make her stronger. And you? Well, you may learn to stick to your marriage vows and to take stock of those 'values' you were telling me about." Again, she laughed mockingly. "Although, it's highly unlikely.

"No, John, I'm saving *myself* from you, and if by chance your happy marriage is forfeited, I view it as reparation."

His whole body shook. "Name your fucking price! This was premeditated wasn't it? You're a fucking whore."

She ignored him. "I'll have to think about how much; it has to be worth my while."

"Don't call me until you have a figure." John threw his phone on the bed before slamming his way into the bathroom to wash his face, brush his teeth, anything just to cool down. The mirror reflected dark rings under his eyes. It was clear he needed sleep.

He heard the phone ring. "Jesuuuuus!" he cussed aloud as he walked back into the bedroom. It was Brigit.

"Brigit, I'm sorry, love, I was on another call. No, Brig, don't speak about Mom like that, please. She's your mother."

There was a rustle behind him. He jumped on seeing a shadow at the door. Frankie. How long had she been standing there?

"I can't talk to you now, Brigit. Frankie's come to visit." His phone fell as he tried to stop Frankie from lunging towards him.

Nine

The spa was an outrageously expensive retreat for the locals. Jen's lifestyle was above average and, although the price of a stay in the lodge included treatments, it cost much more than even she had anticipated. She had nowhere else to go. *This is becoming my mantra!* She gave the young lady John's platinum credit card and hoped the amount would go through. It didn't.

"Try budget," Jen suggested, not flinching; nothing could make her flinch anymore.

"Six or twelve months, Mrs Pearce," she politely enquired.

"Let's try six."

It was accepted. The receptionist launched into her welcome: "Welcome to our lodges and spa, Mrs Pearce. Please help yourself to a glass of Moët on your way to the golf cart. Gerard, your butler, will drive you to your lodge. It has a private pool." Jen turned to a young man who bowed his head slightly. "However, if you're feeling sociable, you can use the spa's pool. If you'd prefer to relax at the lodge, Gerard will see to all your needs. Kindly ensure that you fill out the form letting us know what treatments you would like and what times would suit you. We can't guarantee the exact time, but every effort will be made to accommodate you."

Jen was about to follow Gerard when the receptionist stopped her. Her tone was less formal. "Mrs Pearce, could I suggest that you lunch in our restaurant this afternoon? Being in the lodge has its advantages, but you'll have the whole night to retreat. It has a spectacular view and the food is out of this world. There's limited space. Can I book a table for you?"

"I'm not feeling hungry right now. Anyway, it's quite late in the afternoon and I'd like to relax a little before I do anything culinary. How about an early supper? Could you book me in for an early supper?" The receptionist smiled at her. Jen guessed she was the same age as Brig.

"Of course. Perhaps you can have an evening treatment. Say an hour after dinner? I can arrange for it in your lodge. Then you can fall into bed."

"That sounds fabulous, thank you, erm...?"

"We share the same name, except I've kept the extra n and y," Jenny laughed.

"Well, thank you, Jenny, it seems as if this is going to be just what the doctor ordered." She grabbed her glass of bubbly on the way out and downed it. Gerard poured her another before driving her through the manicured gardens. The lawns were so lush it was obvious they were watered at least twice a day. Parts of Stellenbosch belied the fact that the Western Cape was experiencing the worst drought in centuries.

Her lodge looked much the same as the others she had passed: a stone and brick structure with huge windows and sliding shutters operated by a switch from inside, as demonstrated by Gerard. The swimming pool was heated slightly. The fridge was not yet stocked as Jen was required to order her drinks.

No expense had been spared. Jen's inner interior designer

revelled in the styling. Bespoke pieces were carefully and cleverly placed in the lounge, creating an eclectic mix of modern and antique, with the emphasis on luxurious comfort. Instead of colour, the designer had used texture in the soft furnishing, the different fabrics lessened the potential for the creams and whites to create a cold and uninviting space. On one wall stood a bookshelf that held a variety of reading materials. Current magazines were decoratively arranged on the coffee table. Televisions were hidden behind panels in both the bedroom and the lounge, visible only at the flick of a switch. *Oh, a designer's dream to have landed a contract like this!*

"Let's hope there are no power cuts," Jen joked with Gerard.

"Not to worry, Mrs Pearce, we do have generators," he said, as if these were as important as the bomb shelters in World War II.

Gerard showed her to her room, easing up a bit as he explained that it was his first day at work and that she was his first client. The bedroom was the haven Jen had hoped for. In the centre was a four-poster bed: minimalist and not loaded with decorative detail or fabric. The white-on-white dots on the percale sheets gave the room a fanciful and fun feel; the towels picked up the dotted theme in the luxurious bathroom.

"I hope you have a relaxed and enjoyable stay," her butler recited as he took the forms for her drinks and treatments. "Your phone dials me direct, so I'm literally a call away."

Jen walked towards the open sliding door in the lounge and breathed in the fresh mountain air, taking in the spectacular view and the vineyards in the valley below. As she finished her second glass of champagne, the lodge phone rang.

"Mrs Pearce, this is Jenny at reception. I've made a reservation for an early dinner at six this evening. The later sitting is fully booked."

She wasn't hungry, despite not having eaten anything. "Perfect," she said, just in case her appetite returned. Then she remembered.

"Um, Jenny, I don't have clothes! My booking was an impulsive one. I saw a little boutique when I came in."

"No worries, Mrs Pearce. If you'll give me your size, I'll ask them to select a few items and send them up to your lodge with Gerard. You can choose what suits you. Do you have a swimming costume?"

"No, I don't. I don't have underwear either!" she laughed, trying to hide her embarrassment. "And I don't have a toothbrush. I have nothing with me except a bit of make-up."

"Not to worry, I'm sure the boutique stocks costumes and I know they have the most exquisite range of lace underwear. Let me see what the owner and I can arrange." Jen felt relieved. Nothing was too much for this establishment and the thought of having to recycle her clothes was one less thing to worry about.

She sat at the edge of the bed overcome by exhaustion. She organised her pillows so that she could take in the view of the majestic Jonkershoek mountain range in front of her. Then she lay down, processing nothing. The night's events had worn her out, and this was the first time she allowed herself to relax completely. Her body clearly responded, and soon she fell into a wonderful, heavy and drool-inducing sleep.

She woke up at five feeling disorientated and switched on her phone to check for messages. The first was from Frankie: "R u ok? Was there room in the inn? (winking emoji)". Her message had come through at twelve that afternoon. Jen replied that she had checked in and that she was fine. The next one was from John: "How much money do u think I earn?!? I see I'm paying dearly for my sin." Jen noticed that the word 'sin' was in the singular. Her lip curled into a half smile. The clever bastard. The last one was from Patty: "Jen, I just wanted to say how sorry I am. My only excuse is that I was plastered. Hope you can forgive me one day."

Jen threw the phone on the bed just as Gerard arrived at the door to collect her for supper. The last thing she felt like. She wanted to throw up. She ran into the bathroom and lifted the toilet seat and hurled. Only bile came up. She heaved again.

Gerard was calling from the lounge. "Mrs Pearce, I hope it's all right if I let myself in. I've been knocking for quite some time. Are you okay?" Jen didn't answer. He called out politely, "If you're not ready, I'm sure I can come and collect you later." He had waited for an answer and when it was not forthcoming, he continued, "I did leave some clothes in the lounge for you to try on. Oh, and Jenny said to leave a complimentary toiletries bag for you."

Poor guy. He got the worst client for his first day!

She rinsed her mouth in the basin and called back. "Thanks, Gerard, I've just woken up. Please come back later."

She chose a pair of silk black palazzo pants and a black and white cotton top. She managed to tie her bob back neatly into a short ponytail. She applied some mascara and eyeliner and smoothed a little gloss over her lips, grabbed her bag and closed the door behind her. She would walk to the restaurant, she decided.

The walk was longer than anticipated, but Jen was fit, and the fresh mountain air helped clear her mind. When she arrived, the maître d' was extremely apologetic, as it was the restaurant's second sitting for the evening and, unfortunately, Jen had lost her table.

"Not to worry," Jen said. "I'll order room service."

"You're more than welcome to join me at my table. I'm alone, and I wouldn't mind the company. I always feel awkward when I eat by myself in a restaurant."

Jen turned around; she wasn't sure if the person was speaking to her or to someone else. A tall woman – very understated but beautiful in jeans, a t-shirt and Tod's on her feet – was waiting for an answer. Jen was starving, and the woman seemed nice enough.

"Thank you. I'm going to take you up on the offer."

They were seated opposite one another at a table near the

window from where they could see the sun finally setting behind the mountain, giving the sky a salmon-pink hue. It was a spectacular end to a very rough day, and Jen marvelled at the fact that she could appreciate such beauty when she felt such emptiness. Her dinner date snapped a pic using her mobile. When she was done, she shook Jen's hand. "I'm Claudia," she said. "That sunset was such a photo opportunity. I always tend to miss these moments."

Jen responded politely, "It is magnificent! I'm Jen by the way."

A moment's awkwardness, then, "What is it that you do, Jen?"

"I'm a housewife. I have two grown-up children, so it seems I'm going to need to find a job."

Claudia laughed. "Nonsense. Just retire."

"I suppose I'll have to. I don't have much work experience. What do *you* do?"

"I'm a psychologist."

What are the odds that I'd be seated opposite a psychologist? "Well, I'll remember to steer clear of all my 'issues'," she said, laughing. "I'm sure that's why you're here: to unwind?"

"Partly true," Claudia conceded. "I have just testified in a child abuse case. I deal with children, so my work is depressing and very draining. This one was depleting. But, trial or no trial, it's my once-a-year treat to myself. And you, Jen, what brought you here?" Her eyes fixed on Jen. Jen felt that if she looked at her any longer, she would uncover the truth.

She swallowed, supressing any emotion that dared to reveal itself to this stranger.

"It was an impulsive decision. I needed to get away, so I climbed into my car and, well, here I am. I've always wanted to come here but it's rather extravagant. But to hell with that, I deserve to be pampered after what I've just been through." She babbled on, trying too hard to sound upbeat. "I even had to buy new clothes at a premium price from the spa's boutique. I didn't pack as much as a toothbrush!" she said, making light of her very urgent desire to get as far away from John as possible.

"Well, you weren't joking when you said 'impulsive'!" Claudia said. "Actually, I was admiring the way you looked. I may just go and buy myself the same top, seeing that we don't know each other. I solemnly promise I won't wear it here."

Jen laughed. "Well, I'm flattered. Nobody's wanted to copy my style for a very long time."

Claudia tilted her head sideways. "I think you're exaggerating. Unless this is the only wardrobe upgrade you've had since the eighties."

Jen pictured herself trapped in the eighties with leg warmers and a perm. The thought made her smile. Then again, there had been those gold leggings.

"No, not exactly; although my daughter may believe this to be true. I don't know if you have children, but girls, it seems, stop thinking that their mothers are cool around about puberty. Mine thought I was embarrassing from birth, maybe even conception. My attempts at being cool…"

The waiter interrupted to take their food order.

"I'm afraid we haven't looked at our menus yet," Jen said, amazed at the ease with which the conversation flowed. "Give us another five minutes, please."

The two women studied the menu. Jen decided on the fillet steak accompanied by a garden salad and baby potatoes, and a side order of mushrooms.

Claudia ordered the same. "Only please see that my fillet is medium. No rare bits."

After their wine was poured, and after they had toasted to "recharged batteries", Claudia said softly, "You said that you needed to get away from home. You don't have to tell me why, but it would be very rude of me not to ask." She paused then said, "I'm not asking to be polite either. It may help to talk. I'm a stranger. It may make talking that much easier."

Jen sighed. "Do you really want to know that I caught my husband with another woman early this morning?" She could see Claudia's eyebrow lift. "I'm not sure if I'm angry with him, that woman or myself."

Claudia leaned towards her. "Why would *you* be to blame?"

Jen swirled her wine around in her glass, took a sip and swallowed before answering.

"It makes me think. Maybe I haven't been the model wife. Maybe I'm boring and I've let a lot go."

Claudia wasn't letting anything go. "What do you mean?"

"Well, I've just resigned myself to the fact that I'm getting old. I sure as hell don't feel sexy or interesting, or needed for that matter, so why should anyone else feel that way about me, especially my husband?"

Claudia smiled at her. Jen liked her smile. It was warm.

"So, what do you do for 'me time and we time'?" she asked.

"Well, my friends and I do book club once a month and we've recently started Zumba class, which is fun. I don't really do anything for myself. I regard it as a little self-indulgent."

Claudia smiled. "Ah, thank you. You've answered my question. Do you think 'me time' is selfish? Yes, you do. Do you think that being selfish is a bad trait? You definitely do. You haven't even mentioned 'we time', so can I just assume that your husband and you don't do much together as a couple?"

Jen looked down to hide the tears that were welling up. She smiled and waved her hand at Claudia to apologise for her emotions. *Have I no fucking self-control?* she thought.

Eventually she looked up.

"I'm sorry, Jen. I was playing psychologist. Maybe I don't know how to engage with people any other way."

"That's fine. You're right. That's the thing. I know we all have choices. I didn't know that my choice would ultimately have a very lonely outcome."

Claudia interrupted her. "What choice?"

"To devote my life entirely to my husband and children," Jen said, knowing she had willingly pushed aside career plans after Brigit was born. "I didn't know how to do it any differently. It just felt like it was the right thing to do. And look at me now," she said, smiling with a hint of self-pity in her voice.

Ten

"What do you think you're doing, Frankie?" John shouted.

"I cannot believe it! You and Patty! You two-timing asshole."

John tried to free himself from her. He pushed her onto the bed, but she bounced back up at him as if she had been catapulted from a sling. Her open mouth exposed a set of bleached teeth. At that moment, she reminded him of the rabid dog his dad had to shoot when he was a kid.

"Since I last checked, I have one wife, and it's not you. You're not my fucking wife!" he bellowed.

John's head bounced sideways as Frankie flat-handed him across the face. The slap had somehow made him realise that Brigit was still on the phone. He lunged to retrieve it off the floor, pushing Frankie aside as he did so. *Fuck!* He picked up the phone and shouted into it, "Brigit! Brig, are you there?"

Silence, then, "I heard everything," before the call disconnected.

Oh Jesus!

At the same time, Frankie was shrieking, "Hit me back. I dare you. Do it!" She was in his face.

"Jesus, Frankie! Brigit. She was on the phone. She heard you, dammit, Frankie." He sat on the edge of the bed, his head in his hands. This revelation seemed to calm her down. "I'm sorry, John, I didn't mean for her to…"

"Please, just go," he said.

She left the room as quietly as she had come in.

Brigit sat on her bed, legs crossed, shell shocked. She couldn't believe her father! This was just too much to absorb, too much to digest. The one person she could count on had failed her, unreservedly. Her heart palpitated. She stared at her phone at the foot of her bed. An unexploded hand grenade. She jumped when it vibrated. Caller-ID read, "best dad". She leaned across the bed to reach it and rejected his call. "Fuck you, Daddy!" she screamed.

She paced up and down her bedroom, second guessing herself. Had she heard right? Did Frankie accuse him of cheating? *Why? Why!* She had to speak to someone! Her therapist was the first person to come to mind and she dialled her number then hung up. She couldn't be certain this constituted an emergency to disturb her on a Sunday. There was only one person with whom she could speak. It didn't take long for him to answer. "Lee!" she cried as she heard his voice. "I need to see you. Something dreadful has happened."

Lee was reading the Sunday papers. He was tired. He'd left the party later than anticipated. Frankie had been fixated on Patty and John. She was hell-bent on keeping an eye on them. And poor Jen; her speech had been caustic. He saw the humour in it, but he knew John so well. He certainly hated when the joke was on him.

He answered Brig's call immediately. He had spoken briefly

to her at the party. But after that awkward afternoon it felt like they had both been avoiding each other; he had to admit, he had certainly been avoiding her.

"Hey, Brig." *That is how the younger generation greet one another?* His son answered all his calls with a "hey".

All Lee heard was, "I need to see you." Brigit's hysteria had made her inaudible.

The last thing he felt like doing was driving to the city. But Brigit had sounded distraught, so he forced himself up from his chair, brushed his teeth, splashed on some aftershave and quickly changed into a pair of chinos and a t-shirt before grabbing one of many sets of car keys. He just hoped this wasn't a ploy to seduce him. *Surely she wouldn't try again, not after he had blocked her advances?* The front door slammed on his way out.

Frankie had left the house early, mumbling something about helping Jen out, so there was no need to explain to her why he was driving to the city on a Sunday. He decided to take the Ferrari. The roads would be quieter, and he could really hit the open road. Driving a sports car at full throttle was something he very seldom got to do, so the drive, at least, was some consolation.

He hadn't even knocked on Brigit's door when it opened. She looked a mess, her eyes red and swollen, her mascara smudged and her hair looking as if it hadn't been combed in a year. He breathed a sigh of relief. She had no intention of jumping him!

"My God, Brigit, what's wrong? Has someone died?"

"Figuratively speaking, yes, someone has just died." Lee knew that Brigit could be melodramatic, and she wasn't holding back. He had forgotten how hysterical young women were. *Thank God I have a son.*

"Okay, make me a cup of coffee, and then we can sit down and chat. Try be calm, Brig. No one's died, thank goodness." He sunk into the sofa.

Brigit didn't move; instead, she blurted out: "It's worse than death. My father is cheating on my mother!"

Lee sat up. "Have you got proof, Brig?"

"Yes," she sobbed.

He needed a whisky, never mind a coffee. He got up from the sofa and went to make espresso for both of them. Handing her one, he asked again, "How do you know?"

"I was on the phone to Daddy this morning. I had WhatsApped him to say I wasn't going to lunch. He hadn't responded. So, I called him."

Lee looked beyond Brig's tear-stained face. He could see a resemblance to Jen. "You're still not telling me how you found out about your dad. Ag, Brig, it may not in fact be true."

"I'm trying to tell you, Lee!" Brigit answered, flustered. "It's true because I heard Frankie screaming at him."

"What! Frankie? My wife?"

"How many Frankie's are there, Lee? She'd interrupted our call. She came in screaming at Dad about being a two-timing asshole." Brigit laughed sardonically. "Dad hadn't dropped the call, so I heard everything." She wiped fresh tears on the sleeve of her dressing gown.

A man's worst nightmare. Being caught out by your wife is one thing, but being exposed as a lying cheat to your children? Eina! Poor John. Poor Brig. And poor, poor Jen! And Frankie? Lee was angry with her for making matters worse. *Why couldn't she have minded her own business?*

"Brigit, do you think your dad knows you know?"

"Of course he knows! He realised I was still on the phone! I told him I heard everything."

Fuck! Lee thought. "Brigit, I, I don't know what to say. Just that we're all human." He could see Brig prepare for battle. "Wait. Let me finish. I'm not condoning what your dad did, but maybe he was drunk. Wait, Brig. Hear me out. Who knows? All I know is, he made a mistake and he was caught. God knows, Brigit, it could be Frankie finding out about us. If we had done something stupid."

That stopped her. "Are you trying to say something, Lee?"

"I'm saying that we all make mistakes. Sometimes we don't think things through. And alcohol can be a very important factor."

"Well, you were drunk, and I didn't manage to seduce you." She was laughing.

If he closed his eyes, it could be Jen he was speaking to. *Brig hated her mom, but she was just like her*. He smiled. "Brigit, I always think things through, drunk or not."

Lee thought about John. *What the hell happened, that's what I'd like to know?* How did he allow himself to be seduced by Patty? He smiled. *Easy. Everyone lusts over Patty*. John was always in control. His mates had often joked with him that he was a dark horse, probably having loads of fun behind their backs. At the club, while the others would lose face, he never once got out of hand. He was a good sport, but that was where it ended.

"So, John, you're not tempted by any of these girls?" Frans had asked him on their way back from the club one night.

"Of course I am, but I can keep my dick in my pants, unlike you motherfuckers!"

They'd all laughed.

"Hey, John," Lee had cut in. "I'm reasonably well behaved."

"Who wouldn't be?" it was Lecherous Larry. "You're married to Frankie."

"Kak, man," John had retorted. "It's his medication; it takes away the desire."

Lee had laughed at John's joke. The fact that it was partly true irritated him. Frankie had an insatiable sex drive which he couldn't keep up with since his diagnosis. He remembered their fight.

"Lee!" she had screamed at him. "I love sex and you're not interested."

"It's the medication, my love. I'm sorry."

"Well you'd better do something, Lee. I can't live like this."

"Are you threatening me, Frankie?"

"No, I'm not threatening you. I'm just telling you that I am young and nubile. So best you get your shit together. That's all."

It was true. Frankie was the babe his friends lusted after. It was Frans who always said that John managed to bag himself the catch of Stellenbosch, and Lee, the sexiest woman alive. "No wonder you're such loyal husbands. You have a lot to lose." This had made Lee do something he didn't normally do: disclose personal stuff to his friends.

"I'm not sure I've still got her to lose," Lee had confessed.

It was John who had asked, "What do you mean?"

"Frankie's been having an affair. But it's over now." The disclosure had stopped their banter.

A considerably sober Larry had carefully probed, "How do you know?"

"I made sure it ended," was all he had been prepared to divulge.

"Lee, are you listening to me?" Lee looked at Brig. "I said okay. You've added a different perspective. But now, what do I say to Mom?"

"Nothing. Don't tell her a thing. Maybe she doesn't know. But if she does, I'm sure she'd want to keep this from you."

"And Dad?"

Lee grabbed his keys from the coffee table and got up to go. "I don't know. Give yourself a bit of time, Brigit. Remember what I said: we're all human."

He saw himself out again, climbed into his beloved Ferrari and pulled off after generously tipping the beggar who had offered to look after his car.

Lee drove home deep in thought. He had left a calmer Brigit, but his mind was racing. Patty was something!

It took someone like Patty to seduce his friend. *Ag, come to think of it, John always had a fascination for her.*

He put his foot down on the accelerator, allowing the car to move at the speed it was engineered to. He would stop at John first. He smiled. *Pay him a visit.*

Eleven

Brig's phone rang. It was Pete. She reluctantly answered, wondering whether he had heard the shocking news.

"What's up?" he said. Brig didn't answer. "Brig? You there?"

"Yes." She didn't feel like speaking to him.

"Dad WhatsApped me. Lunch is cancelled."

She heard her brother yawn. He was always so oblivious to the dramas unfolding around him.

"Mom's apparently fucked off to a spa or something. I love Mom, you know I do, but it's Dad's birthday. A bit hectic of her."

Brigit decided she was sick of being the only child who seemed to be in the loop when it came to their parents.

"I have something terrible to tell you."

"This sounds interesting." He sounded anything but interested. "Bae, can you leave me alone for two minutes?" Brigit knew exactly who he was speaking to. She was horrified.

"Pete!" she scolded. "I thought you broke up with her."

She wouldn't even utter Amanda's name. "She's divorced with children. She can only want one thing!"

Pete mocked, "And so do I. So we well suited."

"Please, Pete, it's really not funny."

"Okay! Okay! I hear you. Now tell me: what drama did you invite into your life this time?" Brigit knew he had no intention of breaking off his relationship, but she had more important things to focus on than Pete's bad relationship choices.

"Patty and Daddy were together last night, at the party!"

Brig jumped as she heard her brother's hand slam down on something hard. "I knew it!" he exploded. "Fuck, Brigit, why you telling me this? What am I supposed to do with this information?"

"I don't know!" Brigit screamed back at him. "What am I supposed to do? It's devastating to find out that Dad cheated on Mom. Who would've thought?"

Pete's rancour came through loud and clear, "Really? You and Dad have formed such an alliance that you haven't even bothered to take your head out of his ass to see that he's not the angel you think he is!"

Brigit found herself pouring a gin and tonic. She didn't give a damn that it was virtually breakfast time. This could be regarded as a special circumstance. It was not lost on her that Lee had left her alone and miserable for the second time. What was lost on her was that she blamed Patty entirely for her father's indiscretion. As far as she was concerned, Patty was the reason her dad had betrayed her mother, and his children in the process.

"What are you implying? Daddy's *not* sleeping around! This is Patty's fault. Patty's a slut. Everyone says so. I bet she's been trying to get into his pants ever since she started working for Daddy. I bet she gets into everybody's pants. Maybe that's why she does so well in sales?"

"You hypocrite!" Pete's voice boomed. It seldom did. "Ms feminist with your constant blah-blah about women having the right to flaunt who they are. Two people are involved here, and you nail one to the cross – the one who happens to be a woman!" There was a brief pause. "You a self-righteous cow! Why don't you fess up about your lover at uni?"

"Pete! What are you talking about?" She didn't expect the conversation to pan out this way.

"The notorious, 'lecherous lecturer'. Is this how you scored your cums, Brigit? Don't you talk about fucking for gain."

She heard Pete's fridge door open. He was downing something. Whatever it was, he always drank straight out the bottle. An annoying habit.

"Are you implying that I got my cum laude because of Pierre?"

"Is that his name? Well, that's what most people think. Patty not too different to you, hey, Brig?" He slammed the fridge door shut.

"How dare you," was all she could say.

"And how dare you, too. Now that your bubble has burst about Daddy, maybe you can focus your energy on Ma, 'cause she sure as hell is gonna need it. And I just want to say that whatever you do, don't tell her. She doesn't need to know, especially from you."

Brigit sighed. "I'm sure she knows. Frankie knows and if Frankie knows then Ma knows."

"Well, just keep *your* mouth shut."

She hated taking instructions from her younger brother. "Of course I'm not going to say anything to her!" Then she did what her mom and Pete accused her of constantly doing: she brought the conversation back to herself. "I can't believe you knew about Pierre."

"Listen, Brigit, forget about it. We've all done things we not proud of. Just don't go tongue wagging if you don't want people to turn on you"

He ended the call claiming he needed to "take a piss". He

really could be awfully crude, but he was kind. A lot kinder than she was, she had to concede.

"Lee," John said as he answered the door. He was the last person John wanted to see.

Lee pushed passed him. "I hear you got caught good and solid. That puts us in a bit of a pickle, don't you think?"

"How'd you hear?" John asked defensively. He ignored Lee's last remark.

"Fuck, John, we're best friends. I can't believe you didn't tell me. But if you must know, I heard from Brigit, thanks to my wife who apparently let rip with you."

John froze. "Why did Brigit tell you?"

Lee sat down on the sofa in the TV room. "I don't know; maybe because I'm her godfather? All I do know is she's very upset."

John walked to the bar to pour himself a scotch. "You want one?" he asked.

Lee nodded. "I spoke to Frankie now-now. I asked what business she had kakking you out. Anyway, I apologise on her behalf. Bloody cheek actually, especially since she's no angel." He scratched his head with his Ferrari key. "She said Jen had phoned her this morning, crying. Ag, you know, I suppose they're friends. Jen would do the same."

John didn't say anything. He handed Lee his scotch. He remained standing.

"She says she's going to Delaire; she's gonna join Jen tonight so she's not alone."

John listened. Lee continued. "Jen's broken, John."

"Do you think I don't know she's broken? I fucking hurt her, Lee. She's a good woman and I hurt her." He pulled on his hair. "But quite frankly, this has got nothing to do with you or your wife." He gulped down his scotch.

"You're right. The major thing that does concern me, though, is Patty. Our group wasn't comfortable about you poaching her from the club. We told you. We were worried, and you assured us everything would be fine."

John refilled his glass. "Jen wants Patty gone, so she'll have to go. Anyway, things would be a little weird with her around."

He saw Lee's eyebrows lift. "So, she's okay to go?"

John threw in some ice. "Not exactly. She's threatening all sorts of things."

"And are we compromised?" John knew what Lee meant by "we". He was afraid that he and their group were going down too. *Well, fuck it. Fuck them all.*

John's tone was resolute. "I don't give a fuck any more what Patty says or does. I fired her because I have nothing more to lose. How much worse can it get? My wife saw us, and Brigit knows about us, so I'm pretty much screwed." He looked at Lee who didn't reply. "So, she'll squeal to our wives about the club. We'll admit to going." John could tell by Lee's facial expression that he didn't quite agree with him. He continued, nonetheless. "We'll get a slap on our wrists like wayward teenagers and maybe the cold shoulder for a while, but it'll be yesterday's news before you know it."

Lee's words were calm but firm: "Here's the thing, John, you're basically saying that we're all going down with you and that you couldn't give a shit."

John finally sat down on the couch opposite Lee. Just last night this very room was filled with friends celebrating his birthday. To try and take his mind off things, he had been watching yesterday's rugby game between the Lions and the Stormers. The Lions had become a team to be reckoned with. He continued to watch the game as he spoke.

"Look, Lee, I'm not saying that at all. I just don't want to be at the mercy of this bitch. Most men go to whorehouses; they're known as strip clubs."

Lee picked up the remote and turned off the television. "Okay, I need to be clear here, John, as I don't think I can say this any other way. You know that the club is one of the best-guarded secrets? Do you know why?"

John shrugged. He chewed on a piece of ice.

"Let me enlighten you. It's run by very powerful okes. They don't want to be exposed, John. This will make the front page of the newspapers if Patty has her way. Christ, do you think she's just going to tattletale to our wives?" Was Lee ridiculing him? "She'll go to the media. She knows if the club is exposed, someone's head is going to roll, and she'll make sure it won't be hers. It would cause a media frenzy if anything should happen to her."

John got up to pour himself another drink. He was starting to feel drunk and, with that, very brave. "So, the club's exposed. What the fuck?"

Lee slammed his empty glass on the coffee table. "When you poached her, I warned you not to because I was instructed to. I got a call this afternoon. Patty has already threatened to expose them. If Patty does anything to jeopardise the club, your head will roll, and they're not speaking figuratively."

John laughed. He couldn't believe the shit that was coming out of Lee's mouth. "You are joking right? Come on, Lee, we're not in Italy. This is not a fucking Mafia movie."

"No, we're not. We're in South Africa, true. But, who do you think runs sex clubs? The boy scouts? The thing is, I'm afraid for your kids' lives. I'm also afraid that you're gonna jeopardise our safety."

John still wasn't buying into Lee's bullshit story. "Kak man."

"How do you think you got into the club?" Lee asked.

"Frans had connections."

Lee smiled at John condescendingly. "It was through me. I got you invited." This is what irritated John about his friend. He liked to flaunt the fact that he was more connected than him. Richer than him. *Fuck him!*

"That's how it works. I know one of the, erm, shareholders, for want of a better word. He's given me business, good business, and I've been a member of his club for a couple of years now. Frans was invited through me, and we thought it would be fun if we went as a group." John carried on drinking while Lee spoke. "You caused major crap when you poached Patty. I had a lot of explaining to do, as I was the one who put you forward as a member. Patty's threat has rattled them. You need to stop her – whatever it takes and no matter how much money it costs. I'm not taking the rap for this, John. It was your blowjob. You pay for it."

The phone rang several times before Patty answered.

"Hello, Patty," John said. She didn't answer. "I feel very cheated out of a happy ending. In fact, the endingsssh been anything but happy."

"You've been drinking, John." She curled her legs under her bottom. This was going to be tedious. She took a sip of her coffee. It was nice and hot.

"That'sh right, Patty. It'sh been a fuck up from shtart to finish. What ju want?" he slurred.

"I beg your pardon?"

"How much ju want to shut the fukup?" He was incoherent. Patty wondered where everyone was. It was his birthday, after all.

She told him the amount she wanted. "Happy birthday, by the way," she added.

"You've got to be kidding?"

Patty was business-like. "No, I'm not kidding. I take it Lee has spoken to you, so I don't have to tell you how serious this is, John."

"Okay, okay," he said, irritated. "That'sh a shiiit load of money. D'you think I have that kind of money lying around in my bottom drawer?"

"No, I don't. But I do know that you'll work something out. You have till Friday." She wasn't sure if he was capable of anything with all the alcohol flowing through his veins. "Why don't you cede one of your insurance policies?" she suggested. "I'm sure Frans will help you." She smiled, knowing that her knowing he had policies to cede would irritate him.

"How do you know...?" He changed direction. "It jush doeshn't sheem fair. I mean, you got to be pleasured and I'm fuucking paying for it."

She really wanted to drink her coffee uninterrupted. It had been a tiring day. She had had a lot of explaining to do, and fixing, for that matter. "You've got until the end of the week, John," she said, wrapping her hands around the warm cup.

"Did you shcrew me over, Patty? I can't help thinking that you fucked me over." Patty ignored him.

"Do *not* put the money into my account. I'll text you an account number." She wondered if John would remember anything tomorrow. "Phone your financial advisor, John." Her sarcasm was lost on her drunk, soon to be ex, boss. "Phone Frans now. I'm sure he'll be able to help you, even on a Sunday night. I don't want cash. Remember to deposit the money, John."

"Yesh, up your arsh!"

Patty laughed despite herself. John couldn't help laughing either. "I'll send you an account number. Now phone Frans. And then go and have a good night's sleep. Maybe you'll dream about me, John, 'cause there never will be a happy ending with me. Ever."

Twelve

Jen and Claudia walked back to Jen's lodge. What a wonderful evening it had turned out to be. There had been an immediate connection between them and, after the initial seriousness of Jen's situation, they had moved on to the issues of men, ageing, children and just living in general.

"So, tell me a bit about yourself?" Jen had said.

Claudia smiled that warm, endearing smile. "I was widowed only five years after my wedding. My husband was killed in a car accident."

"I'm sorry."

"It was the darkest period of my life – his death and the fact that we couldn't have children. Daniel and I had tried to fall pregnant without success. I love children. I guess that's why I work with them; I feel as if I owe it to those kids who haven't been given the parents or the love they deserve."

Gerard had organised for Claudia to share the evening treatment with Jen. On their walk back, Claudia shared that she had been dating a younger man for the last two-and-a-half years. "I met him at a mutual friend's house. Little did we know that it was a set-up! An unusually successful one at that."

He was a well-known Cape Town-based divorce attorney whose clients included many celebrity cases. She nudged Jen: "If ever you want a divorce lawyer, he's your man. He's hellishly expensive, but there's no doubt you will win a very good settlement, especially with what you witnessed this morning."

The moon had risen in the sky, and there was enough light to illuminate the path. It was a perfect summer's evening: crickets chirruping relentlessly and the occasional bat flying low across the night sky, clearly making Claudia a little skittish. *She's definitely a city girl*, Jen mused. There was a comfortable silence as Jen processed the evening's conversation.

"Do you believe in fate?" Jen smiled. "I'm certainly starting to believe that it was written in the stars that I would come here and meet a woman who is a psychologist, who is dating a divorce lawyer. I mean, what are the odds?"

Claudia laughed. "I suppose. Sometimes I see it as just a fluke. I don't know; perhaps it is written in the stars. I mean, I miss Daniel terribly, but I couldn't imagine my life without Leonard. Maybe I was supposed to be married to Daniel for only five years. Maybe I'm one of the lucky few, because those five years of marriage were close to perfect."

On arriving at the lodge, they found it lit by candles. The calming scent of lavender incense wafted through the lounge and generic 'Eastern-style' music played softly in the background. The lounge had been turned into a makeshift therapy room with two portable massage beds placed in the middle. Jen and Claudia stripped down to their panties and lay face down in anticipation of an indulgent hour of pampering. They were silent during their massages. Jen succumbed to her therapist's knowledgeable hands. Her body ached, and the masseuse found every part needing attention.

Before she knew it, Jen had dozed off into a deep sleep. She was dreaming about John. She dreamt that the two of them were making love. He was caressing her breasts, kissing her neck, moving downwards, over her stomach, with his lips. He stood up to face her and he looked longingly into her eyes. "I love you," he whispered.

"I love you more," she answered.

But then his face hardened, full of aggressive lust. "Patty," he said, "baby."

"Mrs Pearce, Mrs Pearce," the therapist was whispering in her ear. Jen opened her eyes. "We're done. Ms Feldman said to say goodnight and that she'd phone you tomorrow."

"Ms Feldman?" Jen asked, disorientated.

"Claudia Feldman."

She began to get her bearings. "Oh! Of course. She's gone already?"

"Yes, you'd fallen asleep. We left you for a while, while we turned down your bed." The therapist handed Jen a white waffle gown. "You should have a very good night's rest."

"Thank you." Jen waited for the door to close.

Waking up from a deep sleep, her dream and the darkness and silence overwhelmed her with an intense emptiness and loneliness. She lay in a foetal position and began to cry. Silent whimpers turned into loud sobs. Her shoulders heaved as she purged herself of the day's trials. Emotions she had suppressed for years came spilling out. She cried for her youth; she cried for her mother; she cried for her children; she cried for herself, but most of all, she cried for her loss. The loss of the man whom she loved and thought she knew. *Who was he? Who is he?*

She was inconsolable, feeling she could not bear to do this on her own. She had to phone someone. But who could she talk to at this time of night? Not Claudia. She hardly knew her, and why would Claudia want some emotional wreck ruining her much-needed rest?

Frankie. *God knows Frankie would call me if she were in a crisis.* Frankie's phone was on voicemail. "Frankie," she sobbed, "I could do with a friend right now. Please phone me when you get this message."

She tried to pull herself together, but she couldn't stand the loneliness, the silence. She would try Frankie's house phone. This was an emergency. *It's late, but Frankie will understand. I would.*

Frankie's landline rang for quite some time until Lee's sleepy voice wafted through the receiver. Jen tried to sound calm. "Lee, I hope I didn't wake you. Is Frankie asleep? I really need to speak to her, please?"

"She said she had booked in at the spa with you. Is she not with you right now, Jen?" He sounded far more awake now.

The room spun. *Oh damn, damn, damn! She probably used me as an excuse to meet her lover! I've just blown her cover.* She thought quickly. "She may have booked in to her own lodge, Lee. I made it very clear with reception that I was not to be disturbed. I took a sleeping tablet, so I haven't been awake till now."

"Have you tried her cellphone?" he asked.

"No, I haven't. I'll try now."

Jen's hands shook as she redialled Frankie's cellphone. Again, no answer. "Frankie, it's me again. I phoned your house. I needed to speak to you desperately. Lee answered. He said you're supposed to be with me at the spa. I'm sorry, Frankie, but I think I've just blown it for you. Please phone me back."

Jen paced, waiting for Frankie's call. This had certainly put an end to her little pity-party. The phone rang and Jen answered immediately.

"Shit, Jen! I should've told you I was using you as an alibi tonight. Sorry." Jen was furious, but Frankie hadn't noticed. "You said that you'd made up some excuse. What is it?" And then as an afterthought, "Are you okay, by the way?"

"I'm fine now. I'll be okay," Jen said. Suppressing her anger, she relayed her conversation with Lee then ended with, "Just sort out your lie, please. I really don't want to be used in your deceit, Frankie. Make sure I'm not implicated in your alibi. I've enough to stress about."

Jen ended their call abruptly. *Bloody self-centred woman!* She got back into bed and lay there in the dark. She was dead tired, but sleep wouldn't come to her. She tossed and turned, mulling over things – things people had said or implied about John. Much of it just didn't add up.

The next morning, she walked to Claudia's lodge for breakfast, wearing a purple bikini – imported from Israel – under a matching sarong selected by Jenny, the receptionist. It was hellishly expensive, but she didn't care. It had been some time since she had worn a two piece or had spent so much on swimwear. But after last night's tossing and turning, she didn't give it a second thought.

Claudia was tall and lithe, with small perky breasts and broad, bony shoulders. She wore a full-piece costume cut high at the hip. "They're coming back," she told Jen. "The eighties' high-cut costumes. Do you remember the girls in the Wham video?"

Jen nodded appreciatively and broke into song, "Club Tropicana drinks are free…"

They packed up laughing. In the background Gerard was preparing their breakfast with a grin on his face, pretending to be invisible.

"You look terrific!" Jen said admiringly.

"How was your night? You were virtually comatose when I left you."

"I hit such a downer."

"Night makes things even bleaker. Why didn't you phone me?"

"I hardly know you, Claudia, and I thought the last thing you needed was an emotional wreck to ruin your holiday. I tried

Frankie, the one who had warned me about Patty."

"Oh, good. At least there was someone you could talk to."

"Only, she used me as a cover." Claudia frowned. "She's been having this affair with a married man for a while now and she lied to Lee, her husband. She said she was spending the night with me at the lodge."

"Oh, that's a bit tricky, and insensitive. Sorry, Jen, I don't know the understanding you have with her. Does she normally use you as an alibi?"

"I wouldn't know. I only found out about this convenient cover-up because I couldn't get her on her cellphone and I was so desperate, I called her house. Lee answered." As she spoke, she realised again the potential trouble she had caused for her best friend.

"Oh my God, I know where this is going!" Claudia said. "So, what happened?"

"I made up some rubbish that I had stipulated I wanted to be alone, and that I had just woken up after taking a sleeping tablet. I told him that it could be possible that Frankie had checked in to her own lodge."

Claudia winced. She took a sip of her orange juice and picked at her fruit salad. "How do you feel about being used in this way?"

"Well, I'm angry! I was feeling this surge of emotion and I needed to speak to my best friend, and she wasn't there for me. For the first time since yesterday morning, I had allowed myself to really feel; and as overwhelming as those emotions were, I had to quell them because I was worrying about Frankie! I hate that she used me, and I hate that I lied to her husband. I don't want to be complicit in her affair."

Claudia was about to speak, but Jen continued with more gusto, "In fact, I feel incredibly angry that she *didn't* spend time with me. Instead, she used me and my situation – my pain – for her own pleasure!"

"Not good," Claudia said. "I do think that you need to have it out with her. Feelings of anger are starting to surface, which is a good thing, but I think that as much as Frankie's behaviour is unacceptable, your anger is misdirected. Start directing it at the person who really deceived you."

Jen agreed, and told her about the things that she had only recently heard about John. In the past, there were nasty whisperings, but Jen had chosen to ignore them. "I have been so focused on my kids and on playing the good housewife that I didn't have time for gossip."

"Is there a lot of gossiping?"

Jen laughed. "Stellenbosch is full of gossips and I grew up with them. My mom had a deceitful husband – my father – and I've learned to ignore people and what they say. I believed that all that mattered was my trust in John. And there has never been any concrete evidence to prove these rumours, until now."

"What about divorce?" Claudia asked. "Is this an option?"

"I'm not sure. I mentioned divorce to Frankie and she said it was ridiculous to even entertain that thought."

Claudia laughed. "Well, that's coming directly from the adulterer's mouth!"

Jen smiled. "Putting that aside, she has a point. Who's going to want me on the brink of menopause? John would move on. Successful men his age will always be sought after, and I'd be a bitter divorcée – lonely and desperate."

Claudia sprayed sunblock on her face. "Perhaps, but it's not about whether he's going to find someone else; it's whether you want to stay in your marriage? Can you stay married to John? Is this what you want?"

Jen burst into tears. "All my married life I've heard: 'You've nowhere else to go,' and it's true. All my inheritance is tied up in the farm. When we first married, I sold my land and ploughed the money into John's – *our!* – farm. The rest of my inheritance is kept in a joint bank account. It might seem short sighted, but at the time, it was the right thing to do. I never married to get divorced. This was a union for life. It was expected of me. It's what I wanted to do."

"And how are you married?" Claudia asked.

"Community of property. There's no way we can halve what we have. And it would mean having to sell the farm. I'd be doing Brigit and Pete a huge disservice."

"As much as you want your children to hold the institution of marriage in high regard, what kind of message will you give them by staying married because you've 'nowhere to go'? Goodness knows, Jen, one is a woman. What is she learning about women and choices from you? And Pete? He needs to learn that women are strong. You are, after all, their role model."

Jen hadn't ever looked at it from this angle. If she had to consider how she had conducted herself over the years, she really hadn't shown her children how to be strong. Although, to be fair, she had shown resilience, and she had shown that marriage needed compromise and commitment. With hindsight, it seemed as if she had been the only one who had done the compromising, although John had always shown commitment. Until now. Jen took a long sip from her cocktail. It was clear this was not going to be easy, whatever she decided to do.

"Look, Jen, I'm serious when I say that Leonard knows a thing or two about divorce and that he'll make sure you get what you deserve. I know it's not in your children's interests for you to cripple John financially, and I don't think you'll feel vindicated by this, but I *do* think that if you are going to leave him, you need to do so with a settlement that you're entitled to. For years you've believed that you've added nothing to your husband's business, yet you've contributed vast amounts of money to the farm. And let's not forget that being a mother is priceless. What's worse is that it seems he hasn't even acknowledged this."

Jen lay back on her deck chair. "No, he has! He has, Claudia. He's always told me he loves me. He's been a good husband and father." She lifted her head to the sun and let the warm rays soak into her skin, as if they would somehow imbue her with strength. "I know it sounds like I'm defending him."

"Do you have *any* money, Jen?" Claudia asked. "The initial cost of going to a good lawyer is huge, but if you do decide to divorce you can claim costs from John."

Jen thought about it. Actually, she did have some money stashed away like a miser in her bottom shoe drawer.

"I do," she said. "I have about fifty thousand in cash. Is this enough?"

"God girl, more than enough! What did you do, rob a bank?"

Jen laughed. She told Claudia about John's poker nights and she felt a resurgence of warmth towards him when she relayed how generous he had been, and still is, by giving her his winnings. Claudia frowned and asked Jen about the seemingly innocent boys' night out.

"Well, it started off at a men's-only drinking spot in Stellenbosch and then they became more serious about the game. For about the past two years they've been going to Cape Town to a poker club. I know they're spending a fortune there, and I think that's why John gives me his winnings; he feels guilty about his indulgence. He said it's insanely overpriced but he's part of the group. It's the way things have always worked with his friends."

Claudia's frown deepened. "Do you know the poker club's name? Have you seen any credit card statements?"

"Yes, it's called something like Boys' Gaming or Boys' Games. Not sure. Why?"

"Jesus, Jen. Your husband and his friends have been going to an upmarket brothel."

"What are you talking about?"

"Jen, there are high-class, highly paid prostitutes strutting their stuff there. The 'gentlemen' play all sorts of card games, yes, but there's a sexual twist to the games. What's more, whatever the sexual fantasy, within reason, will be played out for the client, at a fee, of course."

Oh my God, oh my God, oh my God! How much more of this do I have to take? She tried to compose herself. She was hoarse when she did eventually speak. "How do you know?"

"I told you. My boyfriend rubs shoulders with celebrities and wealthy businessmen. His colleague was invited there by one of the clients whom he had represented. He asked Leonard to tag along. It was the client's way of saying thank you to Ron. Look, this is extremely confidential. Leonard would be really upset if he knew I'd told you about this club. He told me in confidence. It's completely under the radar, and it's owned by top-notch businessmen – men his firm solicits, relies on, for business. Use this information to make an informed decision about your husband, Jen, but please, I beg you not to say anything to anyone about it. No one must know that you know, including John."

Thirteen

It was nine at night and John had eaten nothing the whole day. No wonder he was so drunk. He staggered from his chair towards the kitchen to make himself a sandwich when the doorbell rang. *Who the fuck can it be at this time of night?* If it was Lee again... He opened the door. Frankie stood at the threshold wearing a translucent dress with nothing on underneath. Her Louis Vuitton overnight bag hung from the crook of one arm. Lee bought her a piece of Vuitton luggage every year for her birthday. John knew because Jen had told him this ad nauseam.

"I've come for the night," she purred. Her tone changed. "You've been drinking! You smell of whisky and your dick's hanging out of your pants."

John, too drunk to be embarrassed, shoved John-John back inside his pants, slurring as he struggled to zip up his zipper. "Lishen, Frankie, as much as I'd love to fu...ck you the whole night through, I've had a crrrap day. I haven't eaten and I haven't shlept and pleash don't forget that my wife shaw Patty giving me a blowjob."

Frankie laughed. "That's why I'm here, to remind you that sex with Patty is nothing in comparison to sex with me, you cheating son of a bitch."

"We did not have sheeex," John slurred. He watched as she sauntered passed him and dropped her priceless bag on the entrance table.

Frankie laughed uproariously. "Okay, Mr President." She grabbed his hand and placed it on her crotch. "Feel this. You don't expect to do nothing about it, do you?"

He grabbed her arm and twisted her around. He held both her arms up against the door and pushed up against her, trying to recover his balance. He whispered in her ear, "My wife'sh hurting. Have you no fuck…ing shame?"

Then he released her hands and walked to the bar to pour another drink. "Make me shome shupper," he ordered. She bent over to get some clothes from her bag. "Nah," he said, "make my shupper naked."

Frankie was only too happy to oblige. John knew she loved the idea of domination. Still in stilettos yet naked except for her translucent shift, she opened the refrigerator and looked inside.

John watched as she bent over to get the salad from the fridge. He knew that she knew that he was watching her. *Fucking tease!* John could not resist her.

There was a crash. He had pushed the fruit bowl off the kitchen counter onto the floor. He sat her on the edge of the countertop and nudged her legs open with his head and ran his tongue up her thigh, pressing hard into her flesh with his hands. He was bruising her, but he knew she loved the sensation of pain and pleasure. His tongue reached her as his hands did and she arched her back and allowed him to do as he wanted. John was an expert. If anyone could attest to this, it was Frankie. His desire to please her intensified her pleasure and, after she had climaxed, he slid her backwards across the counter to make room for himself. His mouth was on her breast and he entered her with such force that she screamed in ecstasy. He slammed into her several times and then it was over. He remained inside her. "How am I shupposed to get rid of you? You are shublime."

Frankie's response was a satisfied smile.

"I want to keep you locked up. I'd have you as my shex shlave and do things with you twenty-four-sheven. Lee'sss lucky."

Frankie kissed him on the mouth long and hard.

"There's nothing like marriage to ruin one's sex life, isn't there, John?" She climbed off the counter. "Thanks for the reminder! I'd better turn on my phone. Lee may be trying to get hold of me."

John watched her leave the room. She had a hot body and she knew it. Her legs were the longest of any woman he had ever seen. She had beautifully shaped calves and her thighs were free from cellulite and stretch marks. Her breasts were naturally big, and she showed them off as often as she could. As she walked away from him, he watched how they moved, mesmerised.

"Yourshhh have to be the mosht inviting set of mammary glands I've ever come across," he called at her. She turned to show them off.

He heard her shout from the lounge, "According to your wife, Patty's boobs are real."

John laughed. "I never kish and tell." Frankie returned with her phone in her hand, laughing. "After last night, you're more of a show-and-tell kind of a guy!"

John ignored her. "My wife can be quite a bitsh about you, Frankie. She says the reashon why you only had one child ish because you are vain, and you didn't want to get stretch marksh and sagging boobsh."

Frankie's phone was beeping a slew of messages, but she ignored them. "She's right. I was lucky enough to have escaped them with Clive. There's no way a second sleepless, demanding baby could be any compensation for losing my sex appeal."

"Well, Jen'sh body ishn't bad for a woman who hash carried two children." Frankie nodded in agreement. "I offered to pay for her boobsh, but she said the push-up bra does the job jusht fine."

Frankie made him coffee while he made a simple salad of lettuce and tomatoes with slices of avocado on each plate. "Maybe you should tell her the truth," she said mockingly. "That you're a boob man and the push-up bra isn't doing it for you."

John's tone was defensive. "My wife ish exactly what I want from a wife. She'sh gorgeoush."

"She is pretty," Frankie said.

"There'sh no denying that she'sh not like you and Patty. Women like you are made for shex."

Frankie laughed at him. "I'm not sure if that's a compliment or an insult."

"It'sh the truth." John gulped down his coffee. "You girls love your Hollywood waxes and showing off what'sh on offer. How are we supposed to say no?"

Frankie wasn't listening to him. She was listening to her voice messages. He carried on cooking, lightly oiling the frying pan and allowing the salmon to sear on each side. He ground black pepper and salt and squeezed some lemon over the fish.

He plated the food, but Frankie was in the passage, on the phone.

Fuck that, he thought, *I'm starting without her*. He scoffed down his meal ravenously. He had just finished when Frankie walked in, ashen. Panic was written all over her face.

"What's wrong?" John asked, sounding completely sober.

"That pathetic wife of yours tried to get hold of me tonight! She was depressed and needed a shoulder to cry on," Frankie mocked. "My phone was off, so guess what she did?"

"Hey, Frankie, Jen's been through a lot. Don't be so heartless."

"Defend her all you like, John, but we're about to be exposed for the adulterous couple we are."

"What do you mean?"

"She phoned the house and asked for me. I'm supposed to be with *her*, John!"

John could not believe what he was hearing. He hated Jen for being such a baby; he hated Frankie for being such a tease; and he hated himself for his lack of will power to say no.

Frankie saw the terror on his face. "Let's not panic unnecessarily. Your wife may have been able to salvage the shit she's caused. She told Lee that she had given strict instructions not to be disturbed and that she had taken a sleeping tablet. She said that perhaps I had booked in to my own lodge."

John looked at her unconvinced.

"It could work," she continued. "I'll tell him that that's exactly what happened: that she didn't want to be disturbed, so I decided to go into the city to shop and watch a movie. It is a half truth anyway. I did go shopping earlier this evening when he told me he was on his way to you. I couldn't go back home because I was supposed to be with Jen." She pressed up against him and placed her hand on his front. "And I was hell-bent on spending the night with you." She laughed when she saw the worry on his face. "It's going to be okay. I'm going to phone Lee now to say I'm on my way back from the city and that Jen had wanted to be alone. I just need to take a quick shower."

John was fascinated by how calm Frankie could be. *It must come with years of practise.* He looked at Frankie's untouched meal and decided he'd eat it; she certainly wasn't going to be staying. Although, one never could tell with Frankie.

Lee answered Frankie's call immediately. She could hear the television in the background.

"Hi, darling, it's me. I'm on my way back from Cape Town. I decided to take in a movie."

"Hold on, I can hardly hear you." She heard him rummaging for the remote. Then silence.

"You're sounding upbeat," Lee said. "Jen's trying to reach you. I thought you were with her." His tone was reproachful.

Frankie was defensive. "I know. That's why I'm calling you. She told reception that she didn't want to be disturbed. I tried to persuade them to let me see her, but they refused. So, I thought I'd go to the Waterfront and shop and perhaps go back to the spa later. Except, I decided that it was best for her to be alone. I went to see that show everyone's raving about. The one that won the Oscar."

"I thought we were going to see that together," he said.

"I know, I know, but I was there, and our intentions are always good. It was great, and if you want to see it on the big screen, I'll watch it with you a second time."

There was a pause before he spoke.

"Listen, Frankie, Jen sounded pretty distraught."

"Ya, I know," she said, as she took out her clothes and toiletries from her overnight bag, in preparation for her shower. "I saw her messages as soon as I switched on my phone."

"Did you manage to speak to her?"

"Ya. I did. She'll be okay." Frankie's voice echoed in their friends' bathroom. "She just needed a shoulder to cry on. She's fine for the time being, I guess."

Lee unpaused the programme he was watching.

"Okay, darling. Drive carefully. I'll see you in about forty-five minutes."

Frankie showered and dressed in the clothes she had laid out in Jen and John's bathroom. She walked into John's kitchen smelling of her signature perfume, Tom Ford's Black Orchid. Her scent wafted in before she did.

"You greedy little pig!" she teased when she saw that he had eaten her food. He was sitting on the counter stool and she pressed up against him from behind.

"I could have you over and over again," she said, cupping him until he was hard. She whispered, "I can feel that you concur. Well, at least John-John does."

He turned around and pulled her towards him. "Do you think it's ridiculous to give my dick a name?"

Frankie laughed. "I think it's quite sexy. You were adamant I address your cock by its name. Why are you asking?"

John shrugged. Reluctantly, Frankie broke free. "I have to go, darling. Wifely duties an' all."

John laughed, and then became serious. "We have to stop this, Frankie. It's getting too dangerous. We have to lie low for a while."

"You see what you've done, John?" she said. "I'm actually pissed off with you. Why did you go and shag another woman? Especially Patty? The last thing we needed was for Jen to find out!"

John was taken aback. "How the fuck does this affect you?"

"Don't be a fool, John. A paranoid wife becomes a snoop, which now makes our meetings more difficult."

He kissed her. "I'm sorry. I suppose I never thought this through."

Frankie loosened her hair from its high bun, letting it spill over her shoulders.

"I mean, seriously, do you think I'm jealous of Patty? I really don't give a shit except that it affects us. I'm Jen's best friend; you had to have known that meeting you on the pretext that I was visiting Jen was the only way we could do this? Especially since Lee apparently knows about my previous little dalliance."

John pulled her towards him. "No, don't," she said. "I have to get back. The last thing I want is a divorce, John. This affair is as good as it's ever going to get for us, and now you've compromised everything."

With that, she pecked him on the cheek and walked out of the kitchen. She closed the front door gently behind her. She didn't need those bloody ridgebacks to start barking at her and alert the staff of her presence; not that they didn't know. Staff had the uncanny knack of knowing everything and saying nothing.

Part Two

Fourteen

Frankie tiptoed into the bedroom in the early hours of Monday morning. She didn't want to disturb Lee, who was lying asleep in bed, a glass of scotch on the bedside table and his glasses perched on the tip of his nose. He had been watching the crime channel, his nightly fix. She undressed quietly, leaving her clothes in a puddle on the floor and climbed naked into bed. She leaned over to remove his glasses and to extricate the television remote from his grip. As usual, as soon as she switched off the television, he woke up.

"You're home," he said sleepily.

"Yip, I am," she said, straddling him to place his glasses and the remote next to his scotch. "Drinking in bed?"

He smiled. Frankie leaned in to kiss her husband, but he turned his face away from her. She'd be happy to go to sleep; she was dead tired. "I see you're not in the mood."

Lee placed both hands on her shoulders. "On the contrary, darling, I'm very much in the mood. I'm a very happy man."

"Ah," Frankie purred. "I love a happy man." Maybe he had scored another million-dollar deal. Who knew? "Care to tell me why you're so happy?"

"I will, in time. But in the meantime, Frankie," she felt his hands move down her body and she had to control her impulse to reject him, "do what you do best."

Frankie knew exactly what her husband meant, and so she remained straddled as she pretended to want him as much as he wanted her. *I'm really tired and I've just had sex with your best friend.* It felt wrong. His eyes were closed, and he had a gratified smirk on his face as his hands squeezed her buttocks while she guided him into her. Frankie thought of being with John, and the almost violent intensity of their sex aroused her. She moved more passionately, more vigorously now, but there still seemed to be no connection between them, so she leaned over to kiss him. As she did, he jerked her head backwards by her hair, away from his face.

"Let's just stick to basics, okay?"

She wondered if it was his intention to make her feel like a whore, but she daren't stop. She knew the rules and how to play by them. It felt like forever for her husband to climax and when he did, she climbed off him and picked up her clothes from the floor before padding to the bathroom to shower. He had humiliated her. He'd been almost cruel, and she couldn't help but feel hurt. She had hoped he would be asleep when she got back into bed, but he had rolled onto his side, head propped up against his hand.

"So?" he asked. "How's Jen doing?"

"Okay, I guess."

"Did you speak to her?"

Why is he asking again?

"I told you I had, love. She seems fine. It looks as if she's considering leaving John. She told me that she had met someone who is dating a very good divorce lawyer. Apparently, he's done some high-profile cases."

Lee seemed interested. He had sat up now. She wished he would go to sleep.

"What's his name?"

"I don't know. Leonard, I think. I didn't ask for details. She didn't seem too keen to chat." *I'm not too keen to chat.* He seemed to know this, but he kept on regardless.

"It must be Leonard Mazwai. If it is, she's going to need a lot of money for him to represent her."

Frankie's tone changed. She sounded aggressive. She was sick of talking about Jen. *I did warn her. It's not as if she hadn't been warned!* Frankie pulled the duvet over her naked body. "Well, I told her that I thought divorce is a bad idea. Really, over some floozy. And it's not like I didn't warn her about Patty. But Jen, she's so trusting, stupid even. I could see Patty was a whore from the moment I laid eyes on her!"

Lee smiled as if he had been waiting to hear these very words. "I guess it takes one to know one," Lee said, rolling over to sip the last of his scotch.

Frankie wasn't sure at first whether she had heard him properly. When she realised she had, she suppressed the panic that welled up inside her. She wasn't going to let it show. Instead she turned victim. "Lee! That's mean! You know my past. I've never hidden it from you."

Lee put his glass back down on his bedside table. He looked at his wife straight in the eyes. "I'm familiar with your past and I know your recent past and I'm very aware of your present."

Frankie battled to breathe. "Wh… What do you mean?"

He held her chin, his eyes softening. "Why don't you try figure it out?" Then he kissed her on the lips. She tried to pull away, but he had a firm grip on her. "I'm going to sleep. I'm absolutely knackered and I need to be in the city tomorrow." He glanced at the clock beside his bed. "Well, today, I guess. I'll only be back Tuesday, so don't expect me home tonight."

He gave her another peck, this time on the cheek, and then rolled over onto his side, his back to her, and switched off his bedside lamp. It was as if sleep was immediate for him.

Not so for Frankie; she lay in the dark in a cold sweat listening to her husband snore. She wasn't exactly sure what Lee had meant, but tonight's mood was an indication that something was brewing. This was typical of him: he would let her agonise over issues until he was ready to confront them. There were many things that could compromise her marriage. *Has he found out about them, or am I just being paranoid?*

The sun had just come up when Lee left for Cape Town. He had made an early start to miss the Monday morning mayhem on the roads. And, as much as he had business to take care of, avoiding Frankie was his main priority. He had said too much, and it was becoming more difficult to remain mute, let alone stay passive.

He had bumped into their helper Faith on his way out. She had his coffee ready and was about to start his breakfast. He gulped down his espresso. "No breakfast for me this morning, Faith," he instructed.

"Is Boss Lee going to work on an empty stomach?"

Lee smiled. He never could stop her from preceding his name with 'boss' and had given up trying years ago.

"I am, Faith. Too much to do, and I want to miss the traffic."

"Madam Frankie says it's bad for your sugar. You must have breakfast."

Lee laughed. "Madam Frankie," he teased, "is not a doctor. You can give her my breakfast. I'll see you Tuesday, Faith. Lots of work to do."

The traffic became heavier as he neared the harbour. He hated driving bumper to bumper, so he weaved in and out of the lanes, knowing that this did very little to shorten the time it took him to get to his destination.

He was a little more stressed than usual. It seemed everything was coming to a head, and he told himself that he had to stay calm for things to pan out as they should.

After stopping at his favourite coffee shop for a quick takeaway cappuccino, Lee parked in the basement in one of his allocated bays and took the lift to the penthouse, coffee in hand. He took a sip of his coffee in the elevator. Some days he would take the stairs, but today he felt sluggish. He had drunk too much over the weekend.

The lift opened to reveal the morning skyline. Seldom did he take the sight for granted. The club, on the other hand, was a very different space when it was not being used for sex, drugs and debauchery. *A sad place, ironically,* Lee thought, sipping the last of his cappuccino. He was a big fan of irony. *I should have been involved in the theatre.* He sat at his desk and pulled the newspaper towards him. The front-page headline read PROF SUSPENDED FOR SEX WITH STUDENTS. He smiled.

Also on the table were four neatly stacked brown envelopes. Lee picked up the top one. It was an A4 size and thick. He tore it open and reached in to pull out a wad of photographs. He drew out a random picture and studied it. His phone rang, and he answered without checking who it was.

"Ya, I'm here. Found them on the table." He swivelled his chair around. "Have you left already? I was hoping to have a meeting with you this morning."

He listened to the reply then laughed. "I'm looking at them now. Have you got copies for Mazwai?" He continued to study the wad of photographs as he spoke. "Jesus. This is enough to incriminate... You need to get to the lawyer's office. Today. Okay, okay! You're onto it. Thank you." There was a long pause as he listened intently, then spoke. "After the potential fuck up, it couldn't have gone any better. Okay, meet at four this afternoon. Thanks again." Lee's mouth turned up into a half smile. He crumpled the paper cup in his left hand and lobbed it against the corner wall. It bounced into the dustbin.

"Bam!" he said with a self-satisfied smirk. The cup had TRUTH printed on it – the name of the coffee shop. The irony was not lost on him.

Fifteen

Much to her relief, Frankie found Lee gone when she awoke. It was Monday. *Zumba class!* She reached for her cellphone at the side of her bed. Faith knocked gently on her door and came in with a tray of orange juice and coffee.

"Morning, Madam Frankie," she said as Frankie was about to send a voice message. Frankie lifted her hand: a gesture to stop Faith from speaking.

"Hi, Shelley, it's me. I'm not doing Zumba today so don't miss me too much. Love you. Mean it."

Faith had already placed the tray at the foot of her bed and was halfway out the door when her employer acknowledged her.

"Thank you, Faith. You're my sunshine." Faith turned and smiled. Frankie broke into song. "You are my sunshine, my only sunshine you make me happy when skies are grey."

Faith laughed at her. "Haai, Madam Frankie! That song you used to sing to Clive when he was a baby."

Frankie laughed as she reached for her juice. "And now I'm singing it to you! You'll never know dear, how much I lo-o-ve you, please don't take my sunshine away."

Faith closed the door gently behind her. Frankie gulped down her orange juice and drank her coffee – black, no sugar – as she did most mornings. She flung off her duvet and climbed out of bed, grabbing her silk gown from the hook in the bathroom.

"Today you will do what you should have done ages ago," she spoke out loud to herself. "Delete any incriminating photos, emails or texts, you stupid woman."

She couldn't believe how much she had been prepared to risk – how much was at stake if Lee ever found out.

She had more to lose than John; maybe that's why he could be less careful. She wasn't from Stellenbosch and she certainly hadn't had an easy childhood. She had come a long way from being Moorreesburg's mattress. She couldn't tolerate losing the windfall of landing Lee as a husband by means of sexual savvy. Which could well be her downfall if she didn't rein herself in. Her mother had always said that Frankie would either be somebody or nobody, but that her inability to control her impulses would probably ruin her eventually.

Or save her.

At ten, her uncle, referred to by her siblings as Creepy Craig, had lured her into a bedroom at a Christmas party. The adults had been too drunk to notice the two were missing, and her mom had been too distracted by her new boyfriend to care. Once he and Frankie were in the bedroom, he gave her a toffee. She put it into her mouth and began to chew. He warned her she would break her teeth, and he popped one into his own fat, jowly mouth, showing her how to suck on it. "That way, my darling, you learn to draw the juice from it."

Frankie knew something wasn't quite right and began to ask for her mother.

"Your mommy's busy with her new boyfriend. She said I must look after you," he had said. "Let's play a game."

"I don't want to play a game," she whined.

Her uncle wasn't listening. He had held up his fingers. Ten little pork sausages. To this day, she still couldn't abide the sight of a pork sausage. He had put his stubby, fat index finger in his mouth and sucked on it. She watched him, revolted.

"Sis! What are you doing?" she asked. He ignored her question. Instead, he held the very same finger up to her mouth.

"Now you suck it."

"What? Your finger?" her mouth had pulled up in disgust.

She could see she was irritating him. "Yes. Like I was doing."

"Why?" she asked.

"Because we're playing a game."

"Well I don't want to play your stupid game," she'd said as she got up to leave the room. He grabbed her arm to stop her.

With hindsight, he was probably grooming her for other things, but she would never know, because when he grabbed her, she had kicked him on the shin, hard. Creepy Craig howled in pain. She remembered that he had tried to smack her, but he was too fat to be quick. The thought made her smile. She had learnt from her brothers that the groin was the most vulnerable and promising place for a girl to strike, so she had kicked him again, this time between his thighs. The adults had heard his screams and they stopped what they were doing to investigate.

Creepy Craig was never seen again, and although Frankie didn't really understand at the time what her uncle was trying to get her to do, on a subliminal level she knew there was something deviant in his behaviour.

She flicked through the cellphone pics she had sent to John. Most of them were sexy pouts and poses, but there were other, more illicit photos that could get her into deep trouble should they ever be found.

She remembered stumbling across her brothers' collection of porn magazines when she was a young girl and showing them to her mother only after viewing every disgusting page. "Where did you find these?" her mother had shrieked. She had explained that she had found them under her siblings' beds.

"What were you doing snooping in their bedroom?"

Her mother had admonished her and not her brothers. "Boys will be boys," she had said after she scolded her daughter for being a snoop.

The phone was ringing. It was Clive.

"What you up to?" he asked.

"Shouldn't you be at lectures? It's Monday."

"Thanks for reminding me what day it is. I only start at ten. Can't a son phone his mother to say hello?" Frankie laughed, knowing that Clive never phoned to just say hello.

"I'm terribly flattered, but I'm also not stupid. What's up, Clive?"

She walked towards the mirror and looked at her reflection, not really seeing anything.

"I'm sorry I missed Uncle John's birthday. Is Dad pissed off?" Frankie straightened up and turned around trying to assess the size of her ass. She did have a beautiful butt.

"He didn't say anything to me. I'm not sure he even noticed, but it is bad manners, Clive, and you know it. Where were you?"

Clive explained that he had meant to come after his digs mate's twenty-first, but he had drunk too much.

"Well, I guess boys will be boys," she said, echoing her mother.

Mom had not felt the same way about girls being girls. Especially when she had been called to the office because her fifteen-year-old daughter had been giving blowjobs behind the school tuckshop. At sixteen she had formally broken her virginity with the head boy.

Her mother did not put it down to her being a girl when she was suspended for a month in her final year at school. She remembered her storming into their house after meeting with the principal and Frankie's teacher.

"You are such a slut!" she had yelled at her daughter. "It's bad enough I've had to deal with your shenanigans with other boys. But now, the teacher! And such a nice young man. He says you have been coming on to him from his first day at school! Have you no shame?"

Slut shaming at its best, Frankie thought; although it was true. She had to admit that she had pursued the poor young teacher relentlessly. When she eventually had Mr Samuels alone in the classroom for extra maths, he had explained at the meeting that "There was nothing I could have done to avoid her advances. I'm not a monk and I wasn't trained how to avoid such situations at college. I'm really, really sorry."

By the time she had left school, her pass was as bad as her reputation. She knew that if she wanted to get anywhere in life, she couldn't rely on her academic record, or on any of the boys in her town, for that matter. No one would forgive a girl for just being a girl.

It was by fluke that she had walked into the bar of the local hotel on a cold Friday night with Jay, her newly acquired and only girl friend. A group of men was seated in front of the bar's television watching the rugby game. Her future husband had turned around to find a waitress and he had locked eyes with Frankie. Although he had seemed a lot older than her, she knew how to lure men, and Lee would be no exception.

They began to chat. She asked him what the hell he was doing in "this dead-end place". He had laughed that beguiling laugh and said that he was just passing through.

"I would love to hitch a ride out of this town and never come back. Maybe you're my knight in shining armour?" she had flirted.

It was never Frankie's style to feign innocence. She told Lee she had been through just about all the men in her town and, if it must be known, "None of them are worth the dicks they're carrying between their thighs."

Before the night was over, Lee had missed the entire rugby game and had taken Frankie up to his hotel bedroom where he proved to her he deserved the organ that defined him as a man. Lee had thought she would be a one-night stand. She hadn't been offended; she knew that her type was born to be one-night stands.

"I don't know why," he had said after three weeks of dating her, "but I think I'm falling in love with you."

Frankie had laughed at him as she punched him gently on the chest. "Is that such a bad thing, Lee? What's so wrong with falling for me?"

"Well, you know…" Ever the gentleman, he had tried hard not to hurt her feelings. "You must meet my folks," he had said, determined. "Once they know you, I know they'll like you."

Frankie was finally introduced to Lee's family. She knew he came from an advantaged background, but she had never imagined just how advantaged it was. Despite her sketchy upbringing and his parents' reservations, they were warm and kind to her, believing Lee would eventually tire of her.

When he asked Frankie to marry him, there was no hesitation, and no expense spared on their wedding.

Lee's friends were ambivalent about the new girl. The girls saw her as a threat because their men found her tantalising. The only girl who was welcoming was Jen. She too wasn't quite part of the group, and the two of them became close. Two people more different from each other you couldn't find, but they shared a bond in that their husbands were best friends, and both were wine farmers.

"You're a stupid, stupid woman, Frankie!" she said, looking at her reflection in the mirror. "You have been so lucky and yet you're hell-bent on destroying everything: your marriage, Clive's happiness, friendships, everything. You phone John right now and you tell him you agree, it's over."

She dialled his number, and, after two rings, she ended the call. She knew the rules: If John were free, he would call her back. If he didn't, she knew it wasn't safe for them to speak. She ran in her bath, waiting for him to return her missed call. He never did, so she sent him a cursory, "We need to cool things between us."

She climbed into the tub. *Why sabotage all of this for John?* she thought.

John had always been fascinated by her, but the fascination had not been mutual. Frankie had initially ignored his sexual innuendos and lingering touches. But it all changed about two years ago. After visiting Clive in Cape Town, she had decided to pop by Jen's house. It was a sweltering day and she had worn the skimpiest of dresses, showing her cleavage and her bronzed, toned legs. Jen had gone to visit her mum, who had broken her hip and had taken a turn for the worse. Frankie found herself alone with her best friend's husband.

She had never encouraged anything untoward with him. She was used to his sexual banter and it had become a joke between them. After recently terminating a very short and steamy encounter with a French diplomat she'd met on a trip to London, Frankie was game for a new dalliance. Since she had decided to seek sexual pleasure out of her marriage, she had found it tricky to find a partner who was discreet, good looking and who would not succumb to any emotion other than lust.

"Ah," John said as he opened the front door, "you're just in time for afternoon sex."

"I take it Jen's in the bedroom waiting for me," she joked as she ducked under his arm to get through. "Jen!" she called out. "It's me, Frankie. Come and save me from your husband's grubby hands."

"She's not here. She was called to the old age home. Her mom's taken a turn; it seems like this is it for the old lady."

"Oh no. Are you going too?"

"I'm on stand by; she said she'd call if she needs me. I think she wants to be alone with her. She was very close to her mom. Dad was a stinker, as you know, but her mom was a real love," he said.

"She's not dead yet," Frankie reminded him.

"I know, I know. But she hasn't been lucid for months. She's all but technically dead. Poor Jen, it's been tough to see her that way."

Frankie moved towards him and gave him a long hug. "You can be very sweet sometimes, John Pearce."

She wasn't sure why John had misinterpreted her very innocent hug, but whatever the reason, he had brushed his lips against her ear and then her cheek, and before she knew it, they were kissing.

"Stop. Please," she had whispered. But she couldn't stop him because she couldn't stop herself either.

They had just ended their first sexual encounter against the entrance hall table when the phone rang. It was Jen. Her mother had passed away peacefully. Could John please help her make the necessary arrangements with the undertakers?

"I'm sorry, Frankie," John said, pulling up his track pants. "Jen needs me at the home. Her mom's just passed."

"Of course," Frankie said, searching for her panties. "Please tell her I came by to visit just as you got the call. Send her my love. I'll call her later." There was a slight hesitation from John – an attempt to explain. Frankie shooed him away. "I'll see myself out. I just need to use your loo."

That was a 'gentle start' to what would become a very raunchy affair. Sure, Frankie felt guilty; she was, after all, Jen's best friend. *But this isn't an unusual scenario*, she told herself. How many people did she know of who had been having it off with their best friend's husband? Frankie was different though. She had no intention of splitting up any marriage, especially not her own. It would be what it should be: uncomplicated but fulfilling, with the emphasis on discretion.

Sixteen

Pete made his way up to the farmhouse to check on his father. John was a creature of habit and would have been in his office in the cellar first thing on a Monday morning, organising his diary and his staff, before going back to the farmhouse for breakfast. But today, he'd never arrived.

He found John passed out drunk on the couch, the television set blaring and a half-empty bottle of scotch on the floor next to two cellphones. He was far too angry at seeing his father drunk on the sofa to question why he had more than one phone. He was about to shake him awake, when one of the phones vibrated. It was Frankie.

Before he had a chance to answer, the call dropped.

The phone beeped a message from Frankie, and the words flashed on the screen long enough for Pete to read it. "We need to cool things between us."

At first, he didn't quite grasp the message, but it didn't take long for the penny to drop.

"What's up?" Pete startled. He was holding John's phone in his hand.

"I came to check if you alright. It's Monday morning and you not at work."

John was too hungover to get up off the couch. Pete knew that the sight of him irritated his dad.

"When are you going to learn to speak properly?" John barked.

Pete loaded his "Sorry" with sarcasm. He looked around, noticing for the first time that something had run amok in the house. "Where's Gladys? Or is she also nursing a hangover?"

John sighed. "Do me a favour? Grab me some water from the fridge."

Pete did as he was told. The kitchen was in complete disarray. The fruit bowl lay in pieces on the floor.

"What happened to the bowl I made Ma? What's going on? Where's Gladys?"

"I gave her time off. She worked hard this weekend. Anyway, I don't need another judgmental woman in my house. Like your mother, I want to be left alone."

Pete handed John a bottle of water. "Well, Ma's going to freak out," he warned. "And she's going to be upset when she sees the broken bowl. I made it for her in primary school." He sounded like a kid.

John mocked, "Well Mommy isn't here, so there's nothing to worry about, is there?" He winced as he moved his head and Pete couldn't help relishing the idea of his father in pain. Judging from the almost empty Black Label that lay beside him, he must have a mother of a headache.

"I guess Patty won't be coming back to work after you were caught with your pants down." *There, that should teach you, you fucking asshole.* John's eyes widened. "You fucked up big time!"

"Listen, Pete, I'm not your child. No, Patty is not coming back. Brigit must've told you, and I'm not proud. Why do you think I'm lying here nursing a hangover?"

Pete said nothing. He felt no sympathy towards his dad and it was obvious to him John wanted to play the victim. Pete would not allow himself to be manipulated by his two-timing father. John loved to show his son who was in power and it didn't stop him now.

"Don't forget who pays your salary and who puts a roof over your head. Go and do what you should be doing. Go sell wine," he ordered.

Pete had had enough of being spoken down to. His life on the farm had been pretty stress free. It was his mom who had always envisioned him working alongside his dad and eventually taking over the day-to-day running of La Vigne Sacrée, a name he found completely pretentious, particularly since they had not one drop of French blood pumping even vaguely through their veins. He didn't want to disappoint Jen or add to her worries, but he just couldn't take it anymore.

"I'm leaving. You won't find me here tomorrow morning. You can tell Ma we had a fight and I've gone. I can't work with you, especially after what you called me."

"Come on Pete, stop being such a girl."

"You doing it again; you called me a cunt, remember? In front of Patty. In front of everyone. As if that's not bad enough you cheat on Ma. I can't keep hiding the truth about you from Ma."

"Mom knows about Patty." John's eyes were brimming with tears, but his son remained unmoved.

"Stop feeling sorry for yourself. I'm not only talking about Patty, Dad!" He shoved his father's phone into John's hand and waited for him to read the message. While he read the text from Frankie, Pete spoke, disappointment oozing from his voice. "Of all the women, you had to screw your best business investment and your best mate's wife. *Now* look who's the cunt?"

Pete watched his father attempt to rise off the couch, *maybe to punch me*, he thought. His father fell back and he watched, unmoved as the tears rolled from his dad's eyes.

"I'm sorry," John said. "I'm sorry I broke your bowl. I'm sorry I disappointed you and hurt your mom. I just don't know what the fuck's wrong with me. Please, Pete. I need you. Mom will fall apart if she hears you've gone. I'll make this right, I promise."

Too late, you old fuck, Pete thought and turned to leave the room.

Pete heard John's phone beep. He would never know, nor did he care who it was from – not anymore. The message happened to be from Frans and it read that the money from the ceded policy would be in John's personal account by Thursday. If Pete had been privy to this bit of information, he would certainly have been tempted to transgress all boundaries and punch him. That money belonged to the family and John had thrown it away because of a paltry blowjob. Pete had seen his father's credit card statements, which were off the charts, and he had known the expenses were accrued because he could not keep his dick in his pants. He had studied finance at university. He had wanted to show his father that this is where he belonged in the company and not in wine sales. In so doing he had stumbled across all sorts of transactions that hadn't added up and that had ultimately pointed to his father's debauchery.

Seventeen

Frankie had tried several times throughout the day to reach John, but he had not returned any of her calls or her messages. Nor had Lee for that matter. After deleting very personal and lewd pictures, texts and emails from her phone and her computer, she had little else to do. She recalled having read in some magazine, years ago, about a woman who had caught her husband cheating. He had been caught out because he was obsessed with keeping mementos: restaurant bills and pictures of his lover – even her underwear. The suspicious wife had also found a drawer full of love letters. Frankie had laughed at the man's stupidity. But after going through her own little 'collection', she had to admit that she was just as foolish and reckless. She had made it very easy for Lee to find damning evidence if he wanted to.

Frankie's phone vibrated, and, thinking it was John, she answered immediately. It was Shelley.

"Why weren't you at Zumba today? And where was Jen? Is something going on?" Shelley asked.

"Why should anything be going on, Shelley? I've been busy and Jen's at Delaire," Frankie said without hesitation.

"Oh, that's very nice! While poor John is asking Frans to cede one of his policies because of financial problems, Jen is languishing at the spa. No wonder the poor guy was so belligerent on the phone to Frans the other night. I read a text John sent Frans. He's even pulled out of poker nights!"

Frankie, despite being Jen's biggest traitor, was her biggest ally too. "Shelley, you should be very careful what you say about people. Firstly, I'm sure John's financial worries are confidential, so I don't know how happy your husband would be about you disclosing classified information to everyone."

"Not everyone. You," Shelley interrupted.

Faith had come into the lounge with mid-morning tea and some fruit for Frankie. She set it down on the coffee table. Frankie mouthed a "thank you", and indicated to her to open the patio doors. February in Stellenbosch could be stiflingly hot. She continued with her conversation. "You know what I'm trying to say. It makes me wonder whether Lee can trust Frans with his business." Frankie was earnest. She really wondered at Frans's professionalism. *Why would he be so open about business matters?*

She heard Shelley scoff. "Frans didn't tell me. Are you daft? The two of us hardly greet each other let alone speak to one another. I was eavesdropping, and I sometimes read his messages."

Frankie poured herself some rooibos as she spoke, phone pressed between her ear and her shoulder. "Even more reason to shut your mouth. You'll lose business for him, so be careful. That business keeps you in the lifestyle to which you're accustomed."

Shelley conceded that Frankie was right. But being an incorrigible snoop, she wanted to know why Jen had not told the group she was going to the spa.

"It has something to do with that embarrassing speech she

made at the party, doesn't it? Poor John, he felt like such a tool! And I know Anne's husband is fuming too." Frankie sipped her tea listening to Shelley go on about her friend without any encouragement. "Jen needs to thank God for John every single day, I tell you. He's a great-looking man, he's a good husband and provider. She doesn't know what a gem she has."

Frankie knew that, given half a chance, Shelley would be in John's bed. Shelley still believed Jen was the reason John hadn't married her and not the other way around.

Frankie sighed. "You're still sore that John dumped you for her," she joked.

"I am not," Shelley protested. "Although I wouldn't mind waking up next to him rather than next to Frans, I must confess."

"Shelley!" Frankie shrieked. "You're incorrigible. And, you're such a bitch, too." She wondered at the same time how Shelley would react if she ever found out about her affair with John.

"I know. I know. We all missed you today, Frankie, but we'll see you on Friday at book club. Don't forget, we have to make up for the one we cancelled 'cause of the party of the year. Don't forget to remind Jen, please, if she's not still being rubbed and scrubbed while poor John is pressing grapes with his bare feet to pay for it."

They both cackled like witches. "Sometimes I love you. Only sometimes," Frankie said.

"Bullshit. You love me always, because I shoot from the hip."

Frankie hung up. *Can you imagine the scandal if my friends found out about John and me?* It wasn't a pleasant thought. But she knew Lee; he would go to great pains to avoid a scandal, even if it meant staying in an unhappy marriage to an adulterous wife.

At 05:00 am, John awoke with a start. He hadn't slept this long since he'd been at university. To be fair, he'd had no sleep on Saturday night, and Sunday had been an interminably long and taxing day. He reminded himself that he had also spent Friday night with the boys at the club. It had been a tiring weekend with too much alcohol.

He struggled to get up off the couch. His back ached and he had a stiff neck from lying in the same position for almost the whole of Sunday night and all of Monday. He also had a pounding headache and his tongue stuck to his palate. It was a matter of urgency; he had to have water and he had to find painkillers.

John went to the kitchen as fast as his body would allow, turned on the tap and stuck his mouth directly under the stream of water until his thirst was quenched. And now: painkillers. As he moved towards the first-aid cupboard, he stepped on a piece of broken fruit bowl. "Fuck!" he shouted out, pulling a ceramic chip from his bare foot. After popping three aspirins, he decided to take a shower; he felt rancid.

He stood shivering under a stream of ice-cold water, hoping the cold would energise him. It was also a way to punish himself for his recklessness.

He didn't often feel guilty about his sexual exploits. Maybe because he had, until Saturday, compartmentalised them so that there was never an overlap. He was a happily married man and father of two grown-up children, a successful wine farmer and a respected businessman in the community. He was also a man who enjoyed sexual encounters with different women and regular illicit sex. If he had to be honest, sex with Jen was like smoking weed after mainlining heroin. He knew that being married was a very effective smokescreen for his addiction. It was only when the one started affecting the other that he had to face the truth about himself, and the guilt that seemed to follow.

Eighteen

It was Tuesday mid-morning when Jen arrived back home. Turning into La Vigne Sacrée, she found herself appreciating the beauty of her surroundings in a new way, despite the knot in her stomach. Summer was always a glorious time, and the tree-lined driveway of dappled shade made the approach to the farmhouse a spectacular one.

The option of leaving her home and beautiful Stellenbosch and moving into an apartment in the city had seemed exciting at first, but Jen had decided to go back and face John head on. There were so many reasons she couldn't just move out – her children, for one. Although they weren't children any more, she felt that if she did leave their father, she would owe them an explanation first.

Fear was another one. "To be completely honest," Jen had confided to Claudia as they sipped vodka tonics at the lodge's main pool, "I'm afraid. I can't muster up the courage or the energy I'd need to move out." She had been married to John for twenty-odd years. She was comfortable, and she enjoyed her lifestyle.

It wasn't just the money; Jen was afraid of being alone. What would it be like to be a divorcée at this stage of her life? Would she be able to keep up her friendships if she were single? Couples' dinners and functions would be awkward. She wondered if she would be the one invited, or whether John would crack the nod. She was, after all, friends with the girls through her husband. No, she could guarantee that except for Frankie, she would be the one excluded.

"And the thought of dating again," she continued. "Sex with a stranger!" she laughed. "As if any men are interested in women my age, anyway."

What Frankie had said to her about marriage seemed to make sense when faced with the decision to leave. She did love John. He wasn't the first man to cheat on his wife, and he wouldn't be the last.

"I need to confront the issues with him and work on fixing what's been broken," she'd told Claudia when she gave her a goodbye hug.

Claudia had left her with three numbers: hers, her boyfriend Leonard's and Sharon's, a relationship specialist. She had, in fact, made an appointment for Jen to see both Leonard and Sharon the next day. "Just go see them, even if you haven't made any decisions." She warned her that Sharon was no "run-of-the-mill" psychologist. "Be warned, your appointment will be long and emotional. She spends at least half a day in consultation with first-time clients."

Jen parked her car and pulled down her visor to check her appearance, pleased with what she saw. She had taken in some sun, which gave her a bronzed and healthy look, and she had to concede that her facial treatments had made a difference. She'd have more faith in the benefits of beauty treatments from now on.

As she opened the farmhouse door, their two ridgebacks came bounding towards her. She gave them each a pat then she called out to John. To her relief, there was no reply. Jen dropped the beautifully wrapped purchases from the spa's boutique on the entrance table. John was going to go crazy when he saw his final bill.

Passing the kitchen on her way to their bedroom, she had to backtrack. It was in a state of chaos. Pete's fruit bowl was smashed into pieces on the floor, the contents strewn all over the kitchen tiles. There were two dirty dishes on the counter and the frying pan lay unwashed in the sink. *Where's Gladys?* she wondered.

"You can see how badly I cope without you, Jen."

She swung around, startled to see John leaning against the kitchen doorway, unshaven, his shirt unbuttoned. It was clear to Jen that he had been drinking and he looked as unkempt as the house.

"Where's Gladys?" Jen asked.

"I gave her yesterday and today off." Jen's eyes widened as they usually did when she was angry. "I didn't feel like moping around with her mopping up after me."

"Well, this is a fabulous welcome home!"

Chaos in her home always put her in a bad mood. She used to scream at the kids when they had left the house in a mess after entertaining their friends. It drove her crazy. At least Gladys had come in after the party, or the house would be in complete disarray.

"I didn't know you would be coming home today. I didn't know how long it would take you to come back to me." John ran his hand through his mop of hair. "This is where you belong, Jen. There's too much at stake, you leaving. I love you, Jen." She studied his face. He seemed genuine. "Jesus, Jen, I don't know what I'd do if you left me. We're meant to be together."

"I know," is all she said as she started picking up the pieces of the fruit bowl.

"Let me help you." An unusual offer. "I lost my temper and I smashed the bowl. I'm sorry."

"It was Pete's first attempt at pottery. He was in primary

school. I loved that bowl."

"I know you did. I'm so sorry."

They were bent over, picking up the pieces together. As they reached for the same piece, their hands touched. John leaned over to kiss her, and she kissed him back.

"You're looking great, Jen. I often don't tell you how beautiful you are."

These were words of affirmation she had longed to hear, and without thinking, she grabbed his hand and led him to their unmade bed. They made love with an urgency and passion that hadn't been there for a long time. But after sex, while they lay next to each other on the rumpled covers, Jen couldn't help but feel deflated. She was a pushover. *Why couldn't I have resisted him for at least a day?* She had yearned for physical contact, and his kindness and vulnerability had made him irresistible to her; but more than ever, she needed to know that she was desirable to him. How was she ever going to get what she wanted from this marriage if she couldn't stick to her guns?

"I saw two plates on the counter. Did you have a visitor?" she asked as he combed his fingers through her hair.

"In fact, I did," John said. "You asked me to get rid of Patty, so I had to negotiate a…"

Jen jumped up before he could finish.

"Tell me Patty was not in my house! I can't believe that you would invite her here."

"Relax, Jen," John said, getting up off the bed. "Frans came over. I have to pay Patty a substantial amount to stop her taking me to the labour court. I asked Frans to cede one of my insurance policies," he said, searching for his jocks.

Jen was enraged. "Don't tell me to relax! Look at the cost of your philandering! You let this whore into your life and now she has you by the balls. And who does it affect? Me! It affects *me*, John, and our children." She threw his scants at him. They landed on his head and then fell to the floor. "And then you tell me to relax?"

John scooped them up off the floor. "I'm sorry. You're right, but I'm trying to make it go away."

"Really! At a financial cost. And let's not mention the cost to our happiness and to our marriage! Why should money from *our* policy go to Patty, for God's sake? Why should Patty benefit from your..." She had become flustered. "Your... fuck up?" Jen started whipping on her clothes, not caring that her t-shirt was inside out.

"Look, Jen, I did what you asked me to do. I got rid of her, and it wasn't easy. She threatened to take me to court and to make a huge hoo-ha about it. Do you want that?"

At that moment she could have punched him. Her fists were at the ready, but she screamed at him instead, "I didn't want any of this! If you had kept your fucking pants on you wouldn't have to ask me this stupid, stupid question!"

This is why you left him in the first place! Jen chastised herself. *His inability to genuinely see the shit he's caused. And don't forget the so-called poker nights. Are you going to allow these debauched evenings to continue now you know the truth?*

Overcome by exhaustion, she longed to crawl into bed. She could not face the mess, literally or figuratively. "I'm going to lie down in the spare room." He moved towards her, but her hand came up in a gesture to stop him. "Please don't disturb me. I want to be alone, to think."

"But you've been alone thinking since Sunday," he protested.

"Do me a favour, John, clean up the house and the rest of the mess you've made. And, John, just because we had sex, all is not forgiven or forgotten. We have a lot to talk about."

"So, let's talk, Jen, please."

"I just can't face it right now." She turned her back on him and walked out of their bedroom.

The spare room was on the other side of the house, and

sometimes, if they had had a fight, John was usually relegated to the spare bed. Jen opened the French doors leading to the rose garden and the neighbouring farm's vineyards beyond. She pulled back the duvet and crawled into the double bed still clothed. Suppressing the urge to cry, she told herself this was no time to turn into an emotional wreck. She breathed in deeply and exhaled, trying to release the tension in her body. Soon she felt her eyes become heavy, and after a short while, she was asleep.

She didn't hear John tiptoe into the room or feel his kiss on her forehead.

Nineteen

J en woke up just after four in the afternoon to an immaculately
clean house. It was obvious that John had asked Gladys to
tidy the mess, as everything was spotless – something he
was unable to accomplish alone. He wasn't home, but he had
left a message on the fridge door saying he was in the cellar if she
needed him.

The sheets in their bedroom had been changed and Gladys had
sprayed vanilla room mist and had opened the curtains and the
windows, allowing the hot summer sunshine to stream through.
Jen's parcels had been placed neatly on her bed. She unpacked
and hung up her unworn purchases and threw the worn ones in
the wash basket. She kept aside a stone linen shirt dress, imported
from Italy, to wear to her appointments the next day. She certainly
did not want to look like a woman who was falling apart. No
matter how she felt inside, from now on she would project a
strong and confident persona.

A warm, relaxing bath was what she needed. That's one thing

she'd missed when she went away: her own bath. She never bathed in hotels – even in upmarket places like the lodge.

After she had undressed, she studied her naked body in the mirror. Two days of stress had made her shed some unwanted weight. *Well, at least something good has come from this fiasco.* She climbed into the warm water and submerged herself to just under her chin and lay soaking. She washed her hair and she took the time to exfoliate her tired body.

Jen didn't usually spend long in the bath, but she had resolved to indulge herself from now on. She remembered the body butter Pete had bought her for Christmas, which she had packed away in her bathroom cupboard with her fragrances and toiletries. Today was as good a day as any other to use it. She opened the cupboard to search for it and as she did, an unfamiliar perfume bottle caught her eye. *Tom Ford.* Maybe Brigit had left it behind. Her hands shook as she pulled off the lid and put her nose to it. Instantly she knew to whom the distinct fragrance belonged. It was her best friend's signature smell!

The room whirled and, crouching, she held onto the cupboard door to steady herself. "Gladys," she called out, "could you come in here, please."

Jen was on the bathroom floor, towel wrapped around her wet body, holding the bottle of perfume in her one hand and the cupboard door in the other. She stood up and pulled her towel firmly around her when she saw Gladys standing in the doorway.

"Gladys, did *you* pack this perfume away?" she whispered.

"Yes, Jen. Sorry, were you looking for it?"

Jen ignored the question. "When? When did you pack it away?" Her voice was louder now, more demanding.

"When I... cleaned the bathroom?"

"Today?"

"Yes, today."

The truth: a singular, well-aimed blow to her stomach. And

instead of feeling rage and anger, calm descended upon her – a calm that comes with clarity. She sat down heavily on the tiled floor.

My husband is screwing Frankie. John is cheating on me with his best friend's wife. With my best friend. Oh my God! Of course! It all makes perfect sense now.

It wasn't as if the perfume was proof beyond a reasonable doubt. It had acted more as a catalyst: a stimulus to wake her up to the possibilities and suspicions that lay dormant within her subconscious.

"I know you were off yesterday and today, Gladys, but do you know if John was alone last night?"

"Yes, Madam. I saw no one." Gladys had worked for the family since Brigit was born and she hardly ever called Jen Madam. It was obvious she felt unnerved.

Gladys, like many of the workers on La Vigne Sacrée, lived in a cottage on the farm. Her cottage was close to the main house and Jen knew that she missed nothing.

"And Sunday night?" Her eyes searched Gladys's for the truth.

"Sunday? I'm not sure, Madam. You left and then…"

Jen interrupted her. "So, you're not sure. Okay. So, who was here last night?"

"Boss was alone last nght."

"But he wasn't alone on Sunday?"

Gladys's eyes danced around. "I saw Frankie's car. She came late morning, now I remember. Soon after you left." Jen knew she was holding back the truth.

"Don't hide things from me, Gladys. I'm asking you a question. What's going on?"

"Frankie's car was parked here on Sunday, late morning. And Sunday night, Lee was here, but not for long. Then Frankie came back after Lee had gone. It was very late."

"John said Frans was here." There was a long pause. Gladys

looked down at her feet.

"I didn't see his car."

Jen smiled at her helper, her babysitter, her wingman. She knew that she had put her in an awkward position. She knew that Gladys had been reluctant to divulge information for fear of losing her job. Domestic staff didn't involve themselves in the affairs of the madam and the boss.

"Thank you, Gladys." Jen closed the bathroom door before the tears streamed down her face.

Claudia had warned her that after her initial discovery, more truths would be revealed, whether she wanted them to be or not. "And when they do, Jen, you need to explore their validity, but try not to act immediately. Start to gather more and more evidence. Put the pieces together as you would a puzzle. It's important to remain as 'normal' as you possibly can, because if you do reveal what you've discovered too soon, you will blow your one chance at finding the whole truth, perhaps for good."

Jen closed Frankie's perfume bottle and hid it at the back of her closet. She also took out the accumulated winnings that she had 'earned' from John and hid them more securely in her wardrobe. "This is it. It's time to put on those big girl panties, darling," she told herself as she dialled Claudia's number.

Claudia was clearly not surprised. "It's fairly obvious with hindsight, isn't it? Frankie saying she was with you, knowing full well you wouldn't be at home. Instead, she used the gap you'd inadvertently created to spend time with your husband. You now know that John cheated on you with Patty, his boys' night poker games are actually visits to a brothel, what he is buying on his credit card is dubious to say the least, he lied to you about Frans being there last night and you know for sure that Frankie was 'visiting' while you were at the spa."

She reminded Jen of what she had set out to do. "You have two very important appointments tomorrow. For God's sake, Jen, please just go to them."

Another call came through. "I need to take this call, Claudia. It's Pete." Jen added, "I will go, I promise. And thanks for everything."

"Hang in there, Jen," Claudia said, before hanging up the phone.

"I've been worried about you," Pete said, not giving Jen a chance to say hello. "Dad told me you two came to blows after his party. Can't comment on your speech. I was too pissed to say *my* speech, never mind listen to yours."

Jen changed the subject. "Where are you? Are you still at work?" she asked.

Jen could hear Pete inhale deeply before answering. "I'm done working for him."

Jen paused before speaking. "Don't be impulsive, Pete," she advised. "Dad needs you. The farm needs you."

Pete tried to sound convincing, but Jen knew her son too well. "Ma, don't worry about all of this shit."

"I worry about you."

Pete laughed. "Well, don't. It's time you start thinking about yourself, Ma. We all fine. As for me..."

"Does Dad know?"

Pete hesitated. "I'll let you know what I decide. I'm pretty sure Dad's not gonna expect me back after what went down yesterday, and I'm not sure I want to work for him any more. But I don't want you to worry, okay?"

"Just give yourselves a little time." The growing rift between Pete and his father was apparent to all. She shifted the focus again. "Tell me about Brig. Have you heard from her? I see she tried to get hold of me."

"Brig is Brig," he said. "I must admit, she's been quite upset. I think she feels bad about her histrionics at Dad's party. But you never can be sure with her. Phone her back, Ma. Maybe she wants to say sorry."

Jen couldn't face speaking to Brigit, although she knew she must. Pete ended the conversation.

"Ma, got to go. Phone Brig back, Ma. Love you."

Jen sighed. How she loved both her children. But Pete, he had a very special place in her heart.

Twenty

Lee sat in his armchair, feet on the coffee table, reading the paper when Frankie walked in from her afternoon's pampering at Radiance salon in Technopark. She carried a month's supply of creams, tonics, oils, cleansers and polishes – the bare necessities for her beauty regimen.

"You're home. I was worried about you. I've been trying to reach you the whole day," she sang, trying to sound jovial.

He grunted back at her, his eyes still scanning the business section.

"Have you eaten? I asked Faith to make her lasagne you love, and a salad."

He didn't answer but she served up his meal anyway, sitting opposite him at the kitchen table, an empty plate in front of her.

"I'm not eating alone, Frankie. Dish up for yourself. I'll wait."

Usually, she would argue, but Frankie sensed that this would be a bad idea tonight. They ate in silence.

"I need some wine," Lee barked, scraping his chair back. He

selected his farm's flagship, the Cabernet Sauvignon 2001, from the cellar just off the kitchen. One of their best years, but older than Frankie would have thought appropriate for a simple supper at home.

Lee sniffed the cork. He poured a little wine into his glass, swirled it then lifted it to his nose.

"Is it corked?" Frankie asked softly.

He took a sip.

"It *is* corked, isn't it?"

Lee's wine glass hurtled across the kitchen. Frankie shielded her face with her hands as the glass shattered against the wall behind her, red wine dripping down the tiles. Lee's fists hit the table. "Yes, the wine's corked, Frankie. Like our fucking marriage?"

Anger replaced anxiety. She had witnessed too much aggression growing up to not tolerate it in her home. She mocked, "What's with the ridiculous comparison? Feeling poetic, darling?" Lee's breath heaved. Frankie continued regardless, "And what's with you throwing your weight around? Does it make you feel more like a man, now that your dick isn't working as it used to?"

Lee shoved his face in front of hers. His fingers dug deep into her arm. Panting he shouted, "Don't *you ever* mock me!" He grabbed the bottle with his free hand. Frankie cringed. "You hear? I won't have it! Our marriage, darling, is like this wine: corked! Spoiled!" He slammed the Cabernet against the wall so that he was left holding only the bottle neck. "Absolutely fucked!"

Red wine was everywhere. *God, it looks like Violet Beauregarde has exploded in the kitchen.*

He let go of his grip on her. The chair took his full weight as he collapsed into it. "We had a great marriage, Frankie, and you screwed it up."

So, there it was. She had been caught out after all. Anxiety resurfaced and, in an attempt to calm her nerves, she began to pick up the broken glass from the floor. A shard tore into her forefinger.

"Sit down, for Christ's sake! What have you got to say?" he asked. "I want to know what you've got to say!"

"I, I don't know what to say," she said sucking the blood from her finger. "What do you want me to say?"

Lee pushed his chair back and it fell to the floor with a crash. The noise shook her to the core. "Damn it, Frankie, you've been fucking around, and you've got nothing to say?" He chucked ice into a whisky glass he retrieved from the kitchen cupboard.

Frankie pushed her plate of food aside. What was she supposed to do or say? How much did he know?

"When I married you, Frankie, warts and all, you agreed to conduct yourself in a manner that befitted a wife and mother." Frankie so wanted to do a Disney Channel eye roll, but she daren't. She was a child again, and Lee was her mother, her teachers, the principal all rolled into one. She was that delinquent kid, the one who would never be good enough. "That's all I asked of you in exchange for everything I have. Everything!"

Before Lee had proposed to her, he had admitted that her past was an issue, especially with his parents. He was a sought-after bachelor and could have taken his pick. And though he loved her, he had told her that he wasn't sure she could be a loyal and steadfast wife and mother.

"You're not royalty for fuck's sake!" she had joked.

"Not true, darling," he had smiled back. "We are as close to royalty as you can get in Stellenbosch. We're known as blue blood." She laughed. "It's true. You've got to know that I've gone against what I've been raised to think and do, by marrying you. You can't fuck it up for me. Tell me you won't fuck it up."

Frankie had wanted him, and she had never hidden the fact that she desired everything he had stood for: status, wealth and a lifestyle she had only dreamed of. She knew what a catch he was, and she had to admit that she had been shocked he would even consider her for his wife. Girls like her very seldom married a man of Lee's standing. They shagged them, yes, but it seldom ended with a ring on their finger.

"That French diplomat you met in London – I see you've ended that relationship."

Frankie did not respond. She knew he knew about the diplomat because John had told her. But this was the first time he had ever spoken to her about him.

"Is the affair over?"

Forgetting to breathe, she gasped for air.

"Well? Has it or has it not ended?" he shouted.

"Yes, it has. But look, Lee, you haven't exactly been meeting *my* needs."

Lee shook his head in disbelief. Frankie cringed at how pathetic she sounded.

"Are you really that cold hearted? I was diagnosed with diabetes. Give me a break. The medication suppressed my libido. I told you it wouldn't be a permanent thing. How disappointing to find that my wife loves me only in health. How's that for a rude awakening? What's worse is that while I'm trying to deal with my illness, Frankie is only thinking about Frankie. Again."

He downed his scotch and poured another. "It's a pattern with you, isn't it? We said we were going to try for two children, but you couldn't deal with losing your figure for a second time. I'm diagnosed with a serious illness, and the only thing you give a shit about is whether you'll ever get laid again. So much so that you screw a diplomat, and at my personal cost. Fuck! I footed your hotel bill!" His anger mounted again. "As if that wasn't enough, you then move on to bang your best friend's husband at the expense of your only real friendship. Was that even a consideration to you? And with my so-called best mate."

There! He knew about her and John. Frankie recoiled. "You don't give a fuck about anyone, do you?"

She looked up. Her husband towered over her as she sat at the table trying to steady her breath. He wanted, more than anything, to slap her. She could feel it, his eyes burnt into her. It was a look she recognised. It was the first time she had seen it in him.

But then he seemed to collect himself. He righted his chair and he slumped back into it across from her. His voice was softer this time. "What a win for you – Jen being away. You could spend the whole night with her husband, in their bed, or wherever it is you prefer to fuck. Pity Jen messed things up. How fucking inconsiderate of her to call you 'cause maybe she needed to cry on her best friend's shoulder." Frankie looked at Lee. He wasn't looking at her. "I'm ashamed for you, for both of you!" His eyes met hers and Frankie's head dropped. "I don't know what a doos you think I am, but I will no longer be made a fool of and I will no longer allow you to make a fool of Jen."

The last time Frankie had seen Lee even nearly this enraged was when she'd refused to try for a second child. Of course she felt remorse about Jen, but it had never been her intention to break up the marriage. What she felt most at that moment was afraid – afraid she would lose Lee, and as a result, lose absolutely everything.

"I'm sorry, Lee," she said in a little-girl voice. "I love you. I didn't mean to hurt you. You're my world."

"Ag kak, Frankie! I'm supposed to believe your bullshit? Don't insult me, please. That's enough. Just shut up and let me speak. You're not in a position to say another word. You hear me?"

Frankie nodded. Her finger throbbed.

"I'll tell you what you're going to do so that your Persian rug isn't ripped from under you; because that's what you're really scared of, be honest, you gold digging, calculating…"

The unspoken word 'whore' hung in the air between them.

He finished his scotch and chewed on the ice as if this would cool his temper. It seemed to work, because when he spoke again, it was with calm control. "You will end this, uh, relationship with

John. I don't care how you do it. Next, my darling wife, he cannot know I know about your affair, d'you understand? I'm warning you, if you want to save what marriage we have, do not tell him I know about you two. And you will continue to be Jen's friend, unless of course she finds out what you've been doing."

Frankie was about to interrupt him, but she knew he'd meant it when he said she should shut up.

"Unless she figures it out on her own, she must never know. She's dealt with enough, what with a cheating father and a fuckhead husband who has no fucking concept of the words loyalty and honesty. Come to think of it, you're kindred spirits, aren't you?" Lee's laugh chilled her. "Except, I think that you were loyal to him. What a crap surprise it must've been to find out about Patty. But Patty is just a drop in the ocean of his lies and deceit." Lee smirked. "Ag, please don't kid yourself into believing that you're the only one besides Patty. John has many, many women." As he spoke, he placed a plain brown envelope in front of his wife. She looked at it but didn't move to see what its contents were. "Aren't you curious? Open it. Look at the pictures of your adoring lover. See how devoted he is to you."

Frankie's shoulders shook as she wept. She couldn't believe how cruelly her husband was behaving. He had never spoken to her like this before. He hardly ever swore at her. And now she was made to open the envelope. She tore off the seal and shook the contents onto the table. Pictures of John with different women, some of whom Frankie knew or had seen around revealed themselves to her. She lifted one, looked at it then put it down replacing it with another. Lee stood over her, his arms crossed, making sure she had seen every one of them. One series of shots captured John sitting at a bar counter alone. A woman joins him, they talk and then there's a shot of him lighting her cigarette. The final shot in the series is of him leaving the bar with his hand wrapped around her waist. Frankie was one of a multitude of women. Despite feeling anger towards John, it was Lee at whom she wanted to lash out; he had succeeded in humiliating her, and what was worse, it was her husband who had been the one to expose her lover's sexual promiscuity.

"Hurts, doesn't it, darling?"

There were no photos of her with John. She couldn't be sure that Lee didn't have any; he just hadn't included them with the others. *He's been planning this for months. He's been planning to hurt and humiliate me and now he's enjoying it.* Frankie did not believe she deserved this kind of humiliation at the hands of her husband.

"I only hope you've been taking precautions," he said as he left the kitchen, "or else you've given yourself and me something more to worry about."

Frankie followed him down the passage. When he emerged from their bedroom carrying an overnight bag, she started to panic.

"Where are you going, Lee?"

He ignored her as he walked past her to the front door.

"It's late. Please don't go," she begged, running after him, pulling at his shirt. "You spent last night away! Please, don't go, Lee. I love you. Don't leave me alone. Stay. Let's talk things through, please." He shrugged her off, but she grabbed onto him again.

"Don't, Frankie. Don't cause a scene. I'm out of here. I'm giving you time to think about the kind of wife and friend, and in fact, mother, you've been over the last, what's it, two and a half years?"

"I'll sleep in another room. Please, Lee, don't leave me!"

But he had already closed the car door and was reversing down the driveway. She couldn't run after him; the staff would see her. They must have already heard the fighting. Lee hated a scene and tonight had been so out of character. She shut the front door, ran to her phone and tried calling him, but his phone diverted to voicemail.

Frankie's sobbing was guttural, uncontrollable. She couldn't conceive being without him. She knew she had pushed him too far. She had crossed that non-negotiable line, and there was no turning back. Where was he going? Was he checking in to a hotel or did he have someone to go to? She wished she had someone to phone. She didn't want to be alone. She couldn't stand to be alone.

It dawned on her that this is how Jen must've felt so late at night. Jen had phoned her while she was probably having sex with John. The guilt and shame were all consuming. What had she been thinking? What kind of a friend compounds the agony of a husband's betrayal by sleeping with that same husband? Why hadn't she at least done the right thing for just one night? Even if she was screwing John, she could have shown her commitment to her friend by being at her side.

There was no way she was going to make it through the night without help.

She opened the medicine cabinet and took out her "rescue pills" as she liked to refer to them; she swallowed two Xanors. She needed to knock herself out so that she didn't have to think or feel; she didn't want to face what she had done and the potential repercussions of those actions. Frankie could hear her mother's voice echoing as drowsiness replaced anxiety: "Only you will be to blame for your downfall, Frankie. You just don't know when to stop, do you?"

Twenty-one

Lee was furious. Furious he had allowed himself to lose control. *But then again*, he thought, *there's pent up anger that had to be vented*. He had been cautious about having his wife followed and had hired a firm known for discretion and professionalism, and they had charged accordingly. It was easy to uncover her brief affair with the diplomat. Frankie had been reckless in London; he could only assume that she thought that the chances of them being seen together were slim. The two were captured on camera sharing intimate dinners, walking through Hyde Park hand in hand and even kissing at an outdoor concert. The love fest had ended abruptly after Lee had sent (anonymously) incriminating evidence to the diplomat's wife, knowing full well that she would ensure the affair ended without exposing her husband or his lover. She, like Lee, would avoid a scandal at all costs – in her case, for her husband's career. Lee had said nothing of the affair to Frankie. It was in his nature to wait for the right moment. And his gut had told him that it was not quite the right time.

His private investigator had stumbled upon Frankie's next indiscretion – this time with his best friend. After checking that calls between the diplomat and his client's wife had dwindled to zero, he noticed that her account was soon reflecting regular calls to and from an unfamiliar number. Thinking the diplomat may have changed numbers, the mysterious calls were traced to a Mister John Pearce. It took Lee a while to absorb the nasty possibility that Mr John Pearce was his best friend since school.

This had been problematic to prove, as their trysts, it was thought, took place within the privacy and safety of his friends' farm's boundaries. Most of the time, Jen was at home when Frankie visited. The question, *Was Frankie really visiting her friend or was she fucking his?* perplexed Lee.

Although it seemed nothing untoward was happening, Lee's gut, as always, told him otherwise. By nature, Lee let nothing go, and he soon stumbled upon an ingenious (so he thought) way to uncover the truth, yet he still could not prove the affair and was about to give up, until now.

Lee vented his anger on his accelerator as he drove at an ungodly speed at an ungodly hour. *Where to go? Where to stay?* He had a few options, one being a hotel, but he hated everything about hotels. They were lonely places, especially at times like these. He picked up the phone and looked for Brig's number. *Nah, let's not complicate things.* He decided on another option. She was always awake, and she wouldn't mind him crashing at her place at such short notice.

It rang for a time and then Patty picked up. "Lee, what's wrong?"

"I need a place to crash. Can I come over?"

"Of course you can. You know the gate code."

Lee pressed his foot flat on the accelerator. "Just slow down, Lee. I'll be waiting for you."

Lee accelerated as he turned left on to a back road that would take him into the city – a road that was desolate at this time. He thought about his so-called best friend. He was over the angst of loss and betrayal; in fact, nothing much shocked him anymore.

Jen's mother had been right about John all along, Lee mused as he drove. Jen's parents had had their hearts set on a union between Lee and their daughter, as did Lee's parents. Both wine farmers in the area, they had often joked that they would be in-laws one day, "Providing my son isn't seduced by the floozies he loves to hang around with," Lee's father had joked.

Unlike the rest of the girls at the time, Jen's dad had forbidden her to socialise in town, as he knew those girls visited the pubs in the village despite being underage. She wasn't allowed to hang around with boys unsupervised; he wanted her to remain pure and untarnished. He would not have the whole of Stellenbosch skinner about his child and inadvertently question his parenting skills. This made her a suitable candidate for marriage amongst the parents in Stellenbosch.

It was only when Jen's father passed away that many of the rules slackened. Jen's mom did not have the kind of resolve her husband had had. Even Jen's choice of study would have been vetoed by him if he had lived.

It was in her last year at interior design college that Jen had met John. On paper, he was a good catch: heir to his father's farm, vice head boy at school, graduated cum laude from agricultural college, with looks and charm in spades. But the rumours about him and his womanising did not go unnoticed by Jen's mother, Christa.

At the same time, Lee's parents had met his new love interest, Frankie, and although they never let on to the rest of their family and friends and the town's gossips that they were unhappy, they had been concerned about the kind of woman Lee was considering marrying. An intervention was planned between the two families, and Lee and his parents were invited to dinner at Christa's farm in the hope that their two children would fall deeply in love.

The three cohorts mistakenly thought that Lee and Jen were oblivious to their plan and the two young adults had had fun playing along with them. After dinner, Lee's dad had coaxed him to take Jen to the movies. Only too happy to end the pretence, they drove away laughing at the awkward and archaic situation in which they found themselves.

Lee remembered that evening vividly. There had been no way they would have gone to a movie together, knowing this would spark all sorts of rumours around town. Instead, they had decided to drive to the highest point on Jen's farm, park the car and smoke a joint to kill time.

Both stoned, they lay on their backs looking up at the stars. Lee rolled on to his side, arm resting on his elbow, and they began to giggle uncontrollably.

"How awkward was that?" Jen laughed.

"I think it's not such a bad idea, Jen," Lee joked. "You marry me. We make our parents happy *and* your dad, may he rest in peace. We combine our wealth and create an empire, while we secretly shag John and Frankie."

"Separately or together?" Jen asked, causing them to snort with laughter. It had seemed so hilarious. "Oh my God, Lee, you crack me up. Who said you couldn't have your cake and eat it?"

"The town could do with a scandal. They thrive on this type of thing. Let's give them something to talk about."

Then they stopped laughing and looked at each other as if they'd never really seen one another before. As if they had synchronised their movements, they reached for one another and before they knew it, they were kissing, mouths open, tongues probing, wanting to be naked but prolonging the agony of having each other wholly by exploring the other's body. Their mouths were still joined as their hands moved up t-shirts and pulled down pants, touching places that brought bliss and longing simultaneously. Lee didn't remember seeing Jen naked, but he remembered vividly what she felt like and how she tasted. He could recall the absolute desire and the ecstasy of their union after the protracted teasing and the lengthy foreplay, the curious probing and the constant touching. Never again had he been able to replicate that moment of complete and utter abandon and the feeling of being absolutely satiated. Never.

He shifted gears and drove at full throttle. He remembered the heartache that had followed. He had been prepared to lose his friendship with John over Jen, he had wanted her so much. Never had he felt this way during sex and never again was he able to recapture the intensity of that night, despite his attraction to Frankie and her sexual prowess. Jen, on the other hand, had been racked with guilt. She blamed the alcohol and drugs and insisted that Lee forget it had ever happened.

Years later, Jen's mother had asked Lee to visit her in the retirement village. Over tea, she had cried, telling him how she feared for her daughter's happiness. She shared the story of her marriage to her unfaithful husband and how it had saddened her that history seemed to be repeating itself. She was concerned about the rumours whispered around town. Her only hope was that her daughter would have the courage, courage she had never found, to leave the marriage; but she feared that, like her, she was shackled to her husband financially. It was a long afternoon of promises and disclosures, and by the end of it, Lee had sworn he would see that Jen would be fine, no matter what situation she chose to be in, married or divorced.

Had he failed? Frans was the one who had insisted on roping all the guys into the club. Lee could have prevented John from joining, but it would have caused a major rift in his group. As for his wife's affair with Jen's husband, that was beyond his control. John had finally seduced Frankie. It had only been a matter of time.

It was apparent that John had a sexual addiction. Lee felt that he had no choice but to expose his friend; maybe he would've chosen a different, more gentle approach if he hadn't been fucking his wife. He hoped that this exposure would not cause too much collateral damage, impacting on Jen and her children, but he figured he had very little choice. It was the only way he knew to save Jen from John *and* herself, and to keep the promise he had made to Jen's dying mother.

Twenty-two

J en had left the house for the city long before she needed to. She wanted to get to her first appointment on time and she knew that the weekday traffic was hellish. She was also relieved not to have any contact with the man who had been posing as her faithful husband for the last twenty-four years.

She had hardly slept for mulling over John's betrayal. She had spent most of the night joining the dots of Frankie and his adulterous relationship, chastising herself for being so naïve and blind.

She did not appreciate the spectacular scenery as she entered Cape Town. Majestic Table Mountain to her left and Cape Town's already bustling harbour to her right went unnoticed as she negotiated her way through the traffic just before the N1 offramp into the Mother City. An irate motorist hooted at her for cutting in front of him. She raised her hand in apology. How stupid she was to have missed the signs! She would often come home to find Frankie 'waiting' for her when she had known that Jen would be out or would be home late. "I was in the area", or "I forgot that you wouldn't be home", and "Don't worry, John entertained me until you got back", had become regular refrains when she found her friend in her home alone with her husband. John had always offered to walk Frankie to her car on the grounds that he needed to catch up with work in the cellar, and Frankie had always offered John a lift there, which, Jen remembered, he never declined. That's exactly what happened, Jen concluded: they'd had sex in John's office in the cellar. *She must have parked her car on the other side of the cellar, hidden and unseen by trusting old me.* Jen's imagination started to play out different scenarios of their trysts, and her anger escalated.

She recalled how Frankie had often showed her sexy text messages "from her married lover" and realised now that they must have been from John. How cruel! It was bad enough that she had betrayed her with her husband, but to derive a thrill out of sharing his illicit texts with her was beyond comprehension. Why?

She was relieved to find an empty parking bay in Wale Street, the exact street where Sharon, the relationship counsellor, worked.

She ordered a strong espresso at the nearby Bean There, to kill time and to give her a kick after a restless night and very long drive. She then braced herself for the day that lay ahead.

Sharon was not a beautiful woman. Her features were hard and butch – hardened more by close-cropped, peroxided hair and minimal make-up. But what she lacked in looks, she made up for in style. Her tailored pantsuit was well fitted and expensive. Jen also recognised Sharon's jewellery from fashion magazines: handcrafted, quirky bespoke pieces by Lisa Stanton, an up-and-coming local jeweller. Sharon exuded verve as she walked out to greet Jen and direct her to her consultation room.

Knowing that Claudia had met Sharon through Leonard, who always referred his clients to her, and vice versa, made Jen a little more at ease. Leonard was at the top of his game. If he trusted Sharon, then, surely, so could she.

The consultation room was warm and inviting, completely unexpected, given Jen's initial impression of its occupant. There were three comfortable-looking armchairs positioned around an oval coffee table on which were placed a box of tissues, a water jug and three glasses.

Juxtaposing the warmth of the furniture was Sharon's art selection. Two pieces in particular reminded Jen of the Facebook phenomenon Berlin ArtParasites' haunting and thought-provoking art; in fact, they bordered on disturbing – an unusual choice for a space Jen assumed was supposed to bring tranquillity and resolution. One was of a male bust oozing blood from its eyes, the other of a woman hanging naked from a cross. At the far end of the room sat Sharon's desk – a long and overbearing antique printer's desk, burdened with piles of seemingly neglected folders and papers, a telephone, an Apple computer, as well as an open laptop and a glass vase with a print of Matisse's *Dance* circling it, used as a container for stationery.

Feeling a little uncomfortable, Jen shifted in her chair and poured herself some water.

"Have you visited a psychologist before, Jen?"

Jen shook her head, then swallowed.

"Well, I'm not a psychologist, and if you'd ever been to one, you would know that I'm a tad unconventional," Sharon said, while looking for a pen amongst the pile of stationery in the Matisse vase. Having found her Mont Blanc, she moved to one of the empty chairs and sat down, crossing her legs to prop the notepad she held in her right hand. "The burning question everybody is afraid to ask me is, what do I know about marriage and relationships? The answer to *that* would be: what does anybody really know about relationships, period? I'm not here to give you solutions. I'm here to help you on your journey to self-discovery, and to assist with unravelling and making sense of the truth, however painful."

Sharon stopped mid-thought. "This sounds a bit like psycho-babble and I guess it is." She threw her head back and began to laugh, showing perfect molars. "We counsellors can be very convincing because we confuse you with words."

Jen wondered whether she could divulge anything to this strange woman.

"I'm a little unconventional, not only because I can be, but also because we're working against time. We don't have the luxury right now to thrash through months of analysis. We can do that later, through regular hourly sessions, either alone or with your husband, if you like, once you've made a decision as to what you want to do."

"Do you mean whether I want to stay married or whether I want to divorce John?"

Sharon smiled. "Yes, to stay married, or file for divorce or separate. The choice is yours and you need to be sure that you have thought this through carefully. You also need to know that nothing is set in stone. You can change your mind, given that your husband is willing to concede."

Jen listened carefully, trying to process her options.

"Claudia has briefed me as to why you're here, but I want to know from you, Jen. Why *are* you here? What do you hope to achieve from seeing me?"

Jen felt her cheeks burn and her eyes start to fill. Sharon gestured towards the tissues, and Jen grabbed one, dabbing her eyes as she spoke. "Well, I caught my husband in the throes of oral sex with his wine rep." She stopped, expecting to see shock on Sharon's face.

Instead, Sharon said, "Were they performing oral sex on each other, or was John the only one being indulged?"

Mortified at Sharon's candid question, she tried to explain. "He was, um, he was…"

"Go on?"

"She was giving him a blowjob."

Sharon wrote something down in her notepad, then looked up. "Were you watching, or did you stop them?"

Jen shifted in her seat. *What difference does it make?*

"I was watching for a while. I was in shock. At first, I didn't quite register that he was my husband."

There was a long silence. "Can you remember what went through your head at that moment?"

"Honestly? Well, I was quite fascinated, actually, at how *good* Patty was at it. It looked as if she was actually enjoying herself. I remember thinking, *so this is how it's supposed to be done.* And then I tried to scream at them, but really it was a whisper."

"Don't you engage in fellatio, Jen?"

Jen looked down at her hands and noticed she'd been picking at her cuticles. "I don't see how this has any relevance to what happened."

"Maybe it doesn't, but you never know. You just said it intrigued you that Patty was enjoying performing oral sex on your husband. Maybe this was a once-off indiscretion."

Jen stood up abruptly. The nerve of this woman! She had her mind made up to leave, but Sharon stopped her with a raised, quizzical eyebrow and she sank back into her chair.

"I'm not trying to justify your husband's actions, but he may just use the excuse that he was drunk; he was lured by this woman and was exceptionally tempted at the time because you never perform oral sex on him. It's just about every married man's mantra, isn't it?"

Jen knew it sounded peevish, but she couldn't help saying, "The women I know hate oral sex!"

"Which is every *married woman's* mantra," Sharon shot back.

Was this 'counsellor' trying to blame her for John's infidelity?

Sharon chuckled. "See, I know. My poor ex couldn't get my mouth near his dick and now he's pissed off because being a lesbian requires the use of my mouth. Imagine how cheated he feels?"

Jen was stunned into silence and then she began to laugh hysterically. She wasn't sure if it was because she was so emotionally and physically drained, but she needed some relief from this burden she had been carrying around with her since Saturday, maybe longer, she admitted.

Then Sharon joined in and they were unstoppable. When one of them tried to control herself, she was spurred on by the other, and the hysterics would start all over again. Jen hadn't laughed like this in ages, and somehow this shared mirth brought Jen closer to Sharon. A sort of trust had been established.

Sharon got up from her chair and moved towards her desk. She picked up a pile of papers and a pencil and handed them to her client. "These are a series of questions I'd like you to answer. See it as part of my intake interview. It also allows you to reflect and it saves us time, time that we are lacking. Speaking of which, I would like to postpone your appointment this afternoon with Leonard to tomorrow. We're going to need the whole day, if you don't mind?"

"Should be fine, I have all day today and tomorrow."

"After you've answered the questions, you can go for lunch. I believe you're meeting Claudia at the little sandwich shop in Long Street? This will give me time to read through what you've written and to highlight the issues I think are relevant to today's session."

She gestured to Jen to follow her. Sharon led her into a little annex off the reception area. A table and a desk chair filled a portion of the room and against a wall was a long couch framed by four recognisable signed prints.

A sideboard held a coffee station, and Jen was told to help herself, "and there are biscuits if you're feeling peckish".

With that, Sharon walked out of the room, closing the door gently behind her, leaving Jen alone with her emotions, which came flooding back to her in an instant.

She poured tea into a cup and added the sugar and the milk while she worked through the questions.

The intake interview started with the usual information such as name, sex, identity number, date of birth, marital status and profession. Then followed a section regarding her children: their ages and sex and the relationship that she and her spouse had with each child. There was a question as to whether she felt their children had had any adverse effects on their marriage. She also had to write a brief paragraph on her past and her relationship with her parents. The next section was titled Spouse's Details and Relationship Status. In this section, Jen filled out John's name, his age, his occupation, how long they had been married and how long they had dated.

The questions became more personal and probing. Jen was required to state how many times a month, on average, they had intercourse; whether she was happy with this and whether she thought her husband was satisfied. She was also asked whether she enjoyed sexual relations with her husband, and if not, why not? Furthermore, did she think her husband enjoyed sexual relations with her? She had to indicate whether she engaged in any of the following: swinging, ménages à trois, bondage, discipline, sadism and masochism (BDSM); and, if so, was this a mutual decision or was there coercion? Jen breathed a sigh of relief. She felt normal. *At least I can skip this section out.*

This was followed by a subsection about her views on pornography and whether porn was used as a tool during sex.

John had tried early in their relationship to get her to watch porn with him, but she had to admit that pornography didn't really appeal to her. There was always a sense of deviance to porn, which wasn't to her taste, she wrote, adding that she was sure he watched pornography, as most men were wired that way. She then added a big question mark as if to ask, *Am I right?*

By this stage, Jen felt that she must be really dull in bed and wondered if these questions were geared to make her take ownership for John's extramural romps, so she added that she enjoyed using props and performing role-play during sex; after all, she had bought that French maid's outfit, and a nurse's uniform, and crotchless panties in a bid to spice up their sex life.

Next, she was asked whether she had been faithful to her husband, followed by her definition of infidelity and whether both she and her husband subscribed to this view.

The final question in this section was whether she knew or believed her husband was faithful to her. She knew the answer to this question. That was why she was here. She wrote that she had caught her husband with his wine rep and had recently discovered his affair with her best friend. She included that there were many rumours about his philandering, which she had not wanted to believe but which nevertheless made her suspicious.

"List how this makes you feel." She pressed the pencil hard into the paper: "BETRAYED, STUPID, ANGRY, UGLY, HUMILIATED, WORTHLESS", and her last word was "FREE".

Jen was washed out. She needed fresh air, and to escape from the confines of the room. She placed the pages in an envelope, sealed it and left it with the receptionist then walked the fourteen flights of stairs to the ground floor. After sitting the whole morning – probing, thinking, feeling, questioning – she was about to explode and needed to move!

Twenty-three

The sandwich shop on Long Street was bustling with lunchtime custom. All the trendy city slickers were standing or perched on stools around high tables laden with espressos, cappuccinos and other hot beverages, mouths crammed with designer sandwiches, seemingly difficult to eat yet expertly negotiated, while laughing, chatting and calling friends over to tables. Everyone seemed to be in a frenzy to eat and meet before going back to offices and desks providing them with work that could bring them one step closer to their goals and dreams.

This little place had crammed some of the most beautiful people into a small area, making it either a popular place for those who aspired to be trendy or daunting for those who thought that perhaps they didn't belong.

Jen felt like one of the latter as she pushed her way through the throngs of people, hoping that Claudia had found them a table. Her imported linen dress was creased. *Definitely pure linen.* The plunging neckline revealed her cleavage and newly tanned décolletage on which her thong necklace rested, as if to point to where happiness could be found. Jen noticed a few businessmen glance appreciatively at her bust. Someone grabbed the back of her arm.

"Jen," a man's voice said, "is that you?"

She turned and looked into the eyes of a tall, well-built stranger. His broad shoulders were covered in a striped blue shirt, and a dark blue tie hung loosely around his neck. His hair was a curly mop of speckled grey and his reading glasses hid between the curls on his head. Tiny laugh lines framed his dark brown eyes and a Roman nose protruded handsomely from the middle of his face.

Jen recognised him. "I know you, but I can't place you," she said politely.

"It's me, Myron!"

She hadn't seen Myron since high school, since his family had emigrated to Greece when she was in Grade Eleven. She remembered the adolescent crush she'd had on him. In fact, all the girls had been half in love with him, and she had been dizzyingly flattered when he had shown an interest in her. She had even made out with him at the school social. Myron was the first boy who had ever touched her breasts. That was a long time ago, and now she was looking into the eyes of a very handsome, middle-aged businessman.

"Well, blow me away! Myron! What are you doing here? I thought you were living in Greece."

"I've been back for just over a year now. As you know, we took a huge knock in the recession. I could foresee that Greece would be teetering on the brink of bankruptcy, so I came back to find you. And look! Destiny has brought you here to the very coffee shop where I have lunch every day," he teased, his dark eyes creasing endearingly at the sides. "You haven't changed. You are as beautiful as ever."

"Oh, don't be ridiculous, Myron, I've aged. I'm on the cusp

of fifty, and gravity and time have taken their toll, as would be expected. But thanks for the compliment."

"You are like the good vintage wine your father has in his cellar, which gets better with age."

"And you're the cheese that goes with it," she grinned.

He asked how her parents were, which was sweet of him, especially since they had forbidden her from seeing "that bloody Greek". She had been distraught, but her dad had said that no Greek was going to gain his experience from his daughter and then dump her for a nice Greek girl. "I know how 'these people' operate and I will not have it!" he had shouted.

"They're both dead. Both of them have passed on," she said. "They weren't very nice about you, were they? If it's any consolation, I was devastated my dad wouldn't let me see you," she said in a teasing voice, her heart beating overtime with excitement and surprise at her own daring.

"I never did marry, Greek or otherwise," he volunteered.

"Oh, don't talk rubbish! You want to tell me that Myron is incapable of luring a nice hot babe into his web?" She was keen to hear his answer.

"No," he said, with a hint of a Greek accent. "I never said that. I had a very long relationship and when I eventually decided to commit, it was too late. So, I've learnt a very hard lesson. Ah well, that's life. You're young and vain and want to stay single and then suddenly you find yourself old and alone."

"Well, at least you were honest and didn't commit to something you knew you couldn't keep to."

Myron searched her face. "Do I sense a bit of hostility and bitterness? Have you added to the divorce statistics, Jen?"

God! He is an Adonis! Jen steered her thoughts back to the conversation. "No. Not yet. But I really don't want to talk about my personal crap. I've spent the whole bloody morning wallowing in self-pity and I have the whole afternoon of the same to look forward to. I'm hijacking your table, whether you want me to or not. I just hope the lady you're meeting will enjoy our company."

She grinned and as he grabbed her hand and kissed it, she saw Claudia through the crowd. She lifted her other arm to wave.

"There you are!" Claudia grabbed a stool and plonked herself down. "I got you the smoked chicken and herb sandwich, I hope it's all right. I don't have much time for lunch, so I thought I'd get our food to save time. Pardon me," Claudia said, noticing Myron. "I'm Claudia."

She looked at Jen and grinned, her brows lifted as if to say, *Already picking up men?*

"Claudia, this is an old school friend of mine. His name is Myron."

"Are you Myron Christofoulo?" Myron had taken his last bite of his sandwich and all he could manage was a nod. "My boyfriend has spoken a lot about you."

Myron leaned back as if to take Claudia in better. He wiped his mouth on his serviette then crumpled it into a ball. "Ah, you are Leonard's partner. I have heard only good things about you."

"Well, isn't that uncanny? What a damn tiny place this world is!" Claudia turned to Jen. "Myron and Leonard are business associates and often cycle together. Is this your table?" Claudia asked Myron. "Because it seems you have company." She smiled at Jen. "Did you just steal Myron's table?" Jen shrugged back at her friend, beaming.

"Yes, it is...it was. But I have to go. It was lovely meeting you, Claudia. And Jen, it was great to see you after all these years." He got up from his stool. "Maybe we can do coffee and a proper catch-up sometime. If you're okay with it; if it's not inappropriate."

"I'm sure she'd love to," Claudia answered for her.

"What's your number?" Jen asked. "I'll quickly dial you and then you can save it on your phone."

Myron gave her his number, and when Jen dialled it, he answered clownishly, "Hello. Maybe I'll see you again soon."

He gave her two strong pecks on each cheek and one on the lips, "For good measure. It was lovely to see you after so many years, Jen."

As they watched him walk away, Claudia commented, "Wow! You really showed restraint there. No 'I'll have to think about it', just a quick 'give me your number'. You're a skank, Jen Pearce."

Jen blushed. "Oh no, is that how I came across? That wasn't my intention," she said as she saved Myron's number to her contacts.

Claudia teased, "You're such a bad liar. Speaking about lies and truths, how has your consultation been? Have you warmed to Sharon or does she scare you?"

Jen recounted her morning with Sharon and how she had been ready to walk out, but that there had been a breakthrough moment. She also told her that her appointment with Leonard had been rescheduled, as Sharon needed more time with her.

"I know. Listen, Jen, Leonard asked me to give you this envelope." She reached down into her lawyer's bag to retrieve a brown envelope. "It arrived at his offices. He doesn't know who sent it," she said as she handed it to Jen. "He was hoping to give it to you at your consultation with him today, but you'd postponed. He thinks that maybe you should take a look at it today, with Sharon around."

Intrigued, Jen was about to open the envelope when Claudia stopped her. "No, don't do it now. I don't know what's in it and neither do you."

Claudia scoffed down her sandwich, gave Jen a peck on the cheek and told her to call her after her session. She had to run as she was appearing in court.

Jen was deep in thought as she finished her lunch, wondering what the envelope contained. Whatever it was, it was sandwiched between two hard boards, and she couldn't resist peeking. She opened the seal and separated the two cards, gingerly pulling out a photograph. It was of John kissing a stranger – a French kiss, for want of a better word. His tongue was deep in a woman's mouth and his hip pushed up against her groin. She slid it back inside the envelope and sealed it again. Her anger and shock dissipated as quickly as it had surfaced, and she grinned. *Got you, you bastard!* She was triumphant.

Two men approached her table and asked whether she minded them joining her. "Not at all, I'm just about done. Go ahead."

"We were hoping that you'd stay." *Are they flirting,* she wondered, *or just being polite?*

"That's sweet," she smiled, "but I have to go. Enjoy your afternoon."

One of the men looked down at her cleavage and instinctively Jen held the envelope over her chest.

"Stay. We'd love to get to know you better," the one man said as he gently touched her wrist.

Okay, she was being hit on (a phrase she had learnt from Pete). She rose to the occasion: "Well, boys, as much as I'd love to stay and chat," she lowered the envelope and thrust out her chest as if to say *look and weep,* "I have to wrap my head around the fact that my husband is an adulterous prick." The stranger jerked back his hand. She smiled, grabbed her bag and walked out of the shop. She began to laugh. *Well if I don't laugh, I'll be suicidal, and John Pearce will never have that kind of a hold on me, ever.*

Clutching her evidence tightly against her chest, Jen pressed the button for the lift to the fourteenth floor of Sharon's building. She had misjudged the distance to the sandwich shop and certainly wasn't going to walk up fourteen flights of stairs. She felt relief. It was empowering to finally know, to have proof, that her husband was a fraud. She had spent twenty-four years admonishing herself for her doubts about him. All those years breastfeeding, rearing and running around her children. Now, for the first time, she had emerged from this haze, and the clarity with which she saw things made her brave and decisive, even excited, to change the course of her life.

Twenty-four

Patty had fallen asleep on the couch. Her phone beeped and she woke with a start. It was morning and Lee had not yet arrived. She checked the message that had come through. It was from John. "I should have the money in my account by tomorrow the latest. Text me the account number. John"

She sent him the account details and checked her phone again for any missed calls. Nothing. Lee would have called her if he had changed his mind. She chided herself for having fallen asleep. Anyway, Lee was Lee. He came and went as he pleased. Who was she to question him or to worry about him? She would shower. It was no use, her sitting around waiting.

After her shower, Patty checked her phone again, and again it yielded nothing. She knew he hated her fussing after him, but she was overcome with worry. It rang and then went to voicemail. By ten o'clock she could stand it no more. Usually he would check in with her by nine the latest. *Bugger it, I know I'm not his wife or mother but...* She phoned security at his work. "No, he hasn't

165

come in today." She could try his house phone, but that would prove disastrous and Lee would be furious, so she dialled the police.

"Has anyone reported an accident involving a Ferrari, or has anyone driving a Ferrari been arrested?" It wouldn't be the first time he had been thrown into jail for speeding. Her call was placed on hold, and after what seemed an eternity, the officer was back on the line.

"Ma'am," he asked, "are you a relative of the deceased?" It took a while for her to process what she had just heard, but when she did, she grabbed the dining room table for support.

"What!"

The detective repeated himself. "I need to know your relationship with the deceased."

Her rapid breath made her practically inaudible. "Is. Lee. Dead?"

"I'm sorry, Ma'am, I can't disclose that until you tell me your relationship."

She knew Lee would laugh his head off when she retold this story to him. "You've just told me he's *deceased*, you moron. You *do* know that deceased and dead are the same fucking thing?" Patty dropped the phone and fell to her knees. She opened her mouth to howl, but she was mute. Her world fell apart.

Frans had texted John that the money would be in his account by close of day, and if not, by Thursday the latest. John hoped that Patty would have payment sooner rather than later – that he'd be able to put this debacle to bed, no matter how costly.

He had woken up early that morning, knowing full well that he had to replace at least one person in sales. He raced up to the cellar, ready to face the day. He figured that good-looking sales reps were a dime a dozen. *You've got to admit, you've been blinded by Patty. You'll find someone easily.* He wasn't so sure whether Jen would approve of another babe near him, but he had to convince her that girls like Patty sold products. The business had to maintain the level of sales that Patty had obtained.

He sent his ex-employee a cursory text demanding banking details before phoning Carina at Human Logic to find a placement for his company. She always had candidates on her books.

"Monday morning, first thing," John insisted. "And I want good-looking girls."

"John, quite frankly, I'm not a modelling agency. I work with candidates who qualify for the job. These women are well presented and come with good references."

Carina herself was a beautiful woman. He had seen her around town – broad smile, tall and well groomed. "Someone like you," he flirted.

She laughed.

"You know what I mean," he said.

"I think I do. John, I'm going to be honest, these women are sales representatives. If this doesn't suit you, don't waste their time, or mine for that matter."

"Okay, okay. I just don't want any old decrepit, that's all I'm saying, or you'll be wasting my time."

After ending the call, he sat behind his desk ready to begin his day. Gladys had come in with a tray of coffee and the newspaper.

"Is Jen up, Gladys?" John asked. "She slept in the spare bedroom last night. She's not feeling too good." Why he felt he had to give Gladys an explanation, he didn't quite know.

"Jen's not home," Gladys answered, not able to look him in the eye. "She left early."

"Oh, of course. I forgot she said she was leaving early today," he lied.

Gladys began straightening up his unusually untidy office.

"And Pete? He should have been here by now," he said, plonking his empty coffee mug back on the tray. "He's sleeping in, is he?"

Gladys looked desperate. "Pete's not in the cottage."

"Well, where is he?"

She shrugged. "His bed is made and his cupboards are empty."

John pushed passed her and rushed from the cellar to Pete's cottage. He yanked the door open. The kitchen was spotless. His bed had not been slept in and cupboard doors were wide open showing empty shelves and hanging rails. "What the fuck's going on?" he yelled.

Pete's number went straight to voicemail. "Where the fuck are you, Pete? You cannot just leave me like this. Phone me when you get this message. I want you back on this farm by the end of today." He slammed his phone down on the counter.

"Gladys!" he yelled. She came running in. "Do you know what's going on around here? 'Cause if you know anything I don't know and you're not telling me, I'm gonna lose my shit."

Gladys looked at him directly in the eyes this time. "I don't know what's going on. I'm just the maid."

The phone rang as Patty rocked backwards and forwards. It stopped and then rang again. She picked up the second time. It was the commanding officer of the police station. He kept asking if she could hear him and she kept whispering, "Yes".

"Ma'am, I'm terribly sorry that you had to learn about the death of... What is your relationship with the deceased?" he asked politely.

Patty whispered back, "He is a good friend."

"The deceased is male, then? I'm sorry I have to ask you this, but the remains are so badly charred we were unable to determine the sex. We have obviously sent the body in for forensic testing to determine identity and whatnot."

Patty closed her eyes and rocked faster at the morbid details. "Maybe it isn't him. Do you have a number plate?"

"We couldn't find the number plate of the car either. Everything was destroyed in the fire. It must've happened late last night or in the early hours of the morning, as the wreck was smouldering when we got to it. We were checking the list of Ferraris in the country, hoping we could find the owner or the driver, but fortunately you called."

Oh God, God, God, please, let it be someone else, please, please, please.

"I need to go. I'm going to be sick." Patty dropped the phone and ran to the bathroom.

The phone was ringing when she returned to the dining room. She reluctantly answered. "Ma'am, are you all right? Would you like us to send someone to speak with you or can you answer questions telephonically? I know this is hard, Ma'am, but we need as much information as possible. It seems you are the only one who can assist us."

Patty spoke slowly. "Look, this is a very delicate situation. The deceased, Lee, is a friend of mine. No one needs to know that. In fact, it would upset his family, particularly his wife. Do you understand?"

"Yes, Ma'am, I do. We will be as discreet as we possibly can, Miss...?"

"You don't need my surname, and if you need me, you have my number. You can phone me any time. Just as I won't lodge a complaint about your officer disclosing personal information about Mr Holms before notifying his next of kin, you are not going to mention that I have any relationship with the deceased. Are we clear about this? I'm only giving you this information so that his next of kin can be notified as soon as possible."

"I understand. Could you tell me his name and where he resides?"

Patty gave the policeman Lee's full name and his details. She gave him Frankie's telephone number and told him that Lee had

169

a son, Clive, who lived in Rondebosch, near the university. She also explained that Lee had seemed distressed and had asked if he could spend the night at her place, which was why she had become worried about him.

"This last bit of information his family need not know. Believe me when I tell you it is innocent, but also understand that it will not be construed as innocent, and surely Mr Holms's family will be hurting enough?"

Twenty-five

S haron was on the phone and gestured to Jen to come in. Jen sat down and pulled out the photograph again, studying it carefully. It awakened a new suspicion: she wondered if the 'small op' – the gynaecological procedure she'd had three years ago to remove atypical cells – related to her husband's philandering? To make things even worse, her gynaecologist, a well-respected man in the community, was a family friend. Had he withheld the truth from her to protect his buddy?

She resolved to march into his rooms and demand to see her file. She was not going to leave any stone unturned; if she had contracted an STI, she needed to know, even though she now was in the clear. This was not so much for vengeance as for the truth. For so long she had been careful to keep the truth from herself, and it was time to expose everything. It had become clear to her that she could not move forward if she didn't.

Sharon put down the phone and looked at her a while before she rose from her chair behind the desk.

"That was Leonard. I see you have the envelope?"

Her answer lay in Jen's lap.

"I'm sorry, Jen, but I'm pleased that you're with me at this time. We can try to handle this together. How do you feel?"

"Glad!" Jen said, before she realised what she was saying.

"Oh! I thought you'd be angry, or hurt. Why glad?"

Jen paused. Why was she glad? "I finally know the truth. John is an expert at covering his tracks. I've always had a feeling, but I've never wanted to probe. If I did upset the status quo, which was seldom, he would accuse me of mistrust, or ask me if *I* was having an affair."

Sharon looked up from her notebook. "That's what guilty people do, they distrust their partners."

"Well, he made me doubt myself, and now I'm glad – glad that my misgivings are founded and that I'm no fool."

"Does this make your decision easier?"

"Most definitely! Divorce. There *is* no other way. No long, protracted visits to marriage therapists to see if we can salvage anything, no questions as to my children and their wellbeing. Finally, there is evidence to prove that he has transgressed every boundary. Divorce is the only answer and I have no choice; there is no alternative."

"How so?" Sharon had moved from behind her desk. She opened the envelope Jen had placed on the coffee table. Jen spoke as Sharon studied the pictures. Her face remained neutral.

"Well, being forty-nine and pretty much lost to job opportunities and relationship opportunities made me question divorce as an option. So many of our friends – including me, I suppose – stay in our marriages because we believe that there is no happy alternative." Jen gestured to Sharon to hand over the picture that she was studying. She looked at it as she spoke. "The thought of divorce made me scared at thirty and terrified at forty-nine – even after I caught John with Patty. Until today, because now there is no maybe." Jen placed the evidence back down on the coffee table. "Do you understand what I'm trying to say? I know that after the divorce, even if I do feel lonely, I won't wonder whether it was the right decision. It's the right decision because there's the proof," Jen gestured to the envelope, "and divorce is the only choice I have."

Sharon leaned back in her chair and observed Jen more closely. "Have you ever cheated on your husband, Jen?"

Jen folded her arms. "No! I haven't. I've been so busy trying to raise children and make our marriage work that I haven't so much as looked at another man."

"Do you think that you would've, if the opportunity had arisen?"

"No. No, I really don't think I would've. For one, there would be too much at stake; for another, it would invalidate what I've subscribed to and lived by. So, no, I can confidently say that I would not have cheated on John if the opportunity had presented itself."

"Okay, so let's try and formulate a plan of action. What are you going to do after you leave this room?"

Jen laughed. "I'm going to get pissed." Jen waited for a response from her counsellor. There was a moment's pause before she continued. "I'm going to pack my bags and check into a hotel, here in the city. I will instruct Leonard to get an interim settlement because, by God, this asshole is going to pay me back for every year I devoted to our marriage."

"Do you plan to engage with him when he sees you tonight? Will you show him the photos? And will you confront your friend, er..." Sharon looked down at her notes. "What is your friend's name?"

"Frankie."

"Will you confront Frankie?"

Jen poured herself a glass of water. Her hands shook, and the water spilt slightly as she tilted the glass jug.

"Leonard can deal with John. I don't want to give him a chance to explain or to reason with me. He can be a very convincing liar. And Frankie. I won't say anything. I won't say anything, more for Lee's sake."

"Lee. Frankie's husband?"

Jen nodded. "Why would you withhold information like this from him?"

"Lots of reasons." Jen fidgeted with the thong around her neck.

"I'd like to know."

"Well, for one thing, I don't want him hurt. Secondly, I've been complicit in Frankie's affair with my husband." Sharon raised her eyebrows. Jen pretended not to notice. "Also, I grew up in the same town as Lee. I know how Stellenbosch thrives on scandals such as this one and how we have been programmed to cover up at all costs. Knowing Lee, even if he has an inkling, he won't do anything that would create a scene."

"Let's go back," Sharon said.

"You want me to tell you why I am complicit in their affair?" Jen shifted, then she took another sip of water before she went on to explain how Frankie had shared her affair with her, and how Jen had all but sanctioned it. She told Sharon that Frankie would show her text messages, "From my husband!", and how she had covered for her on Sunday night.

"Well, there is a very nasty type of nasty in Frankie," Sharon said. "I'm sorry, I shouldn't say things like that, but fuck it. Really, what a bitch!"

Jen ventured, "Well, maybe it's my karma."

Sharon frowned. "What do you mean?"

"I slept with Lee before John and I married." Jen checked Sharon's face, but again it remained neutral.

"Nothing shocks you?"

"I have an excellent poker face," Sharon smiled.

"Well, don't speak to me about poker. That's a story for another day.

"So, Lee's parents and my parents always joked about the two of us getting married. I think there was a family feud of some sort between John's family and mine, and when I started dating John, my mother was very unhappy. It was a Capulet-Montague thing, but Mom had also heard some terrible stories about him. Unbeknownst to me, John was dating Shelley when he started courting me. It was through my mom that I discovered this. By that stage, I was pretty smitten. He was the first guy I had slept with and he introduced me to the joys of sex. There was no stopping me. I loved everything about him."

Sharon had stopped taking notes, Jen noticed. She had her head cocked to one side and was listening intently.

"And although our parents knew one another, Lee and I only became friends through John. He had started seeing Frankie at about the same time John and I started dating. She came with a pretty bad reputation and Lee's parents were beside themselves with worry. My dad had passed on, and though their marriage hadn't been perfect, not by a long shot, my mom was determined to fulfil his wish for me to marry Lee. The two families set up an 'intervention' – supper on our farm. When Lee and I eventually caught on, we played along, and after dinner we drove up to the lookout point, got completely stoned and boom, we were kissing and groping and eventually we were having full-on sex." Jen looked up at Sharon. She could see that she had managed to elicit some sort of reaction from her counsellor whose face was anything but poker. "So, I too had sex with my best friend's husband. Well, sort of," she back-pedalled. "None of us were married, and Frankie and I weren't best friends yet."

Sharon broke the silence that followed. "So, you've carried this guilt around with you?" She put the lid back on her pen. "That is, if you have felt guilty?"

"Yes, I have. I didn't dare tell John! I was the closest thing to perfect and it was no secret that he wanted a 'pure' wife – someone who hadn't been with half the town. There was a time when I was going to tell him about the one-night stand with Lee and deal with the consequences, but then I, I was pregnant. There was no way I could risk being an unmarried mother. I would never find a husband and I had been preened for marriage, so I kept my shameful secret, and now you know, too."

Sharon glanced at her watch. Jen couldn't help feeling that even Sharon must be as exhausted as she was.

"Thank you for sharing this with me," Sharon said earnestly. "Before we end our session I'd like to ask how Lee felt after your... shall we call it passionate encounter?"

"He begged me to leave John."

"Oh." Sharon was clearly not expecting this answer.

Jen went on to explain. "Look, sex with him was pretty awesome, but we were stoned and drunk and young; plus, it was taboo, so all of these things contributed to the ecstasy of it all. I walked around for days afterwards thinking about that evening, and wanting it back again, but I just felt so guilty! I loved John, and respectable girls didn't do those things. I knew that if I left John for Lee my reputation would be questionable; everyone would know what had happened. I also knew that Lee and John had always had a little competition going, and it would have shattered John."

Jen couldn't help thinking that it seemed like she was trying to look like the heroine of this story. Trying to shield John from hurt. How ridiculously empty it sounded when she said it out loud, so she further justified her motives for staying with her then fiancé. "I loved John very much, so it was an extremely confusing time of my life. The decision was made for me when I found out I was pregnant."

"And," Sharon said cautiously, "is there a possibility that

Brigit is Lee's baby?"

Jen wept. She had kept this a secret for so many years.

"Yes," she confessed. "My mother knew about the turmoil I was in, but when she heard I was pregnant, she was adamant that I marry John. She said that neither John nor Lee would want me if they weren't sure whose baby it was. She made it clear to me that Brigit was John's child if Lee ever asked. He never did."

Twenty-six

There was a light knock on her bedroom door. Frankie opened her eyes slightly to see Faith standing over her. She turned on to her side.

"I'm tired, Faith. Let me sleep, please."

"Madam, the police are here."

Frankie's eyes opened. Drowsy from the sleeping tablets she had taken the night before, she hadn't quite grasped what Faith had said.

"I'm a little woozy, Faith. What's the time?"

"Madam Frankie, it's two fifteen." Frankie didn't register immediately. When she did, she shot up off the bed. "Jesus, Faith, have I been asleep the whole morning? Lee, where's he?" She grabbed her robe and wrapped it around her.

"I thought Madam is sick. There are two policemen. They want to speak to you. They say it's very urgent and that I must wake Madam."

"Tell them I'm coming," Frankie instructed. She quickly

brushed her teeth and splashed water on her face.

Two police officers were seated, caps in hand, taking in the lavish décor of the lounge. They jumped up on seeing Frankie. The older officer introduced himself and his colleague.

"Are you Frankie Holms?" he asked nervously.

"Yes?" Frankie said uneasily. These two didn't look like they were carrying a summons for a traffic offence.

"I'm afraid we have very bad news, Mrs Holms." Frankie reacted before the officer could finish his sentence.

"Oh my God, it's Clive, isn't it? What's happened?"

Silence.

"Tell me, for God's sake! What has happened to my son?"

"It's your husband," the younger officer ventured.

Faith screamed, "Boss Lee!"

Frankie looked at Faith and then at the two men.

Calmly, she asked, "What? What has happened to my husband?"

"I'm sorry, Mrs Holms."

"Was he speeding? He's been locked up again, hasn't he?" She searched their eyes. Pity had channelled its way through the faces of both the men. There was an agonising silence as Frankie moved towards Lee's armchair. Her limp body slumped into it.

The officer finally spoke. "His car was found this morning. No other car was involved. It's badly burnt, Mrs Holms." The younger officer handed her a plastic bag with the contents of Lee's Rolex and his gold wedding band.

Frankie heard a groan, but she hardly recognised it as the sound that came from her mouth.

Immersing himself in work had calmed John down somewhat. He had to catch up on Monday and Tuesday's work and he had been in his office behind his computer the whole day. A message that his money had come through flashed across his screen at the same time as his phone began to ring. It was Frans, and he answered immediately.

"Thanks bud. I see the money's come through. Much quicker than I anticipated. I do realise you had to pull some strings to do this for me."

There was no reply from Frans, only what John could decipher as long grunts, as if his friend was choking.

"Frans!" He jumped up from behind his desk, knocking his knee on an open drawer. *Fuck!* He tried to rub the pain away with his free hand. "Are you okay, bud?"

Frans tried to say something, but it came out as garbled – something that sounded like "Lee".

"I'm not hearing you. What about Lee?"

"Lee's dead", was all that Frans could manage.

"What the fuck are you saying, Frans?" he asked with more force this time. "You're starting to scare me."

Forgetting about his injured knee, he paced the office floor.

"I've just spoken to Frankie. The police were at her house about a half an hour ago. They found Lee's burnt-out Ferrari at the side of the road." Frans choked on his words. "His body was found in the wreck. Um, burnt. Our buddy is dead, John. Our buddy." Frans broke down again.

"Why didn't Frankie phone me? I'm Lee's best friend!" John shut his desk drawer and slumped into his chair.

"Is that all you have to say, John? Why didn't Frankie phone you? Who the fuck knows or cares? She's lost her husband, for fuck's sake. I don't know why you never got a call. Jesus! She needs our support. The police are on the way to Clive's digs to collect him and bring him home. We need to get our wives together and go to her house. I've told Shelley. She's gathering the book club girls. You need to let Jen know."

Embarrassed, John said, "I'm sorry, Frans, you're right. Fuck! I'm not quite absorbing this. It was the first thing that came to mind. Lee is dead. Christ! My buddy is dead."

He heard Frans say, "Go and get Jen immediately. She's asking for Jen."

John put the phone down long after Frans had. He was trying to process the enormity of the tragedy. His best friend had died in a grotesque accident. He was overcome by guilt, but also, he felt relief. He was intrinsically sad, but Lee's death was, in fact, going to be his deliverance. He was in the clear. His relationship with Frankie would go with Lee to his grave. If, indeed, he had found out. Thoughts rushed at him now. He couldn't help wondering if his friend's death had anything to do with the club's 'bosses'. Lee had made it quite clear that they had meant business. Paranoia engulfed him. He slammed his fists on his desk. *Fuckfuckfuck!* He shoved his fingers through his hair. *Jesus!* He hoped he wasn't in danger of the same fate. He shook in his rush to transfer the money into Patty's bank account, then messaged her: "Money transferred. I stuck to my side of the deal, now you stick to yours."

He ran to the farmhouse calling Jen's name. There was no answer. She still wasn't home.

"Gladys!" he hollered.

Gladys was out of breath when she got to the spare room.

"Where's Jen?"

"I don't know," she said, annoyed.

John dialled Jen's number while Gladys hovered.

"Lee is dead," he told her matter-of-factly. "I need to tell Jen to get to Frankie's house."

His employee's hand suppressed a gasp. "Lee? Dead?"

"Yes. If Jen phones, please, don't tell her. Just ask her to phone me urgently."

Twenty-seven

It was dark and raining when Jen stepped out of the building. Exhausted both physically and emotionally, she couldn't face the drive back to the farm. Claudia had texted Jen that afternoon to offer her apartment for the night, as she was staying over at Leonard's: "We have some catching up to do since my visit to the spa."

Jen phoned Claudia. "Does your offer still stand?" she asked. "It's been one hell of a day and I can't face the drive back."

"Of course it does, darling. You sound exhausted. It would be ridiculous to drive back in the rain then risk some sort of altercation with John, and then come all the way back to the city and still look for somewhere to stay. Go to the Waterfront, get yourself some clothes. You'll have a brand-new wardrobe by the time your divorce goes through!" They both laughed. "Go chill at my place. The spare key is with the caretaker. Ring her bell and she'll let you in. My apartment is on the second floor." Claudia gave Jen directions to her building in the most prestigious locale of Clifton.

"It will do you good to be alone."

Grateful, she entered Claudia's apartment laden with shopping bags. The apartment was as tasteful as Jen had imagined. An enormous window boasted a breathtaking view of the Atlantic Ocean. A few boats were visible in the distance, their lights twinkling through the rain. A passage led off from the left of the entrance hall to a separate studio for houseguests and on the right, an open plan Moroccan style kitchen, tiled in mosaic with brass fixtures. The kitchen led into a dining room furnished with a round marble table surrounded by a mix of upholstered dining room chairs.

In the lounge, two roomy velvet sofas spilled over with cushions. A large gold ottoman, laden with coffee table books, was placed at the opposite end of the room. The wall separating the room from the bedroom area was covered with framed pictures of Claudia and her family and friends. Jen noticed a picture of a much younger Claudia on her wedding day, standing next to a handsome young man. Daniel. He was robust, blond and tall.

Judging by the landmarks of canals, gondolas and Greek tavernas it was evident that she was well travelled. There were several photos of her kissing, dancing closely and standing together in front of the Eiffel Tower with a man Jen assumed must be Leonard. Jen chided herself for having imagined Leonard as a white Jewish man just because of his name and because Claudia herself was Jewish.

There was a picture of him on what Jen knew for certain as the unmistakable black beach of Santorini's Paradisos. Leonard had one of the most beautifully shaped, chiselled bodies she had seen on a man this side of forty. His board shorts hung just under his hipbones and she had to stop herself from staring too long. *Lucky girl, Claudia.*

She helped herself to a vodka tonic from the bar in the corner of the lounge and sat on the couch facing the Atlantic. Her phone beeped another message which she chose to ignore. She wanted time out from everyone. It had been a long day. Anyway, she wasn't obliged to speak to anyone, especially not John. This new sense of emancipation gave her courage and she WhatsApped Myron before she could change her mind. "Where do you live? Do you feel like catching up this evening? I'm staying at Claudia's and I can pop over if you're not busy."

She decided to shower. She wasn't going to sit at her phone waiting for a reply. His answer would determine the evening's outcome. She stripped and threw her used clothes in one of her packets. *A real bag lady I've become!* She lingered in the shower, allowing the water to cleanse her. When she was done, she checked her phone.

A missed call from John. More importantly, Myron had texted the address and directions to his house in Llandudno and a short "would love to see you". She jotted the address down in her notebook and switched off her phone, deciding to leave it behind. Tonight, she was unreachable.

She moisturised her body and carefully dried her hair. After getting into her new underwear, she admired herself in the mirror. *What are you expecting to do tonight, you vixen?* She turned around to check her derrière. *Not the best bottom, Ms Pearce.* She wore her new wrap dress she'd bought that evening and applied a little mascara and eyeliner. She took one final look at herself. Her dress plunged at the neckline, nipped her waist and opened to show a hint of thigh as she walked. Very unsubtle, she concluded. She dabbed on perfume and left the apartment with a palpitating heart.

Myron's home in the upmarket suburb practically hung over a cliff. It seemed to be constructed entirely from glass. Jen wondered what the hell she thought she was doing as she rang the doorbell. She had had another vodka tonic before leaving, the effects of which seemed to be wearing off fast.

Before she could retreat, Myron had opened the door and his

friendly welcome put her at ease.

She burst out, "I lied!"

"You did?" Myron responded, still standing in the open doorway.

"Before I make a complete ass of myself, I need to ask if you're gay?"

He laughed, "I'm Greek, single and have immaculate taste."

Jen's shoulders sagged. Maybe it was too good to be true. How could he have possibly been straight?

"Okay, then I didn't lie. It is what I said it was: a catch-up," she said as she stepped over the threshold and took in her surroundings. *This is definitely a gay man's abode.* It was impeccably furnished with modern, industrial elements enhancing the structure of glass, stark concrete and iron beams running from ceiling to floor. Items were placed for impact rather than practicality and there were numerous paintings and artworks – three pieces unmistakably by Madi Phala, renowned for his 'herd boy' theme.

"A Dylan Lewis bowl! I've always hoped that one day I'd have one on display in my home. Pity my bag is so tiny," she joked.

Myron leaned against the front door and watched her take in the vastness of the place. She could hear a grin in his voice as he said, "I'm not gay, Jen. You are so presumptuous. I am a single man who hired an interior designer who was given carte blanche as I have no fucking idea about interiors and I'm too bloody busy to care."

"Ohhhh. Then I'll have to go back to my introductory confession. I did lie." She walked towards him, close enough to feel his body's warmth.

"Mmmm, well, 'fess up. What's the lie?" he teased as he closed the door.

"I didn't come to catch up. I came to pick up where we left off at school."

"It's the same thing, isn't it?" She could tell he was trying to play the innocent.

"No," she said, as she moved her body even closer. Pressing her groin up against his, she could feel him stir. "I really don't want to know anything about you, Myron. I just want to... What's the word my kids used to use? Hook up with you. Bag you."

"I think the word you are looking for is 'shag'."

"I think shag is less explicit than what I had in mind, but let's go with that. Are you okay to be used and abused?" She hardly recognised her seductive voice.

"Jen, that's what every man dreads: an easy lay."

They both smiled, and Jen leaned in to kiss him, feeling that familiar urge: the forgotten lust of youth. She never imagined she could ever feel this way again. After a time, she pulled away. "I think your hand was here when we were last together," she said as she placed his hand on her breast.

He cupped it, and her nipple rose. "Where was my other hand?" he asked, feigning innocence.

"I don't know, Myron, I honestly can't remember," she said hoarsely, aware of the intense stirring in her loins. "What I do remember is that my arms were around you. Like this."

She placed her arms around his shoulders, clasping her hands behind his neck, and, pouting, said, "Sadly, I'm not that innocent any more, and I was thinking of placing one hand here." She touched his groin. He sucked in air as her hand pressed harder against him. She lowered herself, her face in line with his crotch, as she unbuttoned his jeans and slid his zip down, excruciatingly slowly. She wasn't as slow with his jocks. There was a need to unveil him. He was hard, yes, and very well endowed.

Myron leaned back against the door and closed his eyes as she nuzzled him. "I see you have very little to be embarrassed about," she murmured. He smiled, his eyes still shut. "Before I go any further, does your 'member' have a name?"

"What?" Myron asked, his eyes now wide open and looking down at her quizzically.

As if she were speaking into a microphone at an information kiosk, she repeated more clearly, "Do you have a name for your dick? Do I address him by name?"

He snorted. "No, I don't. If you want to christen my shaft, feel free, but please hurry up. I need your mouth."

Jen moved her lips up against his nameless member. "Oh good. If you had named it, I would have had to go back to Plan B, which is to…"

Before she could finish her sentence, he was in her mouth, and she was turned on by his urgency. *I think you're enjoying this, Jen. You're a bad girl! Years of withholding from John and now you've all but swallowed Myron whole.*

Jen ran her finger along the line leading to just under Myron's butt. He groaned with pleasure and pushed her head closer to him so that he could get deeper into her. She couldn't believe she wasn't gagging! This was one thing that she and the girls would bitch about: 'the helping hand'.

"I mean really," Shelley would scream with laughter. "It's bad enough having to cram a whole bratwurst down my throat, let alone have that 'helping hand' to guide me!"

Jen had to rein in her thoughts or she was going to burst out laughing.

Then Myron stopped her, pulling her to her feet. "I'm going to explode without having pleased you," he said. "Unless that's what you want? You've made it very clear that you are in control tonight."

He suggested moving away from the door, but she shook her head and untied her wrap dress, which fell open exposing her lace underwear. Her brown nipples were pert and peeked through the lace of her bra and she knew that her pubic hair, thankfully waxed and trimmed at the spa – at great expense to John – cast an enticing dark shadow under her knickers.

"You are a beautiful woman, Jen," Myron whispered. He

couldn't seem to take his eyes off her. "Oh my God, you are just beautiful."

Okay, fabulous. The practical underwear in my wardrobe will have to go to charity. The French should be canonised.

"Take your dress off," he said.

Is he kidding? He wants to see the whole of the moon? Not sure I will look as good without the dress framing my silhouette. But then she remembered her meeting with Leonard in the morning and decided to do as she was told. The last thing she needed was love stains all over her one and only item of clean clothing.

She took a deep breath and removed her dress as sexily as possible, remembering to suck in her tummy. But Myron hadn't noticed. He pulled her towards him as he expertly unclasped her bra. His hands were on her as he hungrily felt her up, squeezing her nipples and weighing each breast in his hands. *It's obvious they're ample*, she thought, as his head dived into them. Parting like the Red Sea, Myron allowed himself time to frolic between them before coming up for air. She closed her eyes and began to relax and enjoy the idea that he may just find her absolutely tantalising. Her body began to rock against his and she was coaxing his hand to touch her between her thighs. It was clear that he was now in charge, and, instead, he grabbed her butt and squeezed, gently at first and then again with more pressure. She groaned.

"Please, please, I want to feel you inside me."

He kissed her hard, stopping her from saying another word while he ran his fingers under the elastic of her knickers. She moved her hips longingly. *Touch me,* she pleaded to herself. *Touch me.* His fingers skimmed over her, teasingly, while his teeth bit gently into her nipples. She thought she was going to burst when she felt his fingers move under her panties.

Her body convulsed. He pulled her panties to the side, lifted her up, her legs wrapped around his waist as he entered her. They stood still for a moment, enjoying the newness of each other.

Before long, their bodies started to move, pounding the front door.

Jen wanted him deeper inside her and she ordered him to put her down.

"Lie on your back," she whispered. She stood over him, her back to him as she removed her knickers and he writhed with desire at what he saw. She slowly sank onto him, riding him feverishly, and before long they were both panting and crying out.

She eased off him, put her knickers back on, clipped back the clasp of her bra and tied up her dress. She noticed that she was still wearing her sandals. Grabbing her bag and her keys, she blew him a kiss and opened the door.

"Thank you," she whispered, as she closed the door behind her, a broad grin on her face.

Part Three

Twenty-eight

Although Faith had covered Frankie's shoulders with a blanket, she still trembled. Her trusted helper had taken on a supportive role since the tragic news; it was Faith who had spoken to Frans. He had instructed her to tell "Madam Frankie that Madam Shelley was on her way with her friends", and that he would be there as soon as he could.

All Frankie wanted, needed, besides Lee's arms around her, was her friend Jen, and she had urged Faith to phone her. Jen's phone was on voicemail.

Instead, Frankie had found John standing in front of her, a hangdog expression on his face. She glanced at him and then looked away. He was the last person she wanted to see – a reminder of her betrayal. In fact, he was why Lee had stormed out of their house, which in turn had led to his fatal crash.

John's words of condolence echoed through her. "I'm really sorry, Frankie," he said. She ignored him. She wanted to wake up from this nightmare of which John was an integral part.

He tentatively placed his hand on an unresponsive leg. "It feels hypocritical to mourn, I know. But he was my best friend. I'm devastated."

Frankie's face was stained with tears. Her head moved slowly from side to side.

He continued, hand firmer now on her thigh. "If anyone knows, it's me. Cheating doesn't mean you loved him less. God knows, I'm also guilty; I cheated on him too. But I refuse to allow the guilt to get in the way; you mustn't either." When she finally turned to look at him, he was sobbing unashamedly.

Disgusted, she struggled to push his hand from her leg.

"You are despicable, John. Lee's dead because he found out about you."

John's sobs came to an abrupt halt and he wiped the tears away with his hands.

"My husband was in an absolute state when he left the house last night."

John tried to touch her again.

"Don't you dare come near me! Don't touch me!" she hissed.

"Okay," John said, retracting his arm. "It upsets me that you think I'm the cause of all of this. We were both involved, Frankie. But if you want to pin this all on me, do it. If it makes you feel better…"

She spoke over him. Not listening to a word he had to say.

"He uncovered a whole lot more, you know."

John's head jerked back.

"Son of a bitch!" she hissed at him again.

Although she had managed to finally shut him up, the nightmare still played on.

"He drove away last night at such a speed; it's no wonder he crashed. Don't speak to me about guilt. You have no scruples, John. I know I've been a pretty shit wife, but you, you're not only an adulterous husband, you're a cheating lover too."

She began to laugh at this ridiculous notion. The shrill laughter brought Faith running in to check up on her. Both Frankie and John gestured for her to leave them alone.

Frowning, he said, "Look, Patty was a mistake. You know that."

She scowled at him.

"I don't understand," he said as he combed his fingers through his hair.

For the first time since she had sunk into Lee's armchair, she hauled herself out. He followed her, but she swung around and barked, "Stay where you are!"

He complied. She could feel his eyes on her as she shuffled like an old woman to her bedroom, returning with the incriminating images. "You piece of crap," she hissed, throwing them in his face. "Now fuck off out of my house. I never want to see you again, you hear me?"

She saw him wince as a corner of a photo nicked his face, and it gave her pleasure. Sitting back down into Lee's chair, she watched as he picked up each photograph from the floor, studying them one at a time as he did so.

"The fucking bastard!" he murmured with every implicating picture. "He had me followed. All his life he wanted to pin something on me and he couldn't, until now." Frankie glared at him. "Sadly, my friend is dead, but now I've got these pictures it's just your word, Frankie. The word of a two-timing whore. If it gets out that you and I were fucking, you may as well say goodbye to everyone who respects you." Frankie's eyes widened. "And you know better than I do that you will be doing your late husband's reputation a huge disservice. The last thing he would've wanted is a scandal."

"Get out!" Frankie screamed. Then, remembering that Faith was waiting in the wings, she whispered, "Just get out!"

John walked away, evidence in hand, then swiftly turned.

"Remember, you are the devastated widow and I'm the best friend. So far, your performance has been sterling, and I will have a chance to shine at my friend's funeral," John's tone hardened. "Where I *will* be pallbearer and I *will* be given an opportunity to speak. Believe it or not, I am truly devastated, and I will not be made to feel that I have no right to be."

At that moment, Shelley and her friends entered the room bearing dishes of food and concerned facial expressions.

"I'm just leaving," he said to them.

She heard Shelley whisper, "How's she doing?" Not giving him a chance to answer, she quizzed, "Did you manage to get hold of Jen?"

John answered aloud, "No. We haven't been able to reach her as yet."

"I see."

"No, you don't see," John retorted as he lifted the tinfoil from the dish she was carrying. He grabbed a frikadel before he walked towards his car. "Focus on what matters, ladies," he said, his mouth full of fried mincemeat. "Lee is dead. That's why you're here remember?"

Before rushing off to Frankie, John had called Brigit to relay the tragic news. She was inconsolable. She didn't care if her father might think her reaction over the top. *My godfather is dead!* It felt so surreal. Death's unpredictability had become a reality to Brigit and it frightened her. She had spoken to him only yesterday. *He was alive only yesterday!*

Yesterday's morning paper's headline had read, PROF SUSPENDED FOR ALLEGED SEX WITH STUDENTS. Shaking, she had opened the paper, searching for the article that read: "The dean of faculty has taken firm action against Professor Pierre Renoux, English department head and professor, for allegedly fraternising with students from the university. According to the statement, many have felt aggrieved by his alleged misconduct and are happy that action has finally been taken against him."

Without thinking, she had dialled Lee's number.

He answered immediately. "Brigit?"

"Have you seen the headlines of the papers?" her voice could not contain the rush she felt.

"No, I haven't had a chance."

"Well, do yourself a favour and read it. Seems like the horny professor has been suspended! Finally, he's got his comeuppance."

She remembered the silence that followed. Lee hadn't asked her how or why. And then it had dawned on her. "If I didn't know different, I would think that you had something to do with Pierre's suspension, Mister Holms."

Lee laughed. "As much as I'd love to take responsibility for this, I'm afraid I had nothing to do with it. Wish I was that kind of guy."

"Well, whatever. I'm glad!" Brigit said vehemently. "That should make finding his next appointment very, very difficult."

"You are a vengeful woman, Miss Pearce," he teased. "I'm pleased this bit of bad news has made your day and you feel vindicated."

"I *do* feel vindicated."

She would never speak to Lee again. She would never see him again.

John interrupted her thoughts.

"Brigit are you listening to me? I'm going to check up on Frankie. You need to get hold of Pete. Tell him he needs to come to the farm immediately. It's not up for negotiation. We have to be around as a family to show our support and love. Remember there's Clive as well."

Then he said, "Mom's not answering my calls or my messages."

"I spoke to her yesterday. She said she was at home."

"Yes, she was, but she left early this morning without telling me, and she hasn't come back. I've tried calling but her phone is off."

"You can't exactly blame her, can you, Dad? She's angry."

"I know she's angry with me but in the grand scheme of things, this is far more important. I have lost my best friend, Brig. My best friend. How do you think I'm feeling?"

Brigit felt a pang of guilt. She had forgotten that Lee and he had grown up together – that they were practically brothers.

"Anyway, Frankie's been asking for her and it looks bad, me not knowing where she is and her not answering my calls. You know what everyone's like. They're already talking."

"Well, just tell them that she's still at the spa," Brigit advised.

She tried her mother's number immediately after. It went straight to voicemail. She left both a voice message as well as a text message for Jen to contact her urgently.

Now all that Brigit had to do was convince Pete to come back.

"I don't see why I have to. It's not like Frankie needs my shoulder to cry on. I'll be at the funeral."

"You *will* come home. Do you hear me? That's what families do; they support each other. Dad has lost his best friend."

She heard Pete snort.

"Don't underestimate Dad's loss, Pete. Anyway, the reality is that you're needed, so swallow your pride and do the right thing."

Brigit packed a small bag for her stay at the farm. Despite her father's shenanigans with Patty, he needed her, and she needed to be around other people who were grieving. Although nobody knew the extent of their friendship, she could at least openly mourn Lee's death with those she loved. Up until now, the only person she had shared her losses and problems with was her psychologist, and recently Lee, who was now lost to her too.

Twenty-nine

It was past eleven o'clock when Jen walked in to Claudia's apartment feeling extremely satisfied. She had taken herself and her life's experience to a whole new level and she was pleased rather than guilty or embarrassed at the outcome. Her audacity had been out of character. She knew it was a once-off, but after all that she had been through, she felt that she had nothing to lose. John's indiscretions had made her feel stupid and embarrassed, and interminably un-sexy. The evening had empowered and emboldened her, and now she felt ready to take on anything.

Jen sat at the foot of the bed and turned on her cellphone. John had messaged her several times as had Frankie and Pete. Brigit had tried calling her too. *Probably worried where she was.* She had nothing to say to John, or Frankie for that matter, but she ought to let Brig know that she was okay. She could rely on her to relay the news that she was fine. She sent her a voice note. "I'm staying at a friend's place in the city. My appointment finished late and I didn't want to drive back home in the rain. I have another appointment in the morning, so it seemed pointless, driving back tomorrow. Please tell everyone I'm fine."

Her phone rang as soon as the message was delivered. "Mom, have you not retrieved any of your messages? Daddy and I have been trying desperately to reach you."

She had had such a fabulous evening. Did she really need this angst? Brigit's prima donna histrionics would put a dampener on everything.

"Brigit, I'm really tired. I told you not to worry."

She slipped off her sandals and untied her dress.

"Mom, Lee was killed in a car accident! We've been trying to reach you the whole day! It's close to midnight. Where've you been? Frankie needs you. We all need you. Couldn't you tell by all the missed calls that something was wrong?"

Jen had stopped listening. The last thing she had heard was "car accident" and the shock had all but blocked out Brigit's voice.

"Mom, are you listening to me? Are you there?"

Jen slumped onto the bed. Her hand rubbed her forehead vigorously. She didn't know what to say.

"Give me the phone!" Jen heard John bellow in the background, and then he was on the line. "Where the fuck have you been? We've been trying to reach you the whole day. For God's sake, I called you about a thousand times. What's wrong with you, Jen?" His tone softened. "Lee has been killed in a car accident. You need to come home." The words shook her out of her stupor. "Support Frankie and Clive. We all need you right now."

Jen finally spoke, and it sounded to her like her voice was coming from far away. "Who's with you?"

"We're all here. Except you. You know how bad it looks? I didn't know what to say to everyone. Not knowing where you are. Frankie's best friend, so jarringly absent and let's not talk about you being the only wife AWOL!"

"Stop, John. Just stop fucking talking. You are the last person to talk about what things look like." Jen would not allow him a retort. "I have a very important meeting tomorrow morning that I won't cancel."

"What?"

She stood up and walked to the window. The black and turbulent ocean brought a shiver down her spine.

"My driving through tomorrow is not going to bring Lee back," she said resolutely.

"Have you completely lost your mind? Of course, it's not going to bring him back. What it will do is show that you care. If not for me then for your best friend who has lost her husband." He then asked, "What's so important that you can't give your best friend your condolences?"

"Our divorce, John," she said matter-of-factly. "And I'm not going to drop everything now that I have set the wheels in motion. Let me speak to Pete, please."

She heard him say to Pete, "Maybe you can talk some sense into your mother. She's lost her fucking mind."

Then Pete's voice. Her darling ally. "Hey, Ma. How you?"

"I'm fine, under the circumstances. Hun, I need you to do me a favour. You can't tell anyone – Dad, Brig, no one. Can you do this for me?"

"As long as it doesn't mean I'm complicit in your suicide or someone's murder."

"Thanks, darling. Go where no one can hear us, and I'll tell you what to do."

She heard the background sounds change as Pete stepped onto the veranda, the rain pelting down on the tin roof.

After she had issued him with his instructions, she heard him hesitate.

"It's going to be quite hard to scrounge in your cupboard without Dad seeing me, but I'll try, Ma. I'll try."

Once she'd said goodbye, Jen fell into bed. She was shattered, but there were no tears and there was no sleep. Her thoughts raced. She could not make sense of Lee's death, so she tried pushing it aside. She had to disengage from this tragedy, she thought to herself. *I need to try to focus on what needs to be done and that is to move forward without John.* She knew that if she stopped to do 'the right thing', it could change the urgency of her decision, and she knew he would use this lull to persuade her that divorce was not an option, that she had nowhere else to go.

She could not bring herself to console Frankie, even though she knew that Lee would have wanted her to pretend for the sake of appearances. Maybe two days ago she would have, but now she would not compromise herself, even if it meant that she would be the one who would face the wrath of her friends and family.

The next morning, Jen did not feel as resolute. The reality of Lee's death and the way he had died began to dawn on her and an overwhelming sadness made her less determined about what she had to do.

The offices of Mazwai, Mantzel, Opilet and Associates were a few blocks away from Sharon's rooms. They were beautifully appointed and occupied the third and fourth floors. What struck Jen most about the formality of the space was the informality and ease with which the employees negotiated their way around it. The atmosphere was busy but relaxed, and the people seemed friendly and welcoming, which eased her nerves.

Leonard Mazwai's secretary collected her bang on time. She smiled, parting voluminous red lips that seemed to overwhelm the rest of her perfect facial features.

"Mrs Pearce, I'm Angie, Leonard's secretary." Jen stood up and they shook hands. "We're on the next floor. Please follow me."

Jen followed her into the lift. She had contemplated suggesting the stairs, but noticing the heels Angie was wearing, decided against it.

The fourth floor was much the same as the third. Next to the receptionist's desk, which Angie occupied, were two office doors, one bearing Leonard's name and the other Ron Opilet's. Angie worked for both attorneys, it seemed.

Carpets soundproofed the clicking heels most of the women chose to wear. The firm's brand colours were introduced in the cadet-grey and Oxford-blue cushions and the striped upholstery of the couches and office chairs. On one of the walls hung a Kentridge artwork – a charcoal and pastel drawing that Jen studied while she waited to be summoned into Leonard's office. On the opposite wall were framed pictures of what Jen assumed were the company's esteemed clients. She noticed some dignitaries among them and was impressed but also afraid at how much Mazwai, Mantzel, Opilet and Associates must charge per hour. She didn't think being friends with Claudia or the fact that she was just a housewife would hold much sway over her final bill.

After she had filled out her personal details and read and signed the terms and conditions of the firm, she followed Angie to the boardroom. Angie pushed open the glass door and offered Jen a seat on one of the Philippe Starck chairs strategically placed around an antique mahogany table. In front of each chair were neat folders and pens bearing the law firm's name, as well as water and a bowl of mints.

Jen was the sole occupant, and Angie enquired whether she would care for tea or coffee.

"A strong whisky," she joked.

"That can be arranged, Mrs Pearce," she winked. "Anything but narcotics."

Jen laughed. She liked this Angie. "Well, good to know. I'll start with a strong espresso. Double, please, Angie."

Jen recognised Leonard Mazwai from the photographs on Claudia's wall. He was exactly as they had portrayed him: tall and unbelievably handsome with his afro and black-framed glasses.

He is also courteous, Jen thought as he stepped aside to allow Angie to exit before he entered the boardroom. Men in suits didn't excite Jen but he looked dapper in charcoal, the pants tapered at the ankles and the jacket unbuttoned to reveal a finely striped purple shirt with a pin collar; the gold pin held a butter-yellow tie firmly in place. His look was accessorised with an antique Cartier wristwatch, which he glanced at before apologising for being a little late.

"I'm Leonard. I've heard so much about you that I feel I know you well."

Jen shook his hand shyly. She wasn't sure what he knew about her, but she did feel a little self-conscious. She adjusted her wrap dress to show less cleavage and in that instant she had a sudden flashback to her night with Myron, remembering that he and Leonard were friends. She blushed.

Leonard didn't seem to notice, and he gestured for her to sit. "Listen, Jen, things seem to have unfolded at a rapid pace. Sharon said you'd like to file for divorce."

"Yes," Jen said. "I'd like you to work on an interim settlement."

"Okay, we can talk about that in detail later."

Jen nodded, holding her breath. It seemed that Leonard had much more on his mind that he wished to divulge.

"I'm really sorry to hear of the death of Lee Holms. He was a client of ours, so we are distraught, to say the least."

"A client here?" Jen said confused. John, Lee and all their friends used Grant van Rooyen, an old friend and firmly entrenched Stellenbosch local, as their lawyer.

"Well, we are one of the firms that represent him, and this is where things have really 'developed', unbeknown to us. I hope that this isn't a conflict of interest, but another person we represent is Patty Klein." Jen looked back at Leonard blankly.

"Patty, your husband's former employee?"

What? Jen shifted uncomfortably. "I'm not sure how this

would be a conflict of interest unless I want to sue her, which I don't. I want to sue my husband for a divorce. She happens to be one of his many, um, liaisons, and the fact that you represent her is a coincidence to say the least. Why would this be a conflict of interest?"

"Well, we have been instructed by Ms Patty Klein to approach you regarding a matter that involves you. She was instructed to oversee this matter by your late friend, Lee Holms."

Jen didn't have the foggiest notion what Leonard was going on about. She wasn't registering what he was saying, and she wasn't really interested for that matter. All she wanted was to get on with the discussions around her divorce and be done with Patty. She realised that she felt absolutely nothing for the woman; except perhaps minuscule gratitude. If not for Patty, she would still be the pitiful wife of John Pearce.

"You're talking in riddles, Leonard. It's been quite an emotional few days, so I'm not sure if it's that or if I'm just plain stupid. I'm sorry, but I really don't understand what you're trying to say to me."

"Jen, Patty is the one who delivered the photos of your husband to our offices. We didn't know this up until this morning. She was instructed to do this by her employer, Lee Holms. Following his death, she now has the awkward task of handling his 'business' affairs, which coincidentally involves you."

At that moment, Angie walked in with Jen's espresso. Jen gulped it down, scalding her tongue.

Leonard waited until she'd finished before continuing. "I'm really asking your permission to allow Patty to speak with you. If you would prefer another lawyer to handle your divorce, then you are well within your rights. Patty, through Lee, was our client before you, though, so we are legally bound to her. We are able to represent you, but that is only if you do not feel that this will pose a conflict."

Jen squared her shoulders; she needed to get to the bottom of whatever was going on.

"Leonard, I'm still confused. Patty is Lee's employee? How can that be when, up until Sunday, she worked for my husband?"

"It is a little complicated, and that is why it's best if she explains to you directly what has been going on and why she has been instructed to take care of her employer's business, which, as I have said, involves you. When you asked me to represent you, I had absolutely no idea that Lee Holms was a friend, and even if he were, it would've been of no consequence, until his death yesterday."

"God!" Jen exclaimed. "What 'business' could Lee have with me? And why do I have to deal with her? Can I not just deal with her lawyer?"

"I suppose you could. But she has insisted she speak to you directly, with representation of course. That is why I have scheduled our meeting in the boardroom."

Jen sighed.

"Is that an okay?" Leonard asked gently.

"Do I have a choice? She is, as you pointed out, a client of yours. As a matter of interest, where do I stand? Am I still your client?"

"You most definitely are if you decide after this meeting that you would still like me to represent you."

"Well, let's see; if there's a 'conflict', as you put it, then you'll have to refer me to someone else."

As she spoke, Jen could see Patty walking towards the boardroom through the glass panelling along one wall. She didn't look like the Patty Jen knew. She walked with a stoop. Her hair had been pulled back from her unmade face and her eyes were puffy and red, evidence that she had been crying. Jen felt a spurt of sympathy. She knew this was crazy, but Patty looked so alone and sad. So vulnerable. How was this even possible?

Thirty

Pete hadn't expected such a big gathering on Frankie's farm that Thursday; all her book club friends were rallying around her. His mother was conspicuous in her absence. He briefly joined the men, huddled in Lee's den with Rita, Lee's faithful bookkeeper, making funeral arrangements and discussing the future of Holms Wine Estate, trading as HWE Wines, and how they could assist Frankie in organising the running of the business until Clive was ready to take over.

Typical of Lee that everything is already in place, Pete thought. Hennie, the farm's respected and loyal winemaker who had been in Lee's employ for the last fifteen years, and who was very much in charge of production on the farm, would continue to do what he had won awards doing: produce internationally acclaimed wines. As far as the vineyards were concerned, Lee had promoted Sarel to farm manager five years ago, as he had proved to be another loyal and committed worker. He had since done a sterling job taking care of the labourers and the vineyards, making sure that everything – planting, spraying and harvesting the grapes – happened right on time, and to Lee's high standards. As far as the marketing and business side was concerned, Lee had been grooming his son, Clive, for that role, but most of the admin was handled by Rita, a seemingly sweet little old lady, clad in a hand-knitted pastel-coloured jumper, who was not as benign as she seemed. Lee had inherited her with the farm, so she knew how to handle most things independently of her boss. She also saw to the wine reps and the sales and tasting staff, and boy, did they fear her wrath if anything went wrong.

The men agreed that, for the time being, Frankie would be okay. Lee had seen to it that the farm practically ran itself. All Frankie needed was time and a little guidance so that she could steer the boat until Clive had finished his studies.

Pete hadn't had a chance to sympathise with Clive, who suggested that he give up university to take over the business full-time. He could study through correspondence. Most of the men insisted that he complete his studies, that Lee would have wanted it that way.

The discussion over Clive's future choices irritated Pete as he was, after all, old enough to make his own decision. He took this opportunity to make his exit.

His friend acknowledged him by a slight nod of his head as he made his way to the door. Clive was a mixture of both his parents: tall like his dad, yet with an athletic build that Frankie always attributed to her good genes. He was lucky enough to have been blessed with his father's blue eyes and Frankie's sex appeal, which, although she wasn't on Pete's list of favourite people, he had to concede she possessed. The two boys would socialise occasionally, and he had seen first hand how popular he was amongst the girls.

Unlike Pete, Clive had always been very close to both his parents. His father had taught him to show respect to everyone and he had developed a kindness and compassion that was way beyond his years. And, although he was aware of his mother's egocentric ways, he loved her just the same. He had often said that Frankie wouldn't be Frankie if she was the kind and nurturing woman people expected a mother to be.

Clive had told him about Frankie's upbringing and how she had had to fend for herself, how she had learnt from an early age that the world was a tough place and how this is what had shaped her and what had attracted his father to her in the first place.

Pete had liked Frankie up until now. He had always thought that behind the tough façade was a very vulnerable woman. The elite would often gossip about how Lee had refined her so that she fitted in with them. Knowing Clive, Pete knew he would want to be around to help her through this rough time. God knows he would want to do the same for his mom.

There was no way that the gravity of Clive's father's death had quite hit him yet. But already he was showing resilience. Typical of Clive and, Pete had to admit, his adulterous mother.

Pete closed the study door gently behind him and looked around. Frankie was as he had found her on his arrival – seated in Lee's armchair. The morning sun shone on her which gave her an ethereal look. She seemed to derive comfort from her deceased husband's chair, and he'd yet to see her leave its worn leather embrace.

He could hear his mother's friends in the kitchen discussing the funeral tea in low voices and knew that the men would be ensconced in the study with Clive for some time. His sister was on the veranda with her group of friends, and there seemed to be no one else around. Now was his chance. He headed towards the liquor cabinet on the other end of the sun lounge (as they liked to call it) near the big sash windows. "I know it's still morning, but I could do with a drink. Can I get you one, Frankie?"

She lifted her head blearily and nodded.

When he handed her the glass, she looked at him searchingly. "Where is your mom *really?*"

"Truthfully, I don't know."

Frankie's look told him that she didn't believe him. He downed his scotch. "Really, I don't. But I did speak to her last night and she asked me to give you this." He reached into his jacket pocket for the perfume bottle. He studied it as he spoke.

"Mom said to say you left it in her bathroom on Sunday night, and that's why she's sorry she can't be here. She's sure Lee would've understood."

Frankie simply stared at it. Pete tried giving it to her, but she wouldn't take it.

"Your mom is mistaken. That's not mine."

"Frankie," Pete stayed calm. "Mom thinks I haven't the faintest idea what's going on. Except I do. I know you sleeping with my father, and now I guess Ma knows too. Sunday night she was at the spa, so you must've been at our house with Dad."

Frankie's features contorted into a snarl. "Don't you dare speak such nonsense! And at such a time. You should be ashamed of yourself!"

"Shit, Frankie, don't you think you should be ashamed? We like to hide our secrets in this little town. So, I'm prepared to pretend that I don't know that you fucking my dad, but only out of respect for Lee and for Clive's sake and definitely for Ma. I guess, until she's prepared to admit that Dad is a complete fuck up, I'm prepared to go along with this bullshit, so the least you can do is pretend to believe that Ma is at a spa. If you make one more snide remark about her not being here, I swear I will tell everyone exactly what's going on."

They both turned as Faith entered the room. She placed her hands on Frankie's shoulders. "Is Madam okay?"

Frankie clutched her one hand reassuringly. "Yes, Faith, I am doing fine." Faith gave Pete a look, and he knew it was his cue.

He leaned in to Frankie to give her a hug and shoved the perfume into her lap.

As he left, he heard Frankie cry out, "I loved Lee! I did. I loved him. And *he* was no angel!"

He turned to look at her one last time. She was clutching the bottle against her chest. Pete walked away satisfied.

Jen watched Patty as she was ushered into the boardroom by Ron Opilet, but she didn't get a chance to catch her eye before Leonard introduced her to his associate, a stocky, mousey-haired man with a lingering smell of aftershave.

"Mrs Pearce, Jen, I'm very pleased to meet you. I represent Lee on matters personal and confidential. I am going to be completely straight with you, as I don't know how else to proceed. Patty, you now know is here because she has been employed by Lee for the last five years. She's been his personal assistant and taken care of all his business matters that don't involve the farm."

Jen turned to look at Patty who avoided eye contact with her.

"A while back, Lee asked me to be the custodian of some money and gold coins, Kruger Rands, which your mother had left in his care for you. She didn't want you to have them while you were married to your husband because you would be obliged to share this inheritance with him. The arrangement was that these be handed to you should you divorce your husband, should Lee or your spouse pass away, or on your sixtieth birthday, whichever came first. Your mom, bless her soul, felt that if you were still married at sixty, the likelihood of divorce would be miniscule. If you died while Lee was alive, the inheritance would go to her grandchildren."

Patty found a tissue in her bag and dabbed her eyes with it.

"Patty now heads this trust due to the untimely death of your dear friend," said Opilet. "It has been decided to disclose the existence of this little nest egg to you. We need instruction as to

211

how you want us to proceed."

Jen felt bewildered. She looked at Patty, and this time Patty looked her straight in the eye. *What the hell is he going on about?* But Jen couldn't bring herself to ask her.

"I've been told that you're filing for divorce, and our company likes to keep our clients' interests at the forefront of everything. Non-disclosure is a suggestion." Jen looked at him blankly.

"In other words, Mrs Pearce, our company is willing to keep this 'inheritance' in our trust until such time as your divorce goes through – with your permission, that is."

Jen felt the colour draining from her face. She needed time for all of this to sink in: the money, Lee's collusion with her mother, Patty's role in Jen's future. Everything!

"I, I'm not sure what to say." She was shaking.

The four of them sat in silence for what seemed a long time.

Then Jen began to cry. This then was the cathartic moment she had been waiting for. Everything had been building up to this: her mother's shrewdness; Lee's desire to keep Jen's wellbeing at heart; Patty's role, which was confusing and beyond surprising. How had the universe conspired for them to land up at the same firm of attorneys? How had all of this brought her to the place where she could finally move forward, with the financial freedom she would need to do so, at exactly the right time?

Jen looked up, and saw Patty crying too. She leaned over the table and placed her hand gently on Patty's. She barely noticed the two attorneys glancing at each other, nodding, then leaving the boardroom.

Thirty-one

Not long after Pete had left, Grant van Rooyen Esq. entered the lounge. Frankie was still fuming as he gave her a long hug and his condolences. He and Lee had been childhood friends, and Lee had been a client of his since early adulthood. Grant had drawn up their marriage contract, had taken care of legal matters pertaining to the farm, drawn up their will and now, she knew, he was seeing to Lee's estate.

After a few polite exchanges and after Faith had brought him a cup of strong black coffee, he broached the delicate matter of the estate. "I know that you are aware, more or less, what Lee decided regarding his property and his money. He set up a trust for Clive, the farm is yours until your death and all his liquid assets go to you and your son. There is one thing that has changed, though, just recently."

"What?" Frankie was immediately alert. Panicked, even. What if Lee had decided to leave her with nothing after he had found out about her affairs?

"There is a property that he bought in the city. Upon his death, it goes to his goddaughter, Brigit Pearce. He said that he hadn't been the most loving godparent and he wanted to make up for neglecting her."

Frankie's relief that she was still in line to be a very rich widow was soon replaced by irritation at Brigit's little windfall.

"She's living in the apartment at the moment, as a tenant," continued Grant. "She has been paying a substantially reduced rental into Lee's account, and he never spent a cent of it. So that money will go to you, as the apartment has been paid for. He never wanted her to know. He wanted her to feel that she was making it on her own. And she is, I guess, because she never missed a payment. Now that the property is hers, and there is no bond, she won't have to pay rent. Isn't it a lovely gesture?"

"Mmmm," Frankie said distractedly.

"Your husband was a kind man," he remarked, his voice thick with emotion. "He will be sorely missed, Frankie, he really will be."

"I know," Frankie said in a half-whisper. "Although I'm sure Brigit Pearce will be delighted. She's hit the jackpot, hasn't she, now that my husband is dead?"

Grant frowned. "I don't think she has any expectations, Frankie, so don't be sore. Just see it as a wonderful gesture on your husband's part – testimony to the decent man he was."

He followed Frankie's eyes to the sash window where Brigit was huddled together with her friends chatting.

"I will speak to her for you, unless you want to tell her yourself?"

"No, I just want to be left alone with my thoughts. It's been a very sad time for me. I hope you understand, Grant."

Grant clapped his hands gently on his thighs – a gesture that he was done and that he would do as she desired. "Of course, I do. I will see you tomorrow at the memorial service. Stay as strong as you've always been, Frankie."

Frankie watched him leave the room and saw him through the sash window as he approached Brigit and Clive's group of young friends on the veranda. Brigit shrugged her shoulders at the group and excused herself before walking away with Grant. Frankie guessed that they would have a chat under the big oak tree that had seen years of family gatherings.

Last night had been a chilling foretaste of others to come. She had ached for Lee next to her in bed. Knowing she would never have him near her again filled her with intense sadness and loneliness. She could not imagine her life without him. His death had forced her to reflect on her marriage, and the issues that had irked her so now seemed miniscule and ridiculous – except of course this surprise matter of Brigit's inheritance. She hauled herself out of Lee's chair to pour herself a second glass of whisky.

"I can't believe Lee's dead, never mind all the other things that my mind has to absorb," Jen said. "Do you know what kind of a whirlwind five days it's been, Patty?" she asked.

"I do. It's been pretty shocking on my side, too."

"Ever since I caught you and John…"

"I'm sorry," Patty said earnestly. "I really am. You were collateral damage. You weren't meant to catch us. It was never supposed to happen the way it did. Lee was furious with me, but it worked in our favour in the end. I'm… *we're* only sorry that it hurt you so much."

Jen blinked and sat up straight. "What the hell are you talking about, Patty? Are you trying to tell me that you colluded with Lee against my husband? That you *blew* him for a 'noble' cause, and not because you're a…?" Jen checked herself. "Am I expected to believe your bullshit?" She felt ganged up against, angry, betrayed and stupid. The sympathy, which had compelled her to reach out to Patty, had lasted only an instant.

"God, Jen, I can imagine how hurt you are, and I'm sorry. The story is so complicated, even unbelievable, and I don't blame you for hating me. I just want you to give me a chance to explain."

"Well it sounds as if you and Lee trapped my husband. Not only that, you managed to get rich off it, too. I should be exposing you, Patty, not giving you a chance to explain yourself."

"Lee had nothing to do with me, um, and John, in the tasting room. In fact, he was furious with me when he found out."

Jen glared at Patty. Patty held her glare.

"I'm sorry for what I did, but I've done you a favour."

"A favour!"

"All you need to do, Jen, is listen."

There was a silence. Jen noticed Patty's hand shaking as she reached for her water. "Well, tell me, for God's sake. Tell me why I shouldn't go to the cops about this! In fact, I'm interested to know how you're okay with prostituting yourself?"

Patty took another sip of water followed by a deep breath. "I need to start from the beginning – to tell you how I became Lee's good friend and personal assistant."

Jen rolled her eyes. *Can't she just edit her story? It's bad enough having to sit here with her after what she did, never mind having to listen to her justify things.*

Patty ignored Jen's obvious hostility and launched into her explanation. "When I first met Lee, my divorce had just gone through and it was my thirtieth birthday. I had absolutely no money, but I felt a newfound sense of freedom. I also had no friends. My husband hadn't allowed me any, so I was very alone. But that didn't deter me from celebrating, even on my own.

"I went to a club because I wanted to dance. I hadn't danced for as long as I'd been married, and I danced alone, shamelessly. I was just so happy to be free to do exactly as I pleased and to do what I had loved doing so much. Occasionally, guys would join me on the dance floor, and I danced for what felt like hours, lost in the music."

Jen sat back and looked out of the window. It was a beautiful day, belying the fact that it had poured with rain the night before.

Patty finished her water and continued. "I spotted a very good-looking man at the bar. He hadn't looked up once, and it seemed as if he was lost in thought. After a few glasses of bubbly, I felt brave enough to approach him. I've always loved sex."

Jen turned from the window and looked at her reproachfully. "Well, it's the truth. That's why I stayed so long in my marriage. Our sex life was phenomenal, if you can believe that! Anyway, I went straight up to him and propositioned him. The man was Lee, and we landed up having sex in the club's toilet."

"Oh my God! Spare me the gory details!"

"No. I need to tell you the details." She paused, and Jen nodded for her to continue. "We both felt so fucking guilty. Lee more so than me. He'd cheated on Frankie to get back at her."

"What was he getting back at her for?"

"She told him that she'd had her tubes tied."

"That's news to me!"

"It was news to Lee, too. Apparently, when she married him, she promised she'd try for two children. But she changed her mind after having Clive. She said she didn't want to go through it all again. He thought that, with time, she'd come around and they would try for their second, but the more time passed, the *less* keen she seemed."

Jen crossed her arms and snorted.

"So anyway, that day, Lee had brought it up with her. Time was running out. They had a fight, and that's when Frankie told him that it didn't matter what he wanted because she'd had her tubes tied years ago."

Jen unfolded her arms. "How? When?"

"I don't know the details. Apparently, Lee had booked an overseas trip with the boys. Frankie was furious. She eventually said he could go on condition that she book herself in at a health farm. Seems she checked in to a hospital instead.

"Lee was so angry that he landed up at this club, and my proposition seemed a good idea. His way of getting back at Frankie."

By now, Jen was thoroughly engrossed in the story. "Go on," she urged.

"I told Lee my whole sob story about my abusive husband, my acrimonious divorce and my joblessness. That was when he offered me a job. He was a partner in an upmarket gentlemen's club, a whorehouse really, and they were looking for a well-groomed, clean-living woman to work as hostess, see to the tips and payments and oversee the strippers and prostitutes."

Jen felt sick. "Oh my God, Lee is one of the owners of that 'poker' club?"

"Yes, he was. And I've inherited his share of the business. He was such a generous man. I can't believe my best friend – let's be honest, my only friend – is gone." Patty began to cry again, her sobs washing over her in waves. Jen was intrigued at how easily Patty allowed herself to mourn. She had been raised to stay composed, no matter what.

When her sobs subsided, Patty sniffed deeply, grabbed her tissue and blew into it. "So you know about the club? It's very off the radar, and we're in the process of moving premises as people are getting wind of it. Strangely enough, working there turned out to be fabulous." Jen remained mute as Patty continued. "I had loads of responsibilities and I had a chance to show my managerial qualities. I could handle the men, and I was able to handle the women too. I started organising Lee's personal stuff; he needed someone who could be discreet about his 'other' life – the one that included an illicit business interest. He couldn't trust anyone else with the job. The people involved in the club aren't exactly like you and your townsfolk, but at least they're honest about who they are and what they're doing."

"That's debatable," interjected Jen. "Their whole operation is undercover."

Patty shrugged. "I guess. It *is* by invitation only. That's how I got to meet John and the rest of the group. I'm going to be honest, Jen. John never slept with any of the women at the club, but he pursued me relentlessly."

Anger began to show on Jen's face, but Patty didn't seem to notice. "When he eventually understood my boundaries, we became quite friendly and we spoke often. That's when he offered me a job as a wine rep."

"Oh?"

"Ya. I laughed it off because I was happy working at the club. But Lee, in the meantime, had found out about Frankie's affair with a French diplomat."

"A what? She never told *me* about it!"

"Lee had hired a private detective and he had hard evidence of the affair."

"Photos?" Jen remembered Leonard saying it had been Patty, on Lee's instruction, who had given him the photos of John with other women.

"Exactly. But Frankie's other affair was harder to pin down even by the investigator Lee had hired to tail her. She was often at your farm, but Lee thought nothing of it, for obvious reasons."

Jen wasn't sure what she meant by obvious reasons.

"Well, the two of you were friends. It's only when he found a number Frankie called regularly that he became suspicious. After investigating, he discovered that the number belonged to your husband. Do you know that John has a second phone?"

"It's apparent I'm easy to fool."

"Lee knew their affair was gaining momentum from the number of phone calls, and from a change in Frankie, but he didn't have concrete proof. The only thing he could go on was a hunch. That's when he came up with the idea that I accept John's job offer as wine rep. This way, Lee would have an 'in' because I would act as a private investigator without causing any suspicion."

Jen nodded. "Clever."

"Right? But for a long time, all I managed to dig up was that John was having regular sex with someone in his office in the cellar."

Jen's eyes widened. "What?"

"Sorry Jen, but I'm going to tell you everything, okay?"

Jen nodded.

Patty's voice was softer, more compassionate. "It was impossible to hang around to find out who it was, because John was adamant that everyone leaves by seven at the latest. And the night I did stay later, that night I dropped in to visit you at the house, remember?"

"Yes," Jen said. "You seemed lonely. I even asked you if you wanted to go to a movie with me."

"Yes, you did. It was that night, on the way to my car, that I decided to do a quick snoop, and that's when I heard him in the cellar."

"Bastard!"

"I'm sorry."

Jen looked at Patty. "Stop saying you're sorry. And finish your story. I need to know everything. Every goddamn thing."

"Okay." Patty tried to squeeze her hand, but Jen jerked it away. She paused before continuing. "Meanwhile, John started harassing me. He was becoming very touchy-feely. One afternoon, he had me up against the cellar wall, his face close to mine."

Jen could hear herself saying, "Oh my God!" repeatedly.

"I managed to free myself by kneeing him, and I thought that if he didn't fire me then, I needed to find a way to leave, as it was becoming impossible to work under those conditions. The only problem was that I was working for Lee."

"Come on! The Lee I know would have let you leave," Jen said.

220

"Yes. He kept telling me to resign. But I told him that if I left, we would never have a chance to uncover the truth. That's when I decided to become, er, creative. Lee knew nothing about this. In fact, it was never meant to go that far."

Angie knocked gently on the boardroom door. She opened it and looked in. "Are you ladies all right? Can I get you anything to drink?"

They both asked for coffees, and when Angie had gone, Patty continued.

"I wasn't sure how or even *if* it was going to work. I thought, naïvely, that if I could get some sort of jealous reaction from Frankie, something might unravel. I wasn't sure what. I knew she didn't like me. Maybe on some level, she knew how close Lee and I were, or that she felt I was a threat to her when it came to John, but I knew that if I flirted with John in front of her, something was bound to happen."

Jen put her elbow on the table and leaned in towards Patty. "What about me? Did you not for one moment think what *I* may have done if you flirted with John in front of me?"

"I hadn't given you much thought, I must admit," confessed Patty. "Your absence from the party made what I had set out to do so much easier. I thought my plan had backfired on me. Instead of Frankie, it was you who caught me, which made Lee so angry and obviously upset me."

Jen allowed her to touch her hand this time. "I really am so sorry about it. Worse, it seemed that Frankie just ended up protecting you."

Jen nodded for her to go on.

"So, I thought I had blown it. I guess that's not a good word to use?" Patty said ruefully.

"It certainly isn't," Jen said, with a slight grin.

"I mean, it seemed as if I'd ruined Lee's chance of ever finding out the truth. It was Lee, by the way, who came up with the idea

221

that I sue John. He saw it as compensation to you for the pain we caused you."

Jen leaned back and crossed her arms again. "I don't understand. How does suing John for money make me feel any better? Half of that money is mine by virtue of marriage."

"Don't you see, Jen? Lee organised for the money from John's ceded insurance policy to go into your little nest egg, along with your mom's undisclosed inheritance. He felt that it was the least he could do after what happened."

Thirty-two

The sun had set, and silence finally descended on Frankie's farm. It had been a long and tiring two days. Although the noise that had filled her house had been that of caring friends with good intentions, it had been too much for her, and the tranquillity was welcome.

After Pete and Grant had left, spurred on by a cocktail of anger, guilt and sadness, Frankie had managed to imbibe at least a quarter of a bottle of whisky, rendering her intoxicated. Her girlfriends, too busy clucking about like mother hens, hadn't noticed.

Faith was the only one aware that Frankie had eaten nothing the entire day. She brought in her supper on a tray.

"Madam, you must eat. You have a long day tomorrow. Madam Shelley made her chicken pie for you, and I know you love it."

"Faith, I can't eat a thing," Frankie slurred. "I just want to drink myself into a coma. Please, be a darling and pour me another," she said as she lifted her glass to her helper.

"I think that's enough for you, Mom. Thanks, Faith, for all your hard work today. I'm sure you could do with a rest. We're going to need you tomorrow, that's for sure."

Frankie hadn't noticed her son's silent entry. Faith seemed reluctant to leave her side, but Frankie caught the insistent look Clive gave her, precipitating her exit.

He stretched out full length on the couch and stared at the ceiling without speaking. They were silent for a while, then he asked, "How are you doing, Mom? Are you okay?"

Frankie spat out, "Did you hear about Brigit's inheritance? She put on a sad face, but I bet she couldn't wait to get home to celebrate her windfall. Dad's death is her jackpot."

"Ya. Grant told me."

"I'm furious," she said.

"I'm not sure why it's such an issue," Clive said.

"Goddaughter, huh? She hardly spoke to her godfather. Why should she get anything? Why?"

Frankie was the most vocal she had been the whole day. She wanted Clive on her side. Maybe together they could fight this ridiculous bequest.

"Mom, don't be like that. It's a drop in the ocean."

Frankie staggered to her feet. "Drop in the ocean? That apartment is worth a small fortune and lavish Lee throws it away. Fuck that! I won't allow it." She felt Clive's hands on her shoulders as he gently guided her back into Lee's chair.

"Come on, Ma. It's what Dad wanted," he said, slouching back onto the couch.

"What Dad wanted?" Frankie was furious. *Why doesn't he see through this bullshit!*

"Dad was always a generous man, Ma. A good man. Stop it, please!"

"Lee, the saint. Let's not forget to canonise him. This just confirms all those rumours about Brigit being his illegitimate child."

Clive sat up abruptly.

"Now he's got the whole fucking town talking and I look like a bloody idiot. He did this on purpose, to get back at me!" she shouted. She knew how drunk she sounded, but she went on, not allowing Clive to interrupt her. "He was like that, you know. He loved to punish me." She looked up to the ceiling and yelled, "You're a fucking bastard, aren't you? You're having a good old laugh at my expense!"

Clive jumped to his feet. "What are you saying, Mom? For God's sake, stop it! Dad's dead. His body isn't even cold yet and you're talking shit about him to me. Stop, please!"

Frankie couldn't hide her bitterness.

"I *knew* he and Jen were lovers before we got married. And his parents were so desperate for him to marry the town virgin! Ha! What a laugh. Jen and the Virgin Mary, both pregnant before they married, and still, everyone believes they're untainted."

"Stop it!"

"She wasn't even here to give me her condolences, to pay her respects! The bitch! But she'll be happy for her daughter to take what rightly belongs to us, Clive."

"Mom, stop it, please!" Clive begged.

Frankie ignored him. "She thinks I'm the bad friend because I slept with her dysfunctional husband. I did her a favour." She burst into tears, sobbing drunkenly. "I tried to keep that asshole on the straight and narrow, so he didn't run around with every whore in town."

"Now you're starting to freak me out completely! Please tell me that you're making this all up. Please, Ma, I beg you, stop it."

Faith walked in and put her finger to her mouth, silencing Clive. Sitting down on the arm of Frankie's chair, she placed the weeping woman's head against her tummy and rocked her gently from side to side. Such a soothing gesture was unfamiliar to Frankie, but she succumbed, nestling her head against the starched uniform that smelled comfortingly of cooking oil and fabric softener. She was completely spent.

"Ssh, Madam, ssh. Faith is going to take Madam to bed now. Here's a little pill for you."

Frankie took the sleeping tablet and swallowed it dry. Faith helped her up and walked her to her bedroom. Her helper pulled back the sheets, removed Frankie's slippers from her feet and helped her lie down. Then she tucked her in gently and stroked her forehead.

"Madam needs to rest. Madam must just relax, please."

Frankie felt herself dropping off to sleep before Faith had even left the room.

The only person who could help Jen sift through all this information and conflicting emotions was Sharon, who was willing to see her early that evening.

"I have to admit that your story has been the most compelling one I've ever been paid to listen to."

Jen adored Sharon: her honesty, and the way she listened. It felt to her that she was more like a friend than a counsellor.

"Well, apparently, I inadvertently played a seminal part in the events that unfolded."

"How so?" Sharon asked.

"Because I insisted that John fire Patty. He was forced to make a financial settlement. And my phone call to Lee's house in the middle of the night asking for Frankie gave her game away. It was the evidence Lee needed to finally point to Frankie's indiscretion."

"It sounds to me like John needs help," Sharon said, her eyes boring into Jen's. "Phew. You have dealt with enough betrayal, haven't you, Jen?" Jen nodded. The tears welled up.

John had betrayed her for years, in every possible way. If she was honest, he had never really been supportive or understanding.

If she had compared John to Lee… She now knew she would have found that Lee was much more caring and supportive of Frankie than John had ever been of her. But then, Jen didn't have much by which to measure a husband's worth. Her parents' marriage hadn't been anything to go by. Her father had openly cheated on her mother. All this time, Jen had felt grateful for John – that he was not like her father. But little had she known. *John was just better at covering his tracks.*

"All I can say now is, thank goodness for Lee. He was a constant, I guess. He had my best interests at heart always, and I can never say thank you."

She began to cry. Her cry became a howl. Lee was dead. She would never see him again.

Sharon allowed her to cry. When Jen finally stopped sobbing, Sharon said, "Jen, I know you don't want to go to Lee's funeral tomorrow, but I think you should. You need to mourn him, you need to pay tribute to him and you need closure. Forget about the other people who'll be there. Focus on why you're there. And mourn; mourn the loss of your friend."

Jen interrupted her, " He was my guardian angel."

"I guess he was. He was the one person who had your back, even though you rejected him all those years ago. You know now that he loved you completely." Jen knew Sharon was right.

After her consultation with Sharon, Jen climbed behind her steering wheel and drove back to Stellenbosch, ready to face absolutely everything and everyone head on. It was dark when she finally arrived at the farm. She had made up her mind. She would attend Lee's memorial service. She would pay tribute to the man who had a hand in unshackling her.

She hadn't felt this brave for as long as she had been alive.

Thirty-three

Jen and Pete were in the lounge talking when they heard John's car pull up. The car doors slammed shut, and John and Brigit's raised voices carried across the vineyards. He was shouting that Brigit was to turn down the inheritance Lee had left her. She was screaming back at him that she would do no such thing, that she was old enough to make her own decisions and that the inheritance was a kind gesture, proving to her how much Lee had valued her as his goddaughter.

"Bullshit! He's trying to make a point. That's what he's doing. At my expense. The conniving son of a bitch!"

Jen jumped from the couch and ran to the entrance hall with Pete on her heels, ready to try to rein in John's temper.

"*Why*? Tell me?" Brigit shrieked. "Is it because *you* can't afford to buy me an apartment? Does this make you look...?"

There was a loud smack as John's hand connected with Brigit's cheek.

Everyone stood stock still for what felt like an age, until Brigit cried out, "You're a monster, that's what you are. Don't you lift your hand to me again, ever!" Jen followed as she ran to her bedroom, but Brigit managed to slam the door before Jen could stop her. Knowing Brigit, Jen thought it best to let her be. She stormed back to the hallway.

John glared at Jen. "Look what the cat's dragged in," he sneered. "To what do we owe the honour?" John motioned to Pete. "I see you have your lackey with you. Why don't you fuck off too!"

"I will not have you speak like that to Pete, do you hear me?" Jen spoke calmly.

"Or what?" John challenged.

"Or it will be your loss; unless of course you want to turn your children against you too."

Pete gave her a look that said, *I'm here if you need me*, then turned and left the room. When she heard the kitchen door swinging shut behind him, she knew he had retreated to his cottage.

Jen went back into the lounge, *her* lounge, which had been photographed all those years ago for an interiors magazine. It was a beautiful cream and pistachio-green affair, with a marble coffee table as the focal point. *I'll definitely take that*, she thought with affection. She had salvaged it from a junk shop and brought it back to its original splendour. Suddenly she was seeing everything in terms of what she would take with her when she left. The couches John could continue to slouch on, but the armoire, too, would find a new home with her. It had been her grandmother's and had been handed down from her mother to her. It had originally been a depressing dark wood but Jen had lovingly repainted it using a French paint technique that was bizarre and sacrilegious at the time, though she'd noticed over the past few years that this had become quite a trend. She had breathed life back into that old cupboard, antique or not. That had been the crux of the magazine article: how Jen had managed to bring modernity into an old farmhouse, on a very small budget.

John had followed her into the lounge. She could feel him seething, but his anger no longer had an effect on her. She sat down on one of the couches and crossed her legs, imagining that she looked almost regal with her arm outstretched across the back.

"I'm here because I'm going to Lee's memorial service tomorrow."

"You've come to your senses," John snarled, "after causing unnecessary crap and embarrassment."

"Yes, I have. With some help, I came to the conclusion that it would be disrespectful of me not to pay my last respects to Lee. And it would be ridiculous to avoid the service because of your affair – with Frankie, I mean. After all, the two of you should be hiding your shameful faces, not me."

"That fucking son of a bitch told you, didn't he? He was always out to get me, because he wanted you and you chose me instead."

"You have clearly underestimated me, John. Give me some credit. I'm not that stupid. I didn't need Lee to tell me. You, on the other hand, are a very, very stupid and careless man. I was bound to find out. All I needed was to open my eyes. For some pathetic reason, I've had them shut for the duration of our marriage."

"Aren't you the brave one suddenly? Sitting there all smug and self-righteous? Do you think I don't know about you and Lee? I rescued you, you fucking whore. Who knows who Brigit's father is? Maybe you can shed some light on your daughter's true identity, huh? All I know is Lee would never have married you if you were pregnant. I did! And I raised her as my own."

She'd expected John to fight dirty and had prepared herself for the abuse that would be hurled her way.

"I slept with Lee. I'm sorry I kept it from you, and I'm sorry if I hurt you. We were stoned and drunk. We were also young and impulsive, and one thing led to another. I admit that keeping it a secret was partly to protect you, but it was mostly to protect

231

me. I was vulnerable, and the thought of living in a community that regards unmarried mothers as outcasts was frightening for me and shameful for my mom. But know this: I always wanted you, John."

John smirked.

"I did! I had resolved to tell you about Lee and face the consequences. But then I found out I was pregnant. Mom was afraid that if I said anything to you, you would leave me. Even if Brigit was yours. I was afraid."

Jen was not weepy; she did not place blame. She just wanted to speak the truth. She wanted no more secrets, no more lies.

"I tried to be the best wife I could be. I committed one hundred per cent of myself to our marriage. To us."

"You're such a clever bitch, aren't you? If I had left you, knowing you were pregnant, can you imagine what everyone would have thought of me? They would never have believed that innocent Jen would fuck another guy. My reputation was already blemished by the pregnancy, so I had to marry you to show people that I was a decent human being. But don't think I'm going to forgive you for trapping me, you cunning…"

"Say it, John. That word seems to roll off your tongue so easily. Do you even realise how jarring it is? I heard you use that word on your own son, and now it looks like it's my turn. Say it. Come on, I know you want to."

John narrowed his eyes at her, weighing up the challenge.

"You cunning cunt," he said after a moment. "There, I said it. And it feels good."

"Lovely. You feel vindicated. I'm happy you do, because I will be divorcing you, John. After the service tomorrow, I'll be packing my things and moving out. Leonard Mazwai, my attorney, will be serving you with papers for an interim divorce settlement. He'll make sure I live in the style to which I'm accustomed. He will also ensure that I am justly rewarded for the pain and suffering you have caused."

John snorted. "You're fucking delusional. You've been watching too many chick flicks, baby."

Jen got up. "I'm not your baby. And don't undermine chick flicks. It's antagonists like you who make the chick flick so popular. Oh, and just a friendly reminder of your huge financial gain when you married me. A little reimbursement at this point would be good." She now looked at him, really saw him. His fists were balled, and he looked like a bull ready to charge.

"Goodnight, sleep tight," she sang cheerily, though shaking with anger. Jen walked out of the lounge and down the passage. She stopped at Brigit's bedroom and knocked quietly on her door.

"Brig?"

"Leave me alone!" Brigit barked. "I don't want to speak to you or Dad."

Then Jen did something she couldn't remember doing since Brigit had been a child. She put her foot down.

"I'm not asking you, Brigit, I'm telling you. Unlock your door. I need to talk to you and Pete."

A moment later, Brigit appeared and reluctantly followed Jen to Pete's cottage. On seeing them, he turned off the television and sat up. "What's up?"

"Mom wants to chat to us. After being unavailable without any explanation for days, *we* now have to make ourselves available when she sees fit," Brigit snapped.

The realisation that Brigit was, without a doubt, John's daughter dawned on Jen. They were two peas in a pod: surly, bombastic and self-absorbed.

"Thank you, Brigit. That's enough," Jen said firmly.

"Please tell me you're leaving him," Pete said.

"Yes. I am. I'm sorry I've made it so difficult for you these past few days. It wasn't my intention, but I needed time away from everyone and everything to try to figure out…"

Jen hesitated. She knew she had to be as honest as she could with her children. Although not everything in life had to be shared, some things needed to be divulged for clarity, and to move on.

"I can't stay married, because your father has cheated on me."

"We know," Brigit said.

"He's a cheating, lying…" Pete interjected. Jen stopped him.

"Don't! Just remember that we're all human. I am not defending your dad, but he is your father." Brigit and Pete looked at each other. Jen continued. "I'm not guiltless myself."

"What do you mean?" Pete asked.

"I have also kept a secret for years. I did want to tell your dad, but then I discovered I was pregnant. I was afraid he would leave me if he knew. So, I kept it from him to save my reputation and our relationship."

Pete paused, a glass of red wine halfway to his mouth. "What secret?"

"I slept with Lee. Once. While Dad and I were dating."

She waited for this to sink in, particularly with Brigit. She wanted to run away and hide, knowing the furore her revelation was about to cause.

"And you got *pregnant*? Oh my God!"

It was just as she'd expected: Brigit was incensed.

"I could be Lee's daughter?"

Jen didn't answer.

"I can't believe you. Pretending to be as pure as the driven snow! You cheated on Dad, and then you married him, knowing full well that I could be Lee's child? I can't believe you! I, I'm going to be sick."

Brigit stumbled out of the room, slamming the cottage door behind her.

Pete called after her but stayed where he was. Then he looked at his mother.

"That's a bit of a mind fuck for Brig, Ma!"

234

"Pour me a glass of that wine you're drinking, Pete." Pete got up, returning with a bottle of wine in one hand and a glass for Jen in the other.

"Keeping it a secret seemed like the right thing to do at the time," Jen told her son. He handed her a full glass of red wine. She took a sip before she continued. "I felt I had no choice. My mother was already ashamed that I had fallen pregnant. My father would've been turning in his grave. I was already a huge disappointment, and I had to make it right. Lee tried pursuing me, but I loved your dad. You must know: I would've chosen your dad over Lee, even if I hadn't been pregnant."

"How did it happen?" Pete asked.

"Lee and I were a little drunk and a bit stoned."

"Stoned?" Pete laughed. "Now I've heard it all, Ma."

Jen looked at her beautiful son. She had to throw him into adulthood whether he wanted to grow up or not. She took a long sip of her wine and savoured the taste before she spoke.

"My lawyer, Leonard Mazwai, would like to meet you tomorrow after Lee's memorial service. It's important. It's about our future and the future of the farm. Will you go?"

Pete nodded.

Thirty-four

J en had to sneak in through a side door of the Town Hall to avoid the book club girls who were waiting for Frankie at the entrance. The hall had been decorated with photographs of Lee from childhood. The most recent picture of him, Jen realised, had been taken at John's party, which was the last time she had seen him.

She noticed Ron Opilet, sitting a few rows ahead of her. Surely he wasn't there as Lee's lawyer? Could it be that they had some other connection? Jen wouldn't be surprised if he was one of Lee's illicit business associates. He had a shady look that made her think he probably had a finger in many pies.

The service had been scheduled for eleven. At half past, Jen heard a commotion behind her at the entrance to the hall and, along with the rest of the congregation, she turned around to see the book club girls, led by Shelley, greet Frankie and Clive at the door with teary hugs and kisses. The congregation stood as Frankie swept to the front row, while the farm workers led the mourners, accompanied by the organist, in singing 'Amazing Grace'.

Jen had wondered how she would feel seeing Frankie. She couldn't help thinking she played a fine grieving widow. *My ex-best friend is an expert at role-play.* Frankie had played Lee's besotted girlfriend and his vixen wife to the envy of everyone. When Clive was born, she took on the role of milf. So much so that Clive appeared to be little more than a wonderful accessory. The role of Jen's best friend had been her best performance to date.

Frankie, appearing distraught but strong, was carefully and alluringly dressed. Patty caught Jen's eye from across the aisle. It was as if she had read Jen's thoughts, and they smiled knowingly at each other.

The minister took to the podium once Frankie, Clive and the group of women were seated. He welcomed the mourners and thanked them for joining Lee's family in "bidding farewell to Lee Holms: respected husband, father, son and friend".

Jen noticed that she wasn't the only one to shift uncomfortably as he went on to remind them of life's only certainty: death.

"You cannot live your life here on earth by *your* rules. God has given you a set of rules to live by. Remember the Ten Commandments?

"Are you living as God would have you live in this life? The party, dear friends, is not here on earth, it is in heaven."

That was pretty sobering, Jen thought. Patty looked at her and pulled a face as if to say, *I guess I'm not going to any party in heaven!*

Jen smiled and shrugged, trying to convey a silent *It seems we're all doomed.*

"Let us pray for the soul of the deceased, Lee Holms, and for the souls of everyone gathered here today."

The congregation rose and sang the hymn 'Be Still and Know That I Am God'.

John then got up to speak. "Pastor Donald would be remiss if he didn't remind us of our own deaths. This is, after all, part of his job, which he has carried out very well. Thank you, Pastor Donald. I speak for myself when I say that I am truly rattled."

There were a few chuckles from the congregation.

"We're here to celebrate the life of Lee, as well as mourn his death. I think we can safely say that we are all sinners. I am counting on God being a loving God and a forgiving God. If, as Pastor Donald says, there's a party in heaven, God would have no guests if he didn't make a few concessions; and I'm sure that Lee will be one God would invite to the celebration. What kind of a party would it be without him?"

Everyone laughed. Even Jen caught herself smiling. *This is why I fell for him. He has a sense of humour and he can get away with being cheeky.*

"I have known Lee ever since we were old enough to be aware of one another's existence. We grew up as brothers; Lee had no siblings and I only had sisters. Our mothers were friends and from an early age we would play while they met for tea. We went to school together and that's where we met the rest of the gang: Frans, Larry, Matthew, Jesse, Dwain and Luke. As a group, we were formidable. Since pre-primary school, we have done just about everything together. The group can attest to Lee's and my competitive streak. We competed for everything. Instead of pushing us apart, it brought us together.

"We have so many fond memories of Lee that we will treasure. He was too young to be taken away from us, and so tragically. He has left an indelible mark on everyone who knew him. A kinder, more compassionate and generous man, you'd struggle to find. You will be forever missed, bud. Cheers, and keep a place up there for all of us."

If I didn't know what John has been up to, I would be moved. Jen was starting to believe that she was married to a sociopath.

How else does he manage to stand up there without flinching?

She felt deeply sorry for Clive when it was his turn to speak. From what she could see, he'd managed to hold himself together until that moment. She could tell from his shaking shoulders that he was sobbing. The mourners waited for him to compose himself before he spoke.

"My dad is my hero. He has been my mentor ever since I can remember. He was there when I took my first steps and he was there to help me ride my bike. He was a father who instilled so many values in me. He taught me kindness. He said it was easy to humiliate those who were supposedly socially inferior, but all this showed, he said, was ill breeding. My dad said there was plenty to be learned from every human being, no matter their status, sex, religion or age."

He took a deep, juddering breath.

"He practised what he preached. He acknowledged the people who showed commitment to their work. Boss Sarel Jenkins is a fine example of a man who started as a labourer, but who worked himself up to farm manager." The congregation turned to search out Boss Sarel, who looked down at his hands. "He has often said that he was lucky to have worked for my father, as he doubted whether he would've been given the same opportunities elsewhere." The labourers and Sarel nodded in agreement.

"My dad saw the diamond in my mom. He saw her beauty and he saw her strength and he defied everyone and married her." It was at this point that Jen heard the devastating gasp and cries from Frankie. Her friends placed loving arms around her, and Jen herself wished that she could do the same. If only. But she checked herself. "He was always in awe of her," Clive continued with a gentle smile. "My dad loved life. I am happy that he has left this world having done just about everything he dreamed of doing, from running one of the top wine farms in our area, to travelling extensively, to buying his dream car. He loved fast cars and to own a Ferrari was his ultimate dream."

The congregation acceded with whispers and nods.

"I will always love him. I will always remember him. And I will always aspire to be like him.

"Rest in peace, Dad. I feel blessed that you are still a part of us when I see those barrels of wine and when I drink our famous Cabernet."

Frankie's quiet sobs accompanied her son's words.

"I would like to end off by playing a song that meant so much to my parents. My mother has asked me to thank you, on her behalf, for your love and support over this trying time."

As the song began, Jen rushed out of the hall. She had come to pay her last respects, and this had been accomplished without too much discomfort. She ran through the foyer and straight into the book club girls, who were preparing tea and eats for the mourners.

"Jen!" Shelley enthused unconvincingly. "You're here. How are you?"

"Hi, everyone," Jen said uncomfortably. "Terrible tragedy, isn't it?"

"It is," Patricia agreed. "Such a tragic thing to happen."

"What's also pretty tragic," Shelley interrupted, "is your absence. Could you not find it in your heart to reach out to your friend?"

Anne added her two cents' worth. "No matter what you're going through, which quite frankly we think is a whole load of shit, the least you could do – the right thing to do – would be to put your angst aside, not only for Lee's memory, but for Frankie, your supposed best friend."

"You're right," Jen said. "It is absolutely unforgivable, at face value. But honestly, ladies, having known me for so long, do you really think I'd stay away unless something very serious had happened?"

They were silent. Patricia stopped arranging the cocktail

sandwiches and Anne raised her eyebrows. They loved a good story and it seemed they were going to get the scandal they craved.

"What could be so bad that you couldn't be here for Frankie?"

Jen looked at Shelley and said, "You and I never really had a real friendship, did we? We're friends because of our husbands. You've always held a grudge, because you think I stole John from you. Well, the good news, Shelley, is that I inadvertently saved you from John."

She then turned to Anne. "As for you, Anne, it seems as if you have finally found an 'in' in the group, now that I'm leaving."

"Leaving book club?" Anne asked.

"No, Anne. John."

Their mouths dropped open at her candour.

"There, that should give you something to skinner about! God knows, your lives would be pretty dull if you didn't have something or someone to talk about. I'm sure that you wouldn't care to phone me. But you know my number, if you do decide to find it in your hearts to 'reach out'." She looked at Shelley. "To quote you, Shelley."

Jen strode out, tears streaming down her cheeks. She had said goodbye to Lee, her friend and silent ally, and she had said goodbye to her girlfriends, who at one time had meant the world to her – who she had thought had made her life worthwhile.

She drove directly to the farm to collect her belongings. True to form, efficient Gladys had Jen's suitcases packed and ready at the front door. With the help of one of the farm labourers, they loaded them into her four-wheel drive. Jen would be happy to trade in her car for a zippier model better suited to the city's traffic. But for now, she was glad to have the boot space.

Gladys seemed to be more upset than anyone else at the idea of Jen leaving.

"I'm going to miss you, Gladys," Jen said, hugging her. "I don't think you realise quite what you mean to me. I would never have managed without you. You've always been a constant help. Thank you so much."

Gladys hugged her back hard.

Jen pulled an envelope from her bag and gave it to Gladys with both hands. "Here's something for you, for all that you've done for me." It was filled with money, all of John's winnings. She also handed Gladys two small boxes, each containing a gold coin.

She didn't wait for Gladys to thank her. She didn't want to be thanked. She wished that she could have given her so much more. And one day, she vowed, she would.

Jen drove out of town with her music blaring. Her phone's playlist was on shuffle and the song that wafted through her speakers first was 'Figure 8' by Ellie Goulding. The lyrics reminded her of her passionate one-night stand with Lee.

She wondered what her life would have been like if she had married him. Until now, she had never allowed herself to entertain these thoughts. The only way to survive her marriage – and be happy – had been to block out the could-haves and the should-haves. But the song was so haunting and full of love and pathos that she allowed her mind to stray to that night.

She accelerated down the highway, listening to the song playing full blast, over and over again. The tears streaked her face. It was such a beautiful memory. Why had she been so hell-bent on trying to forget it? But then she smiled. There was no need to any more. She was free to remember and to recall every moment.

They had fallen asleep on the back of Lee's truck, waking as the sun began to rise. Realising what she had done had filled her with such remorse she'd started crying. Lee had taken her in his arms and kissed every part of her face: her eyes, her ears, her forehead, her cheeks and finally her mouth. He whispered the exact words of the chorus of this song – "I need you" – repeatedly, trying to persuade her that what had happened between them was something special, something to be treasured.

"Remembering is just as important as forgetting," she thought out loud.

Secretly, she hoped that Brigit *was* Lee's child – a testament to their young love.

Thirty-five

John joined everyone for tea and cake in the foyer after the service, greeting the people he knew and making the polite chit-chat that one does. He had caught a glimpse of Patty making an exit from the memorial service soon after Frankie's song had started playing. Jen had also left without giving her condolences. He was livid. She could have at least sympathised with Clive and Lee's parents.

Frankie's friends had organised a substantial spread and the mourners were milling around with cups in one hand and plates in the other.

"We just caught Jen sneaking out."

John turned around, his mouth full of cake, to see Shelley, hands on hips, looking like a school mistress.

He swallowed. "She needed to go somewhere."

"She said that she's leaving you. That she did me a favour by stealing you from me. Apparently, she saved me from you. What did you do this time, John Pearce?"

What the fuck? He didn't know what to say. He was hardly ever at a loss for words, but this had stumped him. Shelley waited for him to say something. It was as if he had to give her some explanation for not handing in a homework assignment.

"Well, then," he said, downing the last of his coffee, "it seems you know more than me." He handed the mug and the plate to her, and then kissed her condescendingly on the cheek.

Shelley visibly seethed.

"You're such a chauvinist. I'm not here to clean up after you. If you wanted me to do that for you, you should've married me." She shoved his plate and mug back into his hands.

John scanned the foyer to see if anyone was looking, then leaned in closer to her and whispered in her ear, "I've lived with that regret all my life, Shelley." He gently bit on her earlobe, teasing her with his tongue. "If Jen goes, then who knows?"

He winked at her and left her gawping after him as he sauntered across the room to find a place to dump his dirty dishes.

Their group of friends had been invited, along with their wives and offspring, to a lunch on Frankie's farm after the service. Frankie had not extended the invitation to John, but he was going anyway, taking Brigit with him.

Faith had set a long table on the veranda, overlooking the Franschhoek mountain range in the background and in the foreground, the farm's vineyards.

All through lunch, Frankie refused to meet John's eyes. When he spoke, she ignored him, snubbing every attempt to include him in the conversation. After everyone had finished their lasagne, Lee's favourite dish so lovingly prepared by Faith, he noticed that she was missing, and he discreetly left the table to find her.

Frankie had retreated to the bathroom to fix her hair and touch up her make-up. She had had an exhausting day, but she felt, somehow, satisfied at how smoothly everything had gone. Faith's thoughtful and unsupervised preparation of the lunch did not go unnoticed. Faith had made sure that the tables were dressed with Frankie's crisp white cloths and the family's finest silver. The lasagne was accompanied by a green salad. The cold tomato soup as a starter was refreshing and light on such a hot day. She was also surprised at how many people, some of whom she had never met, had come to pay their respects. She had even spotted Patty and Jen in the hall.

She jumped with fright as she opened the bathroom door. John was waiting for her. "Get away from me!" she whispered, afraid that somebody would hear her. "What do you want? You have no respect. No remorse."

"I want to say how sorry I am, Frankie." John seemed to be speaking with uncharacteristic sincerity. "I know that this has been a tough time for you, and I'm sorry for everything."

Frankie was taken aback by his kind words but didn't entirely trust him, particularly as he'd obviously been drinking.

"Okay. Thanks," she said, trying to walk around him. The bathroom was through Frankie's dressing room, which made the chances of being discovered slim. As Frankie tried to pass him, John grabbed her arm and twisted it around, pushing her up against the dressing room wall in the way she used to love.

But now it was sinister, and it scared her.

"You make a shit-hot widow," he whispered lustily in her ear.

"Don't! Please!" she begged.

"Are you playing hard to get? Is this the game you want to play, Frankie?" He reeked of alcohol.

"I'm not playing hard to get. I don't want anything to do with you. Do you hear me? We're done. It's over. What don't you understand?" She was desperately trying to break free from his grip.

John's hand moved under her dress and his fingers ran up her inner thigh.

"Stop, you fucking bastard!" She tried again to break free, but he only tightened his grip around her hands.

Pressing himself against her, he kissed the nape of her neck.

She heard a gasp. Someone was there!

"Wha...what are you doing?" It was Brigit.

John quickly withdrew his hand from under Frankie's dress, and let her go. The look on his face told Frankie that he knew exactly how much trouble he was in.

All Frankie could say was, "It's not what you think it is, Brig."

Brigit shoved her father aside and made one of her characteristic dramatic exits. This time Frankie could not blame her; in fact, she was grateful she had saved her from John, who left the room as abruptly as he had arrived. Frankie watched out of her bedroom's bay window as Brigit sped down the driveway in her car, braked hard for a moment to allow a clutch of ducklings to pass in front of her, and then zoomed off, away from the farm.

John stepped back out onto the veranda.

"Boys, let's go," he said, and the men all rose from the lunch table.

"That's enough for one day," Shelley scolded Frans.

"Maybe for Frans, but not for the rest of us. We don't have to ask your permission, now do we, Shelley?"

"I don't have to either!" Frans retorted. "It's my mate's wake. You'll see me when you see me, Shelley."

He heaved his considerable weight up from the lunch table and joined his friends. John knew Frans was making a point: no woman was going to dictate to him, especially not in front of his mates.

The men spilled noisily into the popular pizzeria in Dorp Street that was frequented by students, tourists and families alike. The manager greeted them sympathetically and led them to a table in the bar area where they could resume their drinking. Before long, they had the whole pub singing 'We Are the Champions', much to the chagrin of the residents of the block of flats nearby. Someone – it could have been John, but he wasn't sure – decided they should all drink until they passed out. But by one in the morning, the manager, well known for his no-nonsense style, had closed the bar after they had finished their round of free drinks.

John was far too drunk to drive, but he got behind the wheel anyway. He made his way back to the farm, weaving from side to side along the treacherous sand roads. It crossed his mind briefly that he was way over the limit, but he was John Pearce. He could do anything.

The farmhouse stood dark and empty.

At least Jen was home. No way could she ever leave him. She didn't have enough money to finance a move, and she had no family or friends to run to. She must have come straight home after the service, and she was probably asleep right now in their bed.

Make-up sex with his wife was always passionate. He stumbled to the bedroom and whispered in the dark, "Jen, I'm home. Are you ashleep?"

He fell on his stomach onto the bed.

"I'm home!" he slurred.

He felt for Jen with his hand, but it just swept through air. He pushed himself up to make sure she really wasn't there. He winced as he rolled off the bed, removed his shoes and his suit jacket, undid his tie and finally pulled down his pants. He was standing in a pool of clothing, swaying from side to side, with just his shirt, jocks and socks on.

"Jen! Where are you?"

He staggered past the kitchen towards the spare room. As he pushed the door open, he called out his wife's name again. This room, too, was dark, and there was no answer.

"Come on, Jen," he said. "Let'sh be friends. Fuck it, Jen, life is too short. You fucked Lee and I fucked Frankie. We're even. Anyway, I need you."

He switched on the light to find a neatly made bed. At the foot of the bed was a sealed envelope with his name on it. He grabbed it, tore it open and shook the contents out on to the bed. Out spilled all the incriminating photographs of him, the same photographs Frankie had thrown at him. It had never crossed his mind that there were copies! He fell to his knees, photographs in hand, as he looked at every one of them. He felt as if he'd been punched hard in the guts. Jen had evidence of the life he had kept from her – a secret life he knew was unforgivable, let alone unacceptable. Even in his drunken state, he knew that leaving the envelope was her way of saying 'over and out'.

"I need you, Jen." There was nobody to hear him. "You can't leave me," he moaned.

Never had he loathed himself so deeply. He had pushed his wife away and hurt his children. Everyone had deserted him, even his best friend.

Thirty-six

A distraught Brig had messaged her brother to come to her place as soon as possible; she had just caught their dad and the grieving widow together. Pete had driven as fast as he could through peak-hour traffic to get to her. Overcome by anger, he had phoned Clive.

To his surprise, Clive was not at all shocked. He thanked him for being brave enough to be upfront about Frankie's affair.

"It just endorses what I'm about to do, Pete," he had said. "My mother told me some hectic stuff last night. Some hardcore shit went down. I'm stopping this now and I hope you'll be able to do the same with your dad. This is not good for my dad. For any of us, really. Send love to Brig, and tell her I'm really sorry. I'm really, really sorry," he said, his voice breaking.

When Pete finally got to Brigit's flat, she hugged him tightly.

"Thank you so much for coming, Pete. You have no idea what this means to me," she sobbed.

"I know, I know," he said, wiping her tears from her face.

"You've been through a shitload, Brig. And now Frankie and Dad!"

"Did you know about them?" she asked, searching his face, which – he knew – showed no hint of shock or surprise.

"I did," he admitted. "Look, Ma knows too. This is really the straw that broke the camel's back. They've been fucking each other for months."

"The bitch! And to think that Lee wouldn't touch me because he was married to her!" her voice petered out, and Pete took a step back.

"What? What the fuck you telling me, Brigit? That you made a move on Lee?"

He interpreted Brigit's silence as an affirmative.

"Oh, my fuck! You *must* be Dad's child," he blurted out. They looked at each other, aghast at the tactlessness of what he had just said and, for a second, he worried that she was going to cry, but instead, she snorted. He started laughing, too, and then Brigit was crying and laughing at the same time.

When they finally calmed down, he spoke.

"Look, Brig, if anyone has no right to judge, it's me."

"Well, anyway, I never did sleep with Lee. He was a true gentleman. I now wonder if he batted me because he knew I could be his daughter."

Pete shuddered. "Can you imagine if he, you…"

"Stop it!" Brigit put her hands over his mouth. "I don't want to think about it."

"What are we going to do, Brig? Dad has a problem, let's face it."

Brigit just shrugged.

Pete inhaled deeply before speaking. "Ma and I had a serious conversation last night. She had a proposition she wanted to discuss with me, regarding the farm and her assets. I met with her attorney, Leonard Mazwai, after the service today. I wasn't sure if I wanted to go for it, until now."

He could see Brig had no idea what he was talking about.

"Go for what?"

"Go for the jugular."

The next morning, Pete waited for his father in the kitchen.

"What the fuck do you want here?" he barked.

"I've come to have a conversation with you. One that's long overdue. And I've come back to work here, on the farm."

Pete had been waiting for this day: John's day of reckoning. He was no longer intimidated by him. In fact, his father's misdemeanours had made him lose all respect for him.

"I don't want you back. You and everyone else can just fuck off."

Pete waited until Gladys took her leave before launching into his attack.

"Brigit told me how she ran into you and Frankie yesterday: the grieving widow and grieving best friend." John tried to interrupt, but Pete stopped him. "I'm not finished. I'm really not here to judge you or try to save you from yourself. It's too late for that. What I am here to do is to take over Ma's share of the farm." John was silent and then he was in Pete's face, grabbing his collar. "Don't you fucking think of it, you cu…"

Pete head-butted his father with such force that he fell back against the kitchen counter. "You can fuck whoever," he hissed. "Fling your reputation in the dirt, I don't give a shit. But you won't sink this farm in the process. This, I give a fuck about, so let me tell you about our new arrangement. Partner."

Leonard Mazwai and Jen had come up with a solution regarding the divorce and the splitting of the assets. As Jen and John were married in community of property, John would be forced to allow Pete – who would be Jen's employee from now on – to take over her share of the farm. This meant that Pete would ostensibly hold a fifty percent partnership of the land, the buildings on the farm, the vineyards and the business itself. He would draw a salary from this, and his share of the profits would go to Jen. His mother would open an account for Brigit into which she would split her share of the profits.

John would be "pushed" (Leonard's word) to leave his share of the farm to his daughter. No other spouse or future children, following the divorce, would be entitled to Jen or John's portion of the farm. This was considered a fair exchange in lieu of Jen's capital, which John had used to upgrade the farm and the business during their marriage.

Pete would be employed as Financial Director alongside his father. He would have signing power and they'd have equal say over everything.

"So, you see, Ma's making sure that she's in on the profits of the business while taking care of us and making sure that we will eventually be the rightful owners. She's making sure she gets paid, for a change. And she's got our interests at heart, too. Which is more than I can say for you," Pete finished.

He left John in the kitchen, in his shirt, underpants and socks, to consider how much his life was about to change. But before doing so he said, "By the way, don't you ever call me a cunt again."

Thirty-seven

While spending a week away at a game lodge, Jen had begun to glue together the broken pieces of her life.

It was a rocky start to her so-called freedom, and it certainly hadn't given her the much-needed rest she had hoped for.

The time alone had forced her to reflect on her past. She'd felt bitter about John and the humiliation he had caused her. She'd derided herself for being such a weak and subservient wife. She was to blame for the kind of woman she was – or had become – and she reproached herself for the example she had set for her children. *It's no wonder Brigit has no respect for me. I never once took a stand or showed any backbone.*

Although she knew that John's problem was pathological, she couldn't help placing the blame on her inadequacies. She had never counted sexual prowess as one of her qualities, but she had been sure that she was no dead weight in the bedroom, either. She reflected on her perceived prudishness. She could never measure up to Frankie, who had made it her mission to be sexy. Her body, her clothes, her swagger – everything had been carefully honed to entice and please a man. No wonder John had strayed into her taut, toned arms. Who could blame him?

Especially since she, Jen, hadn't given much thought to her own figure. John had begged her to have her breasts lifted and had nagged her for years to go to gym. He had basically been telling her that she didn't excite him.

God! Had she forced him to stray? Maybe his sex addiction was all her fault?

She thought a lot about her parents, too, remembering how her father had stripped her mom of her dignity and pride. Why had she not shown strength of character by leaving him? Surely, if she had taken a stand against him, she would have shown Jen that women do have choices and, moreover, that women have power? Her mother was also to blame, then; she was the reason Jen had believed she had nowhere to go.

She fell into a deep, dark hole during that week. In fact, she didn't venture out of her suite at all, not even to the restaurant, nor on any of the lodge's complementary game drives or guided hikes she had been so looking forward to.

Jen spent all day in a darkened room, agonising over her past – her lost youth and her sad childhood – all the while berating herself for allowing her mother to persuade her to withhold the truth from John. To marry him, through fear! She hated herself for having been swayed by the expectations of others.

She ignored all phone calls and after the first day, she didn't bother to dress, lying in bed in a foetal position, allowing herself simply to cry and to hate, to weep and to blame. Her desire to move forward had been crippled, paralysed by depression.

She was amazed to see Claudia and Sharon, who had decided to check in on her when she hadn't answered any of their messages or calls. She was overjoyed to see caring faces. They even pretended not to notice her greasy hair and swollen eyes.

Their presence inspired Jen to get dressed and go out. They'd each booked into a suite of their own for the weekend, and the three of them drank in the tonic that is nature: the wildlife, the bushveld, the fresh air. The healing power of friendship and laughter was just what she had needed, and, by the end of the week, Jen was ready to face life as a single, middle-aged woman. She felt a fluttering of excitement at the thought that she was about to embark on a brand-new adventure.

As soon as she returned from the bush, Jen booked a weekly consultation with a "normal, run-of-the-mill" therapist – Sharon's words – and set up regular Friday-night drinks with her two friends. She invited Patty to join them, but Fridays were her busiest nights at the 'gentlemen's club' she had recently re-opened, so she was often unable to meet them.

The most important lesson Jen had learned from her weekly sessions – both at her psychologist and with her friends – was forgiveness. She had realised that anger and bitterness were not helpful if she wanted to forge ahead with her life. She learned to begin to forgive John for his lies and deceit, and to forgive herself, so she could start to love herself.

John had initially played hardball, but quickly realised it would be better not to antagonise Leonard, whose reputation was formidable. Leonard had managed to get his hands on Jen's file from her gynaecologist, and after consultation with another reputable doctor, found that he had, as Jen suspected, agreed to withhold important information from her to protect John, an old friend of his.

Leonard had made it very clear to him that the exposure of his sex addiction, coupled with his collusion with Jen's doctor, made withholding a decent settlement impossible.

Jen found that she was not even vaguely interested in whether her ex was dating or in how he was doing. News, however, did get back to her, as she expected. Soon after the memorial service,

Patricia phoned her. She said that she admired Jen for having the courage to walk away from her marriage. She confessed to having been unhappy with Larry for years but knew she did not have the courage to do what Jen had done.

During one of Patricia's regular phone calls in the time that followed, she got an unsolicited update on John.

"He's really not doing well, Jen," she volunteered. "He's creepy. In fact, I think he's in Larry's league when it comes to being lecherous and crude. People talk about him like he's a dirty old man."

When Jen told Claudia and Sharon about it over cocktails the following Friday, Sharon said, "That's normally what happens. It's weird, but men – particularly the strong, sexy type – lose their appeal after they divorce."

Jen leaned back and shared a look with Claudia.

"How so?" they asked in unison, mimicking Sharon.

"On no, you're exaggerating. Is that really how I speak?"

"That's *exactly* how you speak!"

"Seriously, though, how so?" Jen asked.

"Men are often attractive to women because of the whole package they represent, which includes wife and children. In John's case, he was married to a beautiful wife."

Jen blushed and waved away the compliment.

"It's true Jen, you're gorgeous, and he has two great kids. He owns a wine farm and has an enviable lifestyle. Contrary to what you may think, this is not a deterrent. In fact, all those factors enhanced his attraction. Besides a married man being a 'challenge', they also come across as less desperate, especially after a certain age. It's much more rewarding to bag the guy who has lots to lose than a guy who is middle aged and creepily available. What is John now, other than a middle aged sex fiend whose wife left him because of his promiscuity? Who wants that? It's simply not as enticing, period."

What Sharon said made sense. Why then was it different for Jen, who had become much more attractive to men, contrary to Frankie's warning about older women being less desirable?

"Before, your husband and children defined who you were. In fact, you didn't have an identity separate from them. Now that you are on your own, you are much more desirable. We're talking about you specifically, Jen. There are many women who can maintain an identity separate from wife and mother within their marriages. You, however, were never allowed to, or you never allowed yourself to.

"But now you are independent and confident, and you haven't made finding a man your mission. You are developing interests and friendships because of who you are, not because of who your husband is."

Claudia spoke up. "I remember you telling me about that speech you made at John's birthday. Underneath the wit was evidence that you hardly functioned independently from him. Your day revolved around his day. His hobbies became yours. Not only that, your one shot at doing your own thing socially – book club – was usurped by all the men. They upstaged you and your friends by organising their poker evenings for the very same night."

Jen took a sip of her Sea Breeze. "I never thought of it that way. No wonder I felt so unattractive, and was so unattractive. Putting John's sex addiction aside, maybe if I had maintained my own identity, our marriage would've been more exciting and fulfilling."

Claudia answered, "I agree that you're a little to blame, because you did have choices, but I think that John can take a lot of credit for what you had become. Look at you now, Jen. You're a successful businesswoman."

Sharon and Claudia raised their glasses and toasted Jen's success.

"This makes you extremely desirable to many men, and

women," Sharon winked.

It was true. Jen was becoming a sought-after interior designer. After agonising over the ethics of doing the design of Patty's new gentlemen's club, Jen decided to accept her request for help. As a result, she also landed two projects involving interior design for large corporates in the city, courtesy of a couple of the club's regular guests.

Leonard had, meanwhile, asked Jen to help with his newly acquired beach house in Pringle Bay as Claudia, who had impeccable taste, said she was too busy to be enlisted. Jen had a sneaking suspicion that this had been staged by both Leonard and Claudia to give her a leg-up. She was extremely grateful, especially when the completed house was featured as the centre spread in an interiors magazine whose theme for the month was beach-house living.

Between referrals from the magazine and Leonard's friends who had seen the house, work started pouring in.

She was now so busy that she had hired an assistant and office space in Woodstock and was working long hours and loving it.

Jen had moved into a little Victorian townhouse in Oranjezicht and had just heard the news that her offer to purchase had been accepted.

"And now you are the proud owner of your own house, Jen!" Claudia said.

Jen beamed. "I can't begin to tell you how excited I am. And how beautiful it is going to look when I'm done with it."

"Well, tell us," Sharon said.

"The kitchen, as you've seen, is fabulous – I love the clean modern lines – but I'm opening it up to incorporate the dining room. And there will have to be two bedrooms with bathrooms en suite for the kids, should they feel like crashing for the weekend."

"Sounds exciting. So, when does this project begin?"

Jen wished that it could begin as soon as tomorrow, but she

explained that she had to be patient, for one, as the transfer had to go through, "and my birthday will be at home. There's no way I want a party on a building site." The waitress had brought them another round of cocktails courtesy of two of the men at the bar. They held up their glasses to thank them, then carried on with their conversation.

"And Brigit? How's she doing?" Sharon asked.

"She seems to have made peace with not knowing who her real dad is. The fact that John had chosen to raise her as his own, she says, not knowing for certain that she was his, has made her decide to abandon the idea of a paternity test. This is also why she chose to forgive him: for not being perfect. And she seems to have forgiven me. Well, I assume as much because she's asked if she can help me with my party preparations!"

"No!" Claudia said. "Then all must be forgotten."

"Mmmm. I'm not so sure, she's still in therapy."

Sharon laughed. "Nothing wrong with therapy, am I right, Claudia?"

"Somehow, she relishes the notion that she had two dads who both loved her, despite not knowing whose she was," Jen said. Claudia and Sharon seemed to understand better than she did, but she supposed that they'd heard weirder things as therapists themselves.

"How's Pete coping on the farm with his dad?"

Jen held the straw of her cocktail, sucked gently, swallowed and then spoke.

"It seems to be a little smoother. For a while there, I doubted myself, throwing them in the business like I did. But Pete says that they stay out of each other's way as much as possible and that their relationship is strictly business related."

Claudia had met Pete with Jen over lunch a few times when he had come into the city to follow up with one of the farm's biggest restaurant clients.

"He's a good boy, Pete. Seems to me he's coming into himself." Claudia commented.

"He is. I'm so glad. He really has come a long way, even though he's still my boy."

Sharon downed her cocktail and motioned to the waitress to bring her the bill. It was after sunset and she had a lot of paperwork to finish before the next day. Jen still could not believe how hard Sharon worked.

"Well, you're certainly proof that only good things can happen when people are given the space they need to be themselves," Sharon said kindly.

Jen was almost, but not quite, accustomed to how supportive Sharon and Claudia were of her. Not only were they kind and encouraging, they really seemed to value her. She had never in her life had friends like these. Jen had never felt valued, even when she and Frankie were besties.

She didn't know where Frankie was now, and she didn't care. Frankie had tried calling her, but Jen had blocked her calls. She had heard, through Pete, that Clive had left university to take over his father's business and was doing a good job. He and Pete saw each other quite often, both being in the wine industry. Apparently, Clive had a steady girlfriend whom Frankie despised.

And, of, course Jen's friendship with the book club girls had dissolved since she had left, except for Patricia. Jen knew Patricia needed her more than she did Patricia, so she always answered the phone when she called. She listened politely to Patricia's news, told her a little about what was going on in her life, being considerately careful not to make everything seem too good.

But the truth was, she thought, as she walked towards her beloved little hatchback down Camps Bay's bustling street, festive with Friday-evening revellers, her new life was glorious. She had been given a second chance and she had grabbed it with both hands.

Thirty-eight

It had been just over a year since John's fifty-fifth birthday, with all the ensuing fallout. Jen had now reached the big five-oh she had once dreaded but had come to embrace it. There was no way that she would pass up a celebration to commemorate her transformation and her new beginning. And what better place to celebrate than her new home?

She finished getting ready for the party and examined herself in the full-length mirror. This time, Jen didn't care what Brigit – or anyone else – thought of her outfit. She had chosen a long, Grecian-style gown in emerald green, which showed off her shoulders and long neck. She had splashed out on gold earrings, and her hair had been tied back in a chignon at the nape of her neck. There was a slit up the side of her dress from which a tanned and toned thigh peeped as she walked. She felt – and looked – absolutely gorgeous.

Jen went through to the kitchen to check on the caterers. The guests would start with canapés during the speeches, followed by a sit-down meal of beef fillet or fish with a medley of vegetables. She'd decided on an assortment of desserts to be left on the table for the remainder of the evening, so the guests could tuck into them if they wanted something decadent and sweet. She had her eye on the lavender macarons.

Pete and Brigit were the first to arrive. Claudia, Sharon and Patty had helped her to get the house ready in the afternoon and were now laughing uproariously over a bottle of wine on the little stoep in front. Jen joined them and noticed that Brigit, leaning against the railing with a glass of wine, was resolutely ignoring Patty. Previously, Jen would have fretted about tension between two of her guests, but tonight she didn't let it worry her. *They're both adults. They can sort themselves out.*

Among the fifty guests to arrive were her friends' lovers, followed by Angie, Leonard's secretary, with whom Jen had made a strong connection, as well as Jenny and Gerard from the spa; perhaps they were an unconventional choice, but Jen would forever be grateful for the way they had treated her when she'd been so vulnerable and hurt. She had also made new friends through her work, some of whom she invited to join her celebration. She had included some of her kids' friends, one of which was Clive, who had grown up in Jen's house.

And of course, Myron was there: tall, tanned and handsome and extremely sexy.

He had pursued Jen from the time she blew him a kiss and walked out of his house, closing the front door behind her. But at the time, there had been no place in her life for a permanent romance. Jen was only interested in romancing Jen. She had spent years in self-imposed imprisonment and there was no way she would allow her newfound freedom and energy to be compromised by another relationship. Not then. She had stuck to her guns, and Myron, to his credit, had respectfully, if grudgingly, given her the space that she had needed.

The closest thing she had to a relationship during that time was a brief encounter with a former client, but when he gave her a diamond necklace as a token of his commitment, she ran for the hills.

It had only been Myron she wanted, and when she was ready, she summoned him to her newly purchased home on a Friday evening by way of a hand-delivered invitation. She asked him to meet her at her home address, and wrote, "Expect to wear nothing on entering". He told her later that he had cancelled a date with a woman he had met online.

He knocked on her door at exactly eight o'clock. She had worn a long chiffon dress over a bronze body suit and tied her long hair up in an untidy bun above her head. She had wanted to look sexy, but not as if she had tried too hard.

The first things Jen noticed about him were his trendy glasses and new haircut. He looked even more attractive than she remembered. She breathed in the delectable smell of him as they stood facing each other. She was sure that her desire was radiating off her in waves.

"Hello," he said.

"I'm so happy that you could be here at such short notice. I am the proud owner of this house. The transfer went through today, and I needed to celebrate! The only person I could think to celebrate with was you," she babbled. She had completely lost her nerve on seeing him.

"Well, I must've known, because I bought flowers for your new acquisition."

He handed her the biggest bunch of roses she had ever seen.

"They're beautiful. Thank you."

He couldn't help himself, "*You're* beautiful, Jen. You are even more beautiful than when I last saw you."

The roses never ended up in a vase. They lay on the floor at the entrance as Myron and Jen reached for one another, hungrily and longingly.

This time, they got past the front door. He took her hand and she led him to her bedroom. There, he kissed her, undoing her hairband and allowing her hair to cascade around her shoulders.

He kissed her again and helped her remove her dress.

"Did you not read the invitation?" she asked. "It clearly stipulated that you were to wear nothing."

"No problem," he said as he removed his shirt, revealing a strong torso and a flat stomach. She ran her hands along his chest and down his abdomen. "Very enticing you are," she said.

She kissed his navel and ran her tongue down towards the waistband of his pants. She slowly unbuttoned his chinos. Myron gently held her chin and tilted her head, so that her eyes met his. The longing she felt was tempered with a kiss that was deep and penetrating. She shuddered as he kissed her shoulders and eased the straps of her body suit off, exposing her breasts. He lifted her to her feet and slowly slid off the rest of the clothing that remained between them, moving his hands down the sides of her body as he did so. The feeling was excruciatingly exciting.

Their eyes were still locked. They didn't speak. Jen was swimming in his gaze. He pushed her gently back on to the bed and her legs parted as he lay between her open thighs, enjoying the feeling of him and the anticipation of their long-awaited union. He cupped her breasts. It seemed to pain him to unlock his eyes from hers as he slowly caressed each nipple with his mouth and his fingers. She groaned, and her hips moved, coaxing him. But he resisted.

His head moved down her body, eventually reaching her with his tongue, hands still caressing her breasts, before finding her with his mouth. She arched her back and her thighs clasped him as she felt his tongue and his fingers perform tricks on her she hadn't known were possible. She groaned again, her pelvis bucking as he made her climax with abandon. He then entered her and moaned deeply as they rocked in unison, her legs pointing up like a yogi.

He flipped her over and under and every which way he chose as they danced their tantric dance. And all the while she was aware of only one thing, him. Her hands were all over his body, as were his on hers; their mouths explored every part that was physically possible to explore.

Jen remembered the last time she had felt this way. It was a long, long time ago and she had allowed that person to slip away from her. This time, she knew the value of their connection – that you run with it and not from it.

That was three months ago, and since then, she and Myron had been an item. When Jen looked at him tonight, she felt a familiar stirring. Her desire for him was so intense. As was the thrill of knowing the feeling was mutual.

Once Jen told Pete that everyone had arrived, he tapped on his wine glass to attract the other guests' attention. "Hi, everyone. I don't know why Ma does this to me, but she insists that I speak, knowing full well that speaking publicly is my worst nightmare. Having said that, because you have been the most incredible mother, I will do anything for you, including speaking at your fiftieth. For most people, it's downhill from fifty, but not for this incredibly beautiful person standing here. Most of you have travelled the journey with her that took her from heartbroken housewife to strong and sexy career woman."

Her friends whooped appreciatively.

"I don't have anything much to say other than thank you for being here tonight. It is her wish that I tell you to drink, eat and be merry. I now hand this microphone, gladly, to my gorgeous sister, who will present a slideshow of our mom, depicting a life that spans five decades."

Jen hadn't been happy about a presentation that would include pictures of her ex-husband and her estranged friends. But, during discussions with her psychologist, she had acknowledged that she had a past, and that it included the people who had played an important role in her journey. Jen knew that if Sharon had explained this to her in consultation, the two of them would have had a good chuckle.

The presentation started with new-born Jen in the arms of her mother, whom she had loved and had learned to forgive and appreciate over this past year and a half. There was a portrait of her small family – her father looking stern and full of self-importance, and a tiny scowling Jen sitting on her mother's lap. Brig had included pictures of the farm on which she had been raised. There were photos of her school friends, although Jen had lost contact with every one of them.

There was the image that Jen had dreaded seeing, but had agreed to when Brigit had asked, of a handsome John and a very pregnant Jen on their wedding day. Jen had looked excited and radiant. Oh yes, she had loved him. And they had included a recent picture of Lee wearing a t-shirt that read, "I'll be back". Oh, how Jen wished that were true, and how she knew Lee would have loved the irony were he alive. There were photos of Jen and Frankie on various overseas holidays and of her book club friends lounging in colourful nineties swimming costumes wearing Ray-Ban sunglasses with their hair pulled back in banana clips. How beautiful they all were. They had been happy together, and they were a part of her past, a part of the person she had become.

These were followed by the pictures of her two children, showing them from birth to toddlerhood, from their first days of school, to their gawky teenage years, to the independent young adults they were today.

There was one she'd never seen before of her and Claudia at the spa where they had met. She remembered Claudia asking Gerard to take a photo of them at the pool in their swimming costumes, eating slices of pineapple for breakfast. There was another of Sharon, Claudia and Jen at the game lodge, bent over, just about peeing with laughter. At what, she couldn't remember. Next was a picture of Patty and Jen having drinks at Café Caprice in Camps Bay – Patty soliciting gawks from the arbitrary men in the background, as usual. This was followed by Gerard and Jenny, hamming it up at the spa, serving their day guests, Claudia, Sharon and Jen. And finally – Brig had kept Jen's new love for last – Myron, looking lovingly into Jen's eyes, captured by one of his friends at a party; Myron and Jen, laughing uproariously at being sprayed with champagne at a cycle race; and finally, Jen, happily tipsy on that same evening, being carried to the car, her arms hooked around his neck, their lips locked in a kiss.

Despite her reservations, she loved what had been put together. The slideshow had helped contextualise her life, not only for Jen but for all her guests. It was an overwhelmingly moving and happy display of love, friendship, life and time, past and present, hinting at joy and anticipation for the future. Looking around, wiping her eyes, Jen noticed that pretty much everyone around her had been moved to tears as well.

And then it was her turn to speak. She stood there, clutching the microphone, looking at her guests, taking in the beauty of her children and her new man and her beloved new friends.

"The last time I made a speech, I got into terrible trouble. It was the beginning of the end of a cycle – and the start of something new – and I'd like to thank each and every one of you, because you've all been travellers with me on this new journey.

"I'm not going to pretend that I wasn't afraid. That I wasn't crippled by the past. But I learned, I'm still learning, that the past is something that doesn't exist anymore. In fact, it had stopped existing for a very long time. But my journey has not only been about letting go, it's been about letting go with *love*. It's about acknowledging that whoever was in my life was there for a purpose, and that whatever has happened in my life has happened for a reason.

"I have untold love, gratitude and affection for absolutely everyone whose life has touched mine – even that of my ex-husband, John. The result of our union is our two beautiful children: testimony to a bond and love that once existed." She turned to them. "And it is because of you that I have no regrets."

She continued, hoping to keep the tears at bay for just a little while longer, "As most of you know, I love music. And while I love you Myron," she said, blowing him a kiss, "and you, dear friends, I adore Zucchero. His song 'Flying Away' perfectly encapsulates my journey so far. What life has meant to *me*.

"I hope you'll indulge me while I read a few lines of the song's poignant lyrics, and when I'm finished, Pete will play it for us, because it's so much better sung than read. As I said, this song resonates with me because this is exactly what I have tried to do on my life's journey." Jen swallowed some champagne before she read the lyrics.

"I have 'left the sorrow and the dark memories behind' and I have kept the good, because there has been so much good. And in so doing, I have done what Zucchero urges us all to do: 'Sweep the rest behind'.

"Right now, dear friends, not only am I flying. I am soaring."

As Jen concluded her speech, Zucchero's voice wafted hauntingly through the speakers. Myron walked up to Jen, took her hand in his and led her to the dance floor, where, together, they moved to the slow rhythm of the ballad. His body pressed tightly against hers, their eyes locked. The guests soon followed. They all moved to the music that spoke of her life. And Jen realised that this was one of those moments that would be forever etched into her memory. She had 'blessed her past', but not walked away. She had danced away. And, oh, how she loved to dance.

Epilogue

At 7:28 the next morning, as Jen was slowly becoming agonisingly aware of the hangover, her phone beeped her into consciousness.

Myron lay asleep beside her, his delectable body rising and falling like a baby's in contented slumber. Still facing her man, and feeling 'hashtag-blessed', she grabbed her phone from her bedside table.

Number unknown.

Jen sat up. She glanced at the message, then re-read it. A flush of heat gathered from deep inside. "Morning Jen, Wishing you a happy birthday from beyond the grave. Hope you've been dancing. Remember to tango your way through the next fifty years."

Before she could react, the message was deleted.

Acknowledgements

Melinda Ferguson, my publisher and risk-taker

Thalia, Maria, Catherine and Carina: the fabulous four who read my manuscript from its inception (sagapo)

Penny Hill, my astute grammar guide and grammar geek – your jist the best ;)

Claire Strombeck for her valuable first edit and Jenna Barlow for her invaluable guidance

Shelagh Foster for her final edit and Linda for the final proof

Dom, for believing I could

My team of feisty and sometimes 'wined-up' cheerleaders, as well as my wonderful girlfriends and family (too many to mention) for pushing the should

Simona and Andi for seeing the bigger picture

Sexy Stellenbosch – a backdrop like no other

And to my daughters – strong, feisty and brave, you anchor me always

Join the virtual book club

 Share your saucy insights and thoughts on *Sex, Lies & Stellenbosch* with me, the author, Eva Mazza. It will be fun to join you for a virtual glass of wine and some page-turning gossip. Whether you're an official book club or an unofficial group of friends, set up an online session with me by emailing slsxbookclub@gmail.com.

About Melinda Ferguson Books

Melinda Ferguson began publishing under MFBooks Joburg, an imprint of Jacana Media. Established in 2013, Ferguson published a groundbreaking list of new South African non-fiction, including the 2016 Alan Paton Award winner, *Rape: A South African Nightmare* by Dr Pumla Dineo Gqola. In 2020, a joint venture between NB Publishers and Melinda Ferguson Books was established.

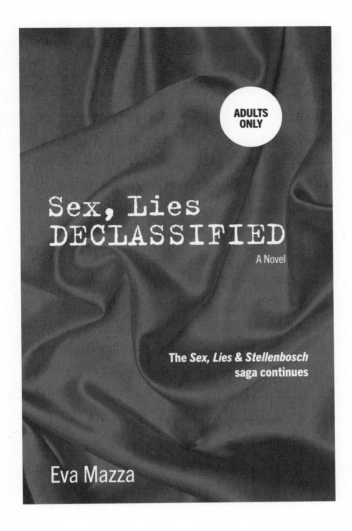

Sex, Lies
DECLASSIFIED

A Novel

The *Sex, Lies & Stellenbosch*
saga continues

Eva Mazza

Social Media
Facebook: Sex, Lies & Stellenbosch
Facebook: Sex, Lies Declassified
Instagram: meklismazza
Twitter: @mazzamaxim EvaMazza

Hashtags:
#SexLiesAndStellenbosch
#SexLiesDeclassified
#SLS
#SLD
#WhatJenWouldDo